Follow Lieutenant Julia Todd in the *Murder In Memphis* series:

The Chartreuse Envelope (2010)

They Gotta Sleep Sometime (2011)

Which One Dies Today? (2012)

Blood Money (2013)

Cast the First Stone (2015)

Check out Jim's short stories in
the Malice in Memphis anthologies
edited by Carolyn McSparren and published by
Dark Oak Press, Kerlak Enterprises, Inc.
Memphis, Tennessee

The Silver Star
***Malice in Memphis: Bluff City Mysteries* (2014)**

The Adventures of Sonny Etherly: Special Powers
***Malice in Memphis: Ghost Stories* (2016)**

The Furnace Room
Malice in Memphis: Elmwood Stories to Die For
(expected 2017)

Five, Six, Seven, Eight
Malice in Memphis: Memphis In Mayhem
(expected 2018)

THE UNSPEAKABLE

Murder In Memphis

a novel by

James C. Paavola

A Julia Todd Mystery

(Book 6)

Published by J&M Book Publishers
Memphis, Tennessee

Website: http://www.jamespaavola.com

ISBN: 978-0-9964571-2-5

Printed in the United States of America

A portion of proceeds from the sale of books in the *Murder In Memphis* series goes to the Memphis/Shelby County Law Enforcement Foundation, a 501(c)(3) non-profit organization to supplement training and equipment.

To Marilyn,
my life partner in our 50 year marriage.
I could never have become
who I am without you.
My forever love.

PART I

Chapter 1

The Journey

*September 23, 2009, Nuhab, Mexico...*The diary of Gabriela Maria Ortiz Delgado:

> *Los Zetas cartel killed many people. Papi says it is not safe to stay here. Tomorrow we start our long journey to the United States. We will go with other families. I will be the youngest. But Mama says I'm a very grownup ten year-old.*

***

Four families—eight adults, five children—gathered outside their village in the Sierra Madre Oriental Mountains, northeast of Mexico City. Each person slung a bedroll and bota water bag or canteen over one shoulder, a bag of dried meats and fruit over the other. Hunting knives hung from the men's belts. The parents made a quick inventory and, for the twentieth time, admonished their children to be absolutely quiet. The group left, soon walking single file down a moonlit narrow trail. Alejandro, Silvia and their daughter Gabriela fell in behind. Alejandro took the last place. Nuhab was five hours behind them before the sun cleared the horizon.

They broke from the trail and hid in the trees to rest and eat. Gabriela heard voices, men's voices. She started to speak but Alejandro shushed everyone, motioning them down. Parents pulled their children to the ground. Five men in military fatigues walked past, automatic rifles slung on their shoulders. She saw one of the mothers mouth the words *Los Zetas.*

They remained still until convinced the men were not returning, and no others were coming. Alejandro urged everyone to gather their things, be quiet, and listen for more Zetas. The trail appeared deserted. The group moved quickly.

A half-hour later Gabriela bumped into the woman ahead of her. She looked back at her mother and whispered, "Why have we stopped, Mama?" Silvia shrugged. Gabriela strained to see. Worried whispers came back through the line. "Los Zetas." Silvia wrapped her arms around Gabriela. The men quickly took the group off the path. They huddled together, spoke in hushed voices.

Gabriela recognized her father's voice. "We have no choice," Alejandro said. "We knew we'd be going through Los Zetas territory and other cartels as we get closer to the Texas border. We must move across the bridge fast. Then get off the path, make our way to Metlaltoyuca."

The men returned to their families. "Hurry," Alejandro said quietly to Silvia and Gabriela. "We must go."

"What is it, Papi?" Gabriela asked.

"You'll see soon enough," Alejandro said, eyes fixed over her head.

No one spoke. Silvia nudged her daughter forward. The trail dropped and angled right. Gabriela saw the end of a primitive walking bridge connected to the far side of a ravine—rope railings and wooden planks. The group slowed, bunched up as it approached the bridge, then stopped. She heard the men, "Don't look down. …Don't stop. …Hold on tight. ...Keep your eyes on the other side."

The woman ahead blocked Gabriela's view till she took her turn on the planks. Gabriela gasped at the full view of the ravine—men, women, children stretched out on an undulating bridge. She felt dizzy, her stomach dropped. She was certain she would throw up.

Silvia gently took each of Gabriela's shoulders and pushed her forward. "Hands on the ropes. Keep looking at the trees on the other side. Don't look down. Not even once."

Gabriela grabbed the upper ropes for balance, stepped out onto the bridge and froze. Her mouth opened, but before she could scream, Silvia's hand smothered the sound. A muffled whine leaked out. "Shh," Sylvia whispered, removing her hand only after every note of Gabriela's cry had been silenced. "You must be quiet. Keep moving," Silvia pushed her gently. Gabriela inched forward. The planks rose and fell in waves. She stumbled.

"Pay attention," Silvia whispered sharply, grabbing a handful of Gabriela's blouse with one hand, holding an upper rope with the other. "Hold on tight. Move one hand at a time. Don't look down."

Gabriela trembled. Keeping her eyes straight ahead, she gripped the ropes tightly, inched forward. Her right hand soon hit the first of two large knots tied around the upper rope. She glanced over. Something moved. Beneath her swung the bodies of two men—naked, hands tied behind their backs, a noose around their necks. Gabriela tried to scream but her throat was too dry. Her breathing became rapid, shallow. Her vision tunneled. Gabriela's knees weakened, her fingers relaxed.

Silvia stepped into Gabriela. One arm wrapped around her chest, pulling her tight. Her free hand squeezed the upper rope just as the bridge rolled. Silvia twisted and fell back, taking Gabriela. Alejandro slammed against Sylvia, catching her with his body, keeping a death grip on each upper rope till the roll calmed. Sylvia regained her balance. Breathed. Adjusted her hold on Gabriela and one rope. "Grab the ropes," she said. Gabriela took the ropes, but did not move. Sylvia pressed her knee into the back of Gabriela's right leg, forcing her to step forward. Then her left leg. She sang rhythmically, softly in Gabriela's ear:

"Right foot…See the trees…Left foot…Hold on tight…
Right foot…See the trees…Left foot…Keep moving…
Right foot…"

Silvia led her young dance partner across the ever moving bridge—rising, falling, rolling. Alejandro pressed against Sylvia, stealing glances behind him. When they reached the other side, hands grabbed Gabriela and Sylvia, pulling them onto firm ground. They collapsed—both in tears. Alejandro came off the bridge, dropped to his knees and wrapped his arms around them.

***

They were well into the foothills as the sun shown overhead. They stopped to rest and eat under a clump of trees. The four men huddled, talking quietly. Gabriela strained to hear.

"We have to stay off the trail," Alejandro said.

"It's slowing us down," said one man.

"There are many snakes and scorpions," said another.

"We've been through all this before," Alejandro said. "The roads and towns are full of cartels. So far it's been Los Zetas, but soon we'll be in the Cartel del Golfo territory. We stay off the roads, and when we must go through a town we split up. Too many people attract unwanted attention."

"Tell us again, where do we find the *coyotes*?"

"We wait till we get closer to the border," Alejandro said. "It will be cheaper. The cartels are watching for coyotes and their *pollos* so they can make them pay every time they cross in or out of their territory."

Bang! Bang! Shots rang out—singles, followed by automatic fire.

The men scrambled back to the women and children. Alejandro half-grabbed, half-tackled Silvia and Gabriela pulling them into the dirt. Two explosions shook the ground. Another burst of automatic gun fire. Men yelled in the distance. Then quiet. Alejandro raised up, looked around. "Down!" he whispered loudly, diving to Silvia's side. Gabriela felt the earth vibrate. She held her breath. Desperately tried to hide her body deeper into the ground. She heard the sound of engines and breaking branches as vehicles ploughed through the shrubbery—two jeeps passed on one side of them and a quarter-ton troop carrier roared by on the other. Gabriela thought her lungs would burst.

The vibrations stopped. Alejandro got up cautiously and looked around. He turned to the group. "There's smoke over the rise. We must go before anyone else comes."

Gabriela could not make her body move. Silvia pulled her arm. Gabriela looked up, her face covered with dirt, lips caked in mud, and her mouth bone dry. "What was that?" she managed.

"Cartels," said Alejandro. "Killing each other. Fighting over turf. Two jeeps and a small truck almost hit us."

That night Gabriela wrote in her diary:

Today was a bad day. I have never been so afraid. What will tomorrow bring? Papi says we have many days before Matamoros. I don't know if I will ever see Tio Ricardo or Tia Leticia in Memphis.

***

Gabriela felt as if she'd been walking forever. Her clothes were sweat-stained, dirty, and needed mending. Her belt—the one her father had made for her to hide her papers and money—now the color of the dust they'd been walking through. She rubbed her bloodshot green eyes, then rubbed them again. She did not believe what she saw—a village, a *big* village.

"That's Metlaltoyuca," said Silvia, removing the dirt from Gabriela's face with a wetted part of her skirt. "Your father says we will catch a bus tomorrow."

"It's so big," Gabriela said. "I've never seen a village that big."

Silvia smiled. "Wait till you see Matamoros."

They camped near town. That night Gabriela wrote:

We are outside a huge village, one I cannot spell—Metla... Mama said we will ride an autobus tomorrow. I have never been on an autobus. It will be so exciting.

Alejandro went into Metlaltoyuca alone to learn where the bus would be and how much it would cost. He walked slowly, head down. He approached an elderly couple.

"One kilometer that way," the old man said, pointing. "The bus leaves in the morning to Tampico. There is always a line. You will need to get there early. Where are you going?"

"Matamoros."

"You will have to find a different bus in Tampico, one that will take you south to Altamira, Victoria, and on to Matamoros."

Alejandro returned to the campsite. He stayed awake through the night and roused the group before sunrise. "We must leave so we'll have time to get to the bus. Take out enough money now for the buses. We don't want anyone to find out we are carrying more."

***

The first bus was old, packed with too many people, even a few chickens. Men and teenage boys climbed atop the bus. Alejandro and two other men from their group rode there as well. Gabriela squeezed in next to another girl from Nuhab.

Gabriela watched the scenery change, but she was more excited about the villages, the cars and trucks. The closer they got to Matamoros the more paved roads and big trucks she saw. She almost forgot about Los Zetas, until jeeps and pickup trucks carrying men with guns whizzed by in the oncoming lane. Her body shivered. They did not wear military fatigues. Gabriela wondered if they were members of the Cartel del Golfo. Maybe there would be more shooting.

***

Their final bus joined the traffic queue as it approached Matamoros, and inched its way to the downtown station. Gabriela pressed her face against the window, looking at the traffic, the crowds of people, and the different styles of clothing. What had been exciting now felt overwhelming. Her mind returned to the bridge, and her hands vice-gripped the seat top in front of her. She did not want to leave the bus. The driver pulled in, made two sweeping turns, and parked. Gabriela heard the sound of the front and back doors squeak open. She closed her eyes, wanting to be invisible. Silvia held out her hand. "Come. We have to get off the bus."Gabriela opened her eyes, slowly reached out and took her hand. Silvia pulled her across the seat.

"You left your diary," Silvia said, pointing. Gabriela turned and scooped it up. They collected their belongings, followed the others down the steps, and joined their group, huddled outside the terminal building.

"This is as far as we go together," Alejandro said. "Now we separate as planned. Matamoros has become a huge city.

My family's going to the east side. Pick a different section of the city, or pick a different city—Reynosa, Columbia, Nuevo Laredo, or Rio Bravo. Find a coyote. They will know the area. They will know how to get us across the border. Some will hide us in cars or trucks, and will charge more for going farther into the States. Others will charge more to use a cartel's drug tunnel, and you'll have to walk. Others will take you across the Rio Grande. May God watch over us."

Chapter 2

Los Coyotes

Bus station, Matamoros, Mexico...The families began saying their goodbyes. Alejandro put one arm around Silvia, the other around Gabriela. "We've come a long way. You have been brave." He paused. "Now may be the most difficult part of our journey. We might get separated."

"No!" Gabriela said, hugging her parents, squeezing hard. She heard voices and turned to see men come across the parking area toward them, walking at first, then almost running. She pulled her father's shirt and pointed. Alejandro stepped forward. The other fathers did the same.

The men descended on the group, cutting off any escape, all speaking at once.

"You want to go to the United States? I'll take you."

"I've taken more folks to the states than any of these jerks."

"I've got the best prices."

"I'll take you anywhere you want to go in the states."

"How much money you got?"

"I'll get you food, a bath, clean clothes."

"I think the coyotes just found us," Alejandro said to no one in particular. "We must have *the look.*"

The talking lulled. "I know who I want," said Alejandro.

"Who?" they demanded.

"Dominic. I know his address."

The men backed away as a teenage boy walked up. "I'll take you to him. I'm Daniel, his grandson."

***

Alejandro sat in the front seat, Gabriela and Silvia in back. Gabriela perched on her knees, hands on the window, her face inches away. Daniel drove through the city, past small businesses and markets, then into neighborhoods. Homes became larger, grander. He turned into a driveway, pushed a button on his visor and an iron gate opened. He parked next to three other cars, and escorted the Delgado family inside.

Gabriela had never seen such a grand house—so large, so shiny, so many leather chairs, so many paintings. "I want to stay here forever," she said.

"I don't know about that, little girl," a man said, smiling. Everyone turned. "But maybe I can get you to a nice home in the United States."

Gabriela looked up. "You're tall. Taller than my Papi."

"Gabriela," said Silvia. "Mind your manners."

"That's quite all right," the man said. He extended his hand. "I'm Dominic."

"I'm Alejandro," he said shaking hands. He gestured. "My wife Silvia. And this little one is Gabriela."

"I'm ten," said Gabriela.

Dominic smiled, shook the girl's hand. "Such lovely green eyes." He turned back to Alejandro. "I believe we have business to discuss. But first, I am certain you would like to clean up. We have an assortment of clothes. I am confident we have your sizes." A woman walked up. "My daughter will show you."

After the family left, Dominic turned to Daniel. "Any problems?"

"No, sir."

***

Gabriela smiled broadly as she followed her parents into the dining room, where lunch awaited them. She couldn't believe her new clothes—a colorful pullover blouse and a long white skirt. Inside the dining room she saw Dominic at one end of the big dining table, Daniel on his left, and a man she had not seen sat across from Daniel.

"Come in, come in," said Dominic. "I must say you look like a whole new family. Please sit. Have something to eat." He gestured. "This is my son Martín."

Gabriela rushed to the table and ate as if she hadn't eaten in days. She barely noticed her parents. Alejandro and Silvia ate slowly, watched their host.

Dominic put down his glass. "Daniel told me you asked for me, Alejandro. How did you get my name?"

Alejandro cleared his throat. "Two years ago, you helped my brother Ricardo and his family get to Memphis, Tennessee. He's been sending money so we could join him. When we finally had enough, he said to find you."

Dominic sat back. "Ah, yes. Ricardo. I remember. Pardon my asking, but one has to be careful in my business. The government frowns on taking people away from Mexico. Well, at least they frown on it whenever the Yankees offer to build another manufacturing plant here."

"We are grateful to be in your care, patron," said Alejandro.

"Please. Call me Dominic. I, too, walked the mountain trails looking for a coyote to take me to the US. I worked for several years in Houston. Sent money back to my wife and family. It wasn't much, but it helped. Then I decided to come back and provide a service—a fair service—helping my countrymen across the border. Me and my family have made a good living and helped hundreds make the journey."

Alejandro squeezed Silvia's hand.

"There are many so-called coyotes clamoring for business," Dominic said. "You no doubt saw some at the bus station. As you've surmised, you looked like *chickens,* a coyote's favorite prey. I hope your friends chose the right coyote." He took a long drink, set his glass down. "You know, the American gangs are no different than our cartels. They are animals. They will kidnap women and children, and kill the men without hesitation. Be careful who you trust."

Alejandro winced, pushed his food around with his fork, looked up. "When do we go?"

"In a few days. We have found there are things we can do to make the journey more successful."

Alejandro started to ask, but remained silent.

"We will use the vehicle checkpoint instead of walking or swimming. In a few hours we will put you in our trunks. This will help you get used to being shut up in a tight place and being quiet." He turned. "Especially Gabriela."

Gabriela's eyes grew wide.

Dominic smiled. "Don't worry, little one, it will only be for an hour or so."

"How long will we be in the trunks when we make the crossing?" Alejandro asked.

"Every day, thousands of cars and trucks of all sizes line up to cross the border. It takes many hours to get through the check point on a good day, and another hour or so before we can find a safe place to open the trunk—usually in a park, just south of San Antonio. The good news for us is that it is impossible for the Americans to check every vehicle. So, we blend in and hope they pick different cars to check."

"Why not tell us when we will be leaving?"

Dominic shrugged. "The Americans rotate the days when they target their searches on more trucks, or more cars. The cartels have spies. They know the Americans' plans. If it's trucks, the cartels smuggle more money, drugs, and people in cars. And vice-versa. We have a spy in the cartel who tells us. Of course, we pay for this service."

"So we wait to hear that the Americans will check more trucks?

"Precisely. But we will have little notice. We must be ready to leave very early each morning."

***

Inside a closed trunk..."Mama," whined Gabriela. "I can't breathe, its smells bad, and the floor is hard."

"Breathe with me, sweetie," Silvia whispered. "Nice and slow." She waited for Gabriela to calm. That's better. Remember, we are hiding. We can't make any noise...for a long, long time. We don't want to be found."

"I don't like this game."

"It's not my favorite game either, but it will only be for one day."

"Is Papi being quiet too?"

"I'm sure he is. I haven't heard a thing, and his car is right beside ours."

"Mama. I have to pee."

***

Martín opened the trunk. Gabriela winced at the garage light. "My neck hurts," she said. "And my leg went to sleep."

"Come on," Silvia said as she climbed out, and helped Gabriela slide to the cement floor.

"It is very hard, no?" said Dominic.

"Si," Alejandro said. "But I'm glad you let us try it before we have to do it for real."

Chapter 3

It's Time

October 1, 2009, Matamoros, Mexico ...Martín knocked hard, then opened the bedroom door. "Wake up! Wake up! We leave now. Make a quick pee stop, grab your things. I'll meet you in the garage in five minutes."

Gabriela held her stomach and watched her parents grab their clothes. "No time," said Silvia. "Go pee. Get dressed. Hurry!"

The little family rushed to the garage. Alejandro hugged and kissed Gabriela, and then Silvia. "I will see you soon," he said. They climbed into their respective trunks and winced as the lids slammed shut. Martín drove Gabriela and Silvia. Dominic drove Alejandro.

***

Martín looked straight ahead and spoke loudly enough to be heard in the trunk. "We are in a long line of cars. It will be hours before we cross the plaza. Remember. No noise. They're checking vehicles with dogs. If they find you, do *not* run. The dogs are vicious. They will tear you to shreds."

Gabriela put her hand over her mouth to muffle her fear. Silvia lightly stroked her back.

"The border guards are pulling out a car in the front of our line. They must have found something." He inched the car ahead.

***

Two hours later. "Here come the dogs," Martín said. "Not a sound."

One dog issued a low, paralyzing growl interspersed with sharp, loud barks. Gabriela jerked. Silvia held her tightly.

"Open that trunk!" ordered an American border guard. The dog barked again, followed by deep-throated growls.

Gabriela visualized the dog, its teeth, even its drool. She wrapped her arms around her knees and tightened the ball she was in, her eyes shut tight. She heard the key go into the lock, the click, and the lid squeak open. She dared not open her eyes.

Silvia dropped her lips to Gabriela's ear. "It's not our car. Just stay quiet. It's not our car."

***

Martín held his credentials out the window. The guard waived him through without inspecting them. He sped up. Seconds later he yelled, "We're through. We're in the United States.

Chapter 4

Plan B

October 1, 2009, Houston, Texas, Traveler's Support Center... "What do you mean, you don't know what happened to them?" Silvia said, almost crying. Then her voice grew stronger, louder. "We left your house at the same time. You said the American border guards would not be checking cars, but they did. He has to be here. We will not leave without him."

Martín held his hands out. "Please, Señora, stay calm. I have tried to call my father on his American cell phone, but there is no answer. He was still in line when we passed through the checkpoint. Highway 37 to San Antonio was closed because of an accident. That's why I drove to Houston. It was our backup plan."

Gabriela cried and clung to her mother. "Where is Papi? I want my Papi."

"Why doesn't your father answer his phone?" Silvia said.

"Sometimes our American cell phones won't work in the plaza. He could still be there. Or...he could have been stopped by the border guards, taken into custody. They could have his phone."

"Into custody! What happens to Alejandro?"

"The Americans will hold him for a few days, then return him to Mexico. He'll be okay."

Silvia clenched her fists and looked to the sky. "This cannot be happening."

A woman approached them, spoke quietly to Martín. "Here's their itinerary and tickets." She looked around. "Tell them they have to change buses in Dallas, board the one with **MEMPHIS** on the destination sign. They must get off the bus when it stops in West Memphis, Arkansas. They will be met there. Their bus leaves in half an hour. You need to go now. Hurry."

***

Martín watched the Greyhound pull onto the street and turn at the light. His cell phone rang. He snatched it up. "Papi! Are you okay?"

"Yes, yes," Dominic said. "I am fine, just late. I have never seen so many trucks and cars pulled over at one time. I don't know what they were looking for, but they were very thorough. My line and one beside me were completely stopped for hours, almost every vehicle searched. I thought surely mine would be as well, but it was not. Mary, mother of God, thank you."

"I've been trying to call you."

"The border guards must have blocked all cell phones. I only got a signal after I cleared the final checkpoint."

"I could not get through on Highway 37, so I drove to Houston as we planned. I found our friend at the Support Center. She pulled the mother and daughter from the line, bought them bus tickets to Memphis, and arranged for them to be picked up in West Memphis."

"Have they already left?"

"Just pulled out when you called," Martín said.

"Did you remind them to be careful around American men?"

"Of course."

"I have been so worried about getting caught I haven't thought about the wife and little Gabriela...I think it best to follow the original plan for Alejandro. I'll take him to San Antonio and get him on a bus to Memphis. The family will be together soon."

***

*Dallas, Texas...*Gabriela wrote in her diary.

I am scared. Papi is not here. I don't know where he is. I think he is lost. Mama won't stop crying. She has papers for the autobus. Mama says we must take a different autobus in Dallas. But I don't think she knows how to do that without Papi.

***

*North Little Rock, Arkansas...*The Greyhound stopped at its terminal. "Everyone off," the driver yelled. "Stretch your legs. Get something to eat. We'll leave in two hours."

A rider asked a question.

"Men's is on the right, Women's to the left," the driver said in English.

"Did he say Memphis?" Gabriela asked in Spanish.

"Sounded like Memphis," Sylvia said.

They followed the passengers into the terminal, looking lost. Strangers in a foreign land, strangers who didn't speak the language. A woman came up to them. "Ustedes necesitas ayuda?" she said, smiling.

"Oh, sí. We do need help," Silvia answered in Spanish. "Are we in Memphis?"

The woman smiled more broadly. "Not yet," she continued in Spanish. "You are in a city called North Little Rock. Memphis will be another three hours on the bus. Are you hungry?"

Gabriel opened her eyes wide, nodded her head.

"Come on. I'll show you."

Chapter 5

Sheep's Clothing

October 1, 2009, *North Little Rock bus terminal*...They sat at a table, eating sandwiches. "Do we need to get back on the bus?" asked Silvia.

"Soon," the woman said.

"I have to pee," said Gabriela.

The woman stood. "I'll take her."

Silvia shook her head.

The woman put her hand lightly on Silvia's shoulder and smiled. "Really. It's no problem. Finish your food. We'll be right back."

Gabriela looked at her mother. Silvia relaxed, nodded. Gabriela took the woman's hand, and the two walked to the restroom. Silvia watched them until they turned the corner.

Gabriela pushed through the restroom door and stopped. Water leaking from the sink pooled, just two steps ahead. A mop stood in a dented bucket on wheels, abandoned in the far corner. She looked for a dry path, ended up tiptoeing through the water. The stall door, hanging by a single hinge, stuck against the frame. She put her finger in the hole where the lock mechanism used to be, then lifted and pushed the door open. Gabriela hesitated, but she had to go really bad...

The woman held a small bottle of hand sanitizer. "Watch

me," she said, demonstrating. She squirted some onto Gabriela's hands. While Gabriela rubbed her hands together, the woman took out her cell phone and texted: *side door now.*

"I want to buy you and your mother some candy for your trip to Memphis," the woman said, taking Gabriela's hand. "Would you like that?"

Gabriela smiled. "Oh, sí."

"Come this way."

Gabriela had not seen this section of the terminal. No drink machines. No tables or chairs. An old man sat on the floor, back to the wall, feet in the aisle, an empty coffee cup in his hand. They turned down a hallway. She felt the woman's grip tighten. She looked up. The woman leaned forward, walked faster, pulling her along. Gabriela sensed danger. "Where's my Mama?" she yelled.

Silvia sat at the table watching the corner where she'd last seen Gabriela, her unfinished sandwich sitting in its wrapper. At the sound of Gabriela's voice, Silvia jumped up and ran through the terminal, calling her name.

The woman looked ahead to the door, hit the panic bar hard, and pulled Gabriela into the night. A black Chevy Impala waited at the curb. Gabriela heard her mother calling. She looked back at the closing door, "Mama!" The woman bent down, wrapped an arm around Gabriela's waist and snatched her up. She yanked open the back door, threw Gabriela inside, followed, slammed the door behind her. The car sped away.

Gabriela punched and kicked her kidnapper. "Let me go. I want my Mama!" She pulled on the door lever, but the security lock was on. The woman grabbed her, pulled her back and slapped her face. Gabriela fell against the seatback, hands pressed against her cheek, crying. She smelled a strong odor and opened her eyes as a cloth was jammed over her mouth and nose. Gabriela struggled. Then…nothing.

***

*Greyhound terminal, West Memphis, Arkansas…*A priest stood at the door, rosary beads hung from his left hand. He watched the passengers offload from the bus, just arrived from Forrest City. He made brief eye contact with a few people and nodded, but no one approached him. After the last rider had passed by, he walked to the bus door. "Excuse me. Are there any passengers still onboard?"

The bus driver looked up. "Everyone's left, Father. You looking for somebody in particular?"

"Yes. A mother and child, maybe ten years-old. But none of the people who just got off the bus."

"I remember a mother and child like that who got off in North Little Rock. Didn't get back on. Maybe missed their boarding call."

PART II

Chapter 6

Lotus and Parsley

Saturday night, Memphis, Tennessee, October 3, 2009...The storm triggered a long forgotten dream.

"No, Mommy! No." Smack! Smack! Smack! Julia's body shuddered with each blow, stiffened when little Wayne screamed. ...The blows stopped. ...She'd be next. She pulled the covers over her head, curled into a ball, waited. Her mother's footsteps got louder, closer. Her bedroom door opened.

Julia Todd jerked awake, heart pounding. She winced when a boom of thunder rattled the house. Sheets of rain assaulted her windows in waves. Lightning flashes lit her room. She buried her face in her hands. "God. I thought I was over all that," she mumbled. She swung her legs over the side of the bed and sat, watching the lightning's flickering patterns of light and shadow. Julia walked to the kitchen, nursed a glass of water. Her father had deserted her and her brother, left them with their abusive mother. It was a long time before she returned to bed.

***

Sunday morning...A sleepy Julia roused. She squinted, trying to focus, listened to the rain—steady but no longer torrential, no lightning, no thunder. She considered going for a morning run to wake up, but opted instead for yoga and meditation.

***

Ninety minutes later, Julia plopped in her oversized beanbag chair, pulled up her holey Dallas Cowboys short-sleeve sweatshirt, dried her face. Her yoga workout had been intense—her range of motion stretched, old injuries soothed, tensions gone. She sipped a glass of water and listened to the rain. Its rhythmic sound on the picture window relaxed her.

The phone rang. Her body jerked, water spilled down her front. "This can't be good," she mumbled to herself. She brushed at her sweatshirt, rolled off the beanbag and pushed up from the floor.

"Hello?"

"Oh, Julia, I hope I'm not bothering you."

Julia recognized the voice—her next door neighbor. "No bother, Mrs. Woozley."

"It's Parsley. The little guy ran off again."

"You want me to look for him? In the rain?"

"Oh, would you please? I just can't get around with my cane."

Julia rolled her eyes. "You see which way he went?"

"He went around the fence, up your driveway."

"And since it's raining, you think he's hiding under my car? Like before?"

"Well…yes."

***

Julia pushed open the back door and squatted, wind-blown spray covering her face. When the puppy heard the door open he moved to the near underside of the Mini Cooper, still sheltered. "Come on, Parsley. Come to me,"

Julia coaxed. Parsley hesitated. Then he burst out, his little legs a blur. He scampered through the rain, leapt over the threshold into Julia's outstretched arms, and squirmed to lick her face. She stood, held the wriggling wet puppy at arms' length. "What am I going to do with you?" She brought him back into her chest. He snuggled into her. "How can I be mad at my lucky charm? Let's go find your mommy." She tucked Parsley under one arm, grabbed an umbrella, and headed next door.

Mrs. Woozley waited, towel in hand. She opened the storm door as Julia climbed the porch steps. "Bad dog," Mrs. Woozley said as she wrapped the towel around him, dried each little paw, and put him down. Parsley zoomed to the food dish, toe nails ticking on the wood floor. Mrs. Woozley turned back to Julia, smiled. "Thanks so much, dear. Come in, come in. You can leave your umbrella outside." Then she noticed. "Oh, my. Parsley got you all wet."

Julia made a face. "What? This old sweatshirt? Nothing it hasn't seen in its storied lifetime."

"Please, sit down. I just fixed a pot of tea. You will have some, won't you?"

Julia hesitated, then sensed her neighbor needed to talk. "Sure."

Mrs. Woozley came back with a tray. "Do you take anything in your tea, dear?"

"Just tea, please."

Mrs. Woozley passed a cup to Julia. "My mind's been elsewhere. That's how Parsley escaped." She poured herself a cup, added two sugar cubes, and stirred.

Julia sipped her tea, waited.

Mrs. Woozley left her cup on the saucer, stared into it. "It's my sister's granddaughter, Ollie." She looked up. "She's missing."

"Missing?"

Mrs. Woozley clutched at her chest. "Rode her bike to the little corner grocery after school Friday. They found the bike in a ditch, outside of town. The sheriff organized a search party. Most of the town showed up. But they haven't found her."

"How old is Ollie?"

"Nine." Her eyes watered.

Julia reached a box of tissues, handed it to her. "Where do they live?"

Mrs. Woozley dabbed her eyes. "Savannah. Here in Tennessee. Where I grew up."

"Did they issue an Amber Alert?"

Mrs. Woozley nodded. "The sheriff questioned my sister's son and his wife, as if they did something to their own child." She picked up her cup. Blew into it, set it down. "When he finally believed them, he said there wasn't much hope if they didn't find Ollie within the first or second day." She set her cup down, tea untouched. "You're a police officer…Are they right? Is that true?"

"The sooner they find her, the better. Each day she's gone makes it more difficult." Julia sipped her tea. She didn't say what she was thinking: *Less likely to find her alive.* "Is the TBI involved?"

"The *T* what?"

"The Tennessee Bureau of Investigation. You know, the state's version of the FBI? They have more resources than the small towns and are particularly good at finding missing children."

Mrs. Woozley shrugged. "I haven't heard anything about that. The sheriff talked about *peedophiles.*" She dabbed her eyes. "That can't be true, can it? She's only nine, for God's sakes."

***

Sunday night. Another dream:

I lean hard left, my squad car squeals around the corner, flashers on and siren blaring, hands gripping the steering wheel, heart pounding in my ears, eyes wide. I slam on the brakes, throw the door open and hit the ground running into the woods. I part two saplings and find the body of a young girl lying on her stomach. I roll her over, then jump back. Julia's hairs stood on end. The face of the dead child is mine—at age eight. I run from 'my' body and search frantically for Wayne, squeezing myself through the dense woods.

Julia snapped awake, wet with sweat, fists clenched, heart racing. She could not stop the tears, the sense of loss and despair. Julia and Wayne Todd had been *throwaway children,* discarded by their parents—a mother who beat them, and a father who, instead of protecting them, walked out of their lives. No rational thoughts calmed her, even the knowledge that Arizona Protective Services had removed her and Wayne to the loving custody of their Aunt Louise in Memphis. A new emotion grew inside her, overwhelming the others—anger. Sleep came only in fits and starts.

Chapter 7

Disposable

*Monday, October 5, 2009...*Julia awoke before the alarm. *A good hard run and workout will burn off these negative juices,* she thought as she laced up her running shoes. Julia needed to regain control, to shake the anger. She ran her usual 4.7-miles, winding through the midtown neighborhood and stopping at the InsideOut Gym. She slid her ID under the card reader, saw her picture pop up. Today's gym workout began with twenty minutes of free weights. Then she assaulted the heavy bag—kicks, punches and combinations echoed off the walls of the back room.

"Somebody got up on the wrong side of the bed this morning," said a small woman in powder blue sweats, holding a towel and a bottle of water.

"Oh, hey, Girty," said Julia. "Sorry. Didn't mean to get so involved."

Girty handed her the towel and water. "Better you hit the bag than me."

Julia smiled, plopped on the nearest bench, and chugged half the bottle. She caught her breath, blotted the sweat from her face. "You have bad days?"

"Of course, but I don't knock myself out punching this big old bag. I just watch you instead." She clenched her fists and threw a few shadow punches.

"Glad I can help." Julia finished the water, said goodbye, and jogged the 2.4-mile direct route home.

Julia peeled off her sweaty clothes, stepped into the shower, and lathered up. She envisioned the vestiges of anger as soap bubbles, and watched them wash away in the rinse water. Julia turned off the water and stood, feeling her body bounce back from the workout, and her self-control return.

She toweled off, shook her short hair into place doggy style, finished with a few finger combs. She dressed and headed for Otherlands coffee bar in midtown for her pre-work ritual—coffee, a Cup of Gold nutrition bar, and a leisurely read of *The Commercial Appeal* newspaper. Then she drove the three-quarters of a mile to the Union Station precinct to begin her workday.

"Morning, Lieutenant," said secretary Teresa Johnson.

"Hey, Teresa. What's the latest buzz on the clerical circuit?"

"Organized Crime Unit requested help from the Sex Trafficking Task Force."

"From the National Center on Missing and Exploited Children?"

"I think that's the place. The talk is the new major—"

"The *former* Lieutenant Ray Ayers," interrupted Julia.

"Yes, that one…Anyway, the talk is Major Ayers is making state and national connections that the old major refused to make. And now that the old major and his kin are behind bars for trying to get you and your family killed…" Teresa stopped and looked at Julia as if worried she may have said too much.

Julia finished her sentence: "…the new major will get the MPD back in the loop."

"Exactly."

Julia turned and walked to her office. Her fingers found the scar on her side, the result of having been shot by a Mexican cartel hitman almost two months ago, courtesy of a set-up by the old major.

***

Julia settled in, reached for the stack of folders on her desk. The phone rang. "The new major's ears must've been burning," Teresa said. "He's on line one." Julia punched the flashing button.

"Morning, Ray. We were just talking about you. That's what happens when you get promoted. By the way, I couldn't be happier. They made a good choice."

"Thanks, Julia. You and your team had a lot to do with my being promoted. Actually, that's why I'm calling. You interested in working together again?"

"Whatcha have in mind?"

"Okay, so we know how important the Memphis transportation system is to smuggling drugs, cash and weapons, right?"

"Yeah, a major distribution route for the Conrios Mexican cartel. God knows who else."

"Right. A boatload of organized crime groups—local and international, big and small. Maybe we put a kink in the cartel's east coast pipeline, but other pipelines are still flowing. Just had a briefing from the Sex Trafficking Task Force about kids being abducted. Gangs across the country are major players. The task force said we're gonna be up to our necks in sex trafficking."

"Sex trafficking," Julia sat straighter. "If that's what this is about, then hell yes!" she said. "Count us in."

"Great. Already touched base with your boss, Major Williams, and his counterpart in the Sheriff's department because I expect this will be a countywide issue." He paused.

"Yesterday, practically in your backyard—across East Parkway from Christian Brothers University, near the railroad tracks—one of my officers was jogging when her dog discovered the body of a young girl, a pre-teen. She called me."

Julia's hand went to her stomach. "I read a blurb in this morning's paper. But for some reason, I thought she was a teenager. So, how old?"

"Doc's guessing nine or ten."

"From Memphis?"

"Probably not. Doesn't match anyone on the missing persons lists—regional or national. You have someone in mind?"

"A neighbor's family member is missing. A nine-year-old from Savannah, Tennessee." Julia exhaled loudly. "She'd have been listed as a missing person."

"This kid could be a new immigrant. Sometimes kids get through the process without being finger printed. Or an illegal, part of a cartel sex trafficking haul, or by a lone coyote. Hell, could be her parents have never reported her missing because they're the ones who killed her. The ME and the lab have been working the case. Doc says the girl died due to complications from chloroform."

"Chloroform? So, she was kidnapped."

"Looks that way. Doc says no sexual assault."

"You thinking she died during the abduction?"

"That's my guess, and I don't think this perp's a gang member. May even be new at this."

Julia paused. "Cause he didn't know how to use chloroform?"

"That, and from what we've seen, gangs do a better job of disposing their bodies."

"Maybe the perp's in this for himself, or he hoped to sell her to a gang that traffics in kids."

"Good thinking," he said. "We'll work the gangs. Y'all

work the homicide. We'll keep in touch. The folder and ME report will be on your desk within the hour."

"How's OCU involved?" Julia asked.

"Tennessee has seen a spike in kidnappings, especially young girls. Like drug smuggling, sex trafficking is a *huge* business worldwide—mostly handled by well-organized criminal groups. The numbers are staggering. More victims are being moved in *and* out of the US, including Tennessee, with an emphasis on younger children—boys as well as girls."

"There're a lot of sick people in the world. Sick people with money."

"You'd think this increase in kidnappings would lead to greater numbers of prostitutes, strippers and addicts. But we don't see it."

"So somebody's killing a whole lot of them."

"These creeps treat people, especially females, like objects," Ayers said. "Disposable objects. Use 'em up. Throw 'em away. Get new ones."

Julia winced.

***

The two members of Julia's homicide team appeared at her door—sergeants Anthony "Professor" Marino and Johnnie "Tag" Tagger. The former white, six foot tall and a little round. The latter black, six foot-four, and well built.

"Hey, guys," said Julia.

The men took seats in front of Julia's desk. "Teresa told us you'd probably want to see us," Tagger said. "You know. One of her *intuitions*. So what's up?"

Julia rolled her eyes. "We've got a new case...probably gonna be *cases*. A young girl, found yesterday in midtown. On Harbert, just east of the athletic field, where it takes that sharp turn down to the Parkway."

"Street's barely two full lanes at that point," said Tagger. "Area's overgrown with trees and weeds on the south side, but it's pretty shallow. Not a great place to hide a body long term."

"This the case OCU's working?" asked Marino. "Runaway?"

Julia nodded. "That's the one. Except they think she was kidnapped. And she might be the tip of an ugly iceberg. Major Ayers says the number of child abductions has gone up statewide. He's wanting to coordinate. Thinks the perp who did this is a freelancer—selling the kids to the highest bidder. We'll work the case as a homicide, while OCU works the gangs who are running the sex trafficking. Maybe we'll find a link, meet in the middle. Major Williams okayed our involvement. He cleared it with the Sherriff's Department in case leads take us into the county. You up on sex trafficking, Professor?"

Marino sat back, eyes floated up and to the left. "Let's see…it's big business internationally. What I've read, one classic business marketing strategy says, 'find out what people want, make it easy for them to get it'. Another is to create a need—make people believe they want what you got to sell. Big organized gangs, like the Mexican Conrios cartel, have turned these strategies into a science and have Fortune 500-level revenues to prove it."

"You're talking about niche marketing for sickos," Julia said.

Marino shrugged. "Sexual appetites of men may not be growing," he said, "but sexual mores in the US have become less prohibitive. Just look at the explosion in internet porn, the increasing sexualization of women on TV and in movies, and let's not forget the ubiquitous commercials for erectile dysfunction drugs—all encouraging men to satisfy their sexual appetites, normal and perverted."

Tagger shook his head. "I'm having déjà vu—Ann Arbor, Social Psych class. When do you have time to do all this reading, Tony?"

"When you like to read, you find the time."

"That's why they call him the *professor,*" Julia said. She opened a folder. "Okay, back to this little girl. No ID. Nine, maybe ten. Black hair, brown eyes, light brown skin. No match on fingerprints or with missing persons. No needle marks and no sexual molestation. Had a parasite in her liver—typical of south Texas and Mexico. Had a rosary in her pocket with *Iglesia de Santa Maria* inscribed. I checked. St Mary's Catholic Church downtown doesn't give out any rosaries inscribed with that. I even checked St Mary's Episcopal in the medical center. But they don't give out rosaries, period. Closest thing they have are Anglican prayer beads."

"So, possible illegal immigrant?" Tagger said.

Julia shrugged. "If so, the part about no needle tracks and no molestation makes me think she came across the border willingly." Julia read from the file—jeans, new Reebok tennis shoes, long sleeve shirt with a San Antonio Spurs logo. Our Jane Doe got in a few licks. Doc found flesh under her nails. Lab's working on the perp's DNA. Found at six-forty Sunday morning by an off-duty OCU officer."

Marino took notes. "Jane's TOD?"

"Doc says between seven and ten Saturday night, in that rain storm."

"Cause of death?"

"Ready for this?" Julia said. "Chloroform poisoning."

"Huh?" Tagger said. "They still use chloroform to knock folks out? Thought it was used to make plastic. And where do you even get it?"

"You're right about the plastic, Johnnie," Marino said. "The stuff's not good for you. But, you can get it where you get anything these days—online."

"And what about chloroform poisoning? She drink the stuff?"

Julia flipped through the ME's report. "Looks like the perp just used too much chloroform, possibly held it on Jane's face too long. Led to cardiac arrest."

"Jesus, Mary, and Joseph," Marino said.

"How long was Jane in the woods?" asked Tagger.

"According to the insects, condition of the body, ME says she was dumped there nine to eleven hours before the dog found her."

Tagger counted on his fingers. "That would mean he dumped her right after she died. Good chance she was abducted in this general area. Anything from the neighbors?"

Julia shook her head. "Not so far. No clear tire tracks. Pretty gravelly just off the street. But the perp must have parked long enough to carry Jane into the woods. Maybe our best hope is to find a driver who squeezed past the perp's car on that narrow turn."

"So...what?" Marino asked. "Creep grabs Jane. Lays on way too much chloroform. Jane has a heart attack and dies. Creep freaks out, drives to *this* spot, parks in the narrow street, carries her into the woods, dumps her, and leaves without being seen?"

"You thinking he's not a pro, just dumb and lucky?" asked Tagger.

Moreno shrugged. "Maybe. But that's not much of a through street. Not a place you'd even stumble upon. You have to want to be there. So I'm betting he's been there before, knows that section of Harbert."

"Good points. We also need information on how legal and illegal aliens come into Memphis. If Jane is the tip of the iceberg, there's another ninety percent below the surface."

***

Music came from Julia's phone and Dr. Mark Sanders's picture smiled at her from the screen. She swiped the icon. "Hey, Babe. Been waiting for your call. How's everything going?"

"The weather was horrible. Good thing the pilot told us to stay buckled up. We bounced around like a rollercoaster ride at one of those Christian fun parks—mega thrills and lots of praying. When we finally touched down everyone broke into applause."

"Glad you made it. We had a frog-strangler here as well. So, how's the workshop?"

"It's been okay. Maybe more for administrators than for us psychologists. But several interesting topics are scheduled. Geriatrics is a major industry down here because Scottsdale has so many retirees."

"Bet another major industry is ripping-off the seniors," Julia said.

"You got that right. A bunch of companies are offering services to protect the seniors. Many by phone."

"I can hear the ad now: Our staff of highly trained professionals is here to help, 24/7. You fall and can't get up, call us. You get a suspicious email, call us. Where else can you get peace of mind for weekly payments of only $19.95."

"You've been watching infomercials again?" Mark said.

"Done your consulting yet? It'd be great if somebody adopted the family support model you developed here at the Haven for Seniors."

"Actually, looks like mental health *is* the latest marketing draw. The community bulletin board posts several positions for psychologists and social workers."

"Don't let them talk you into taking a job. I need you back here."

"You say that as if something happened," Mark said.

"Not really. …Just a few bad dreams."

"Bad dreams? About the shooting again?"

"No, no. Haven't had those for a while. This one's about my mother."

"You mean the beatings?"

"Yeah," she said quietly.

"Any idea what triggered them?"

"Could be a number of things." She paused.

"Wanna talk about them?"

"They're so stupid."

"Triggers often are. Sounds like a couple ganged up on you."

"Don't get upset," she said.

"One of the triggers is me?"

"Well, kind of. Your being in Arizona. Saturday night's storm triggered memories of a storm like when I was a kid…a really bad night. I felt like I was back there. It was so real."

"I'm sorry you're going through this."

"There's more. Kidnapped ten year-old girls—one is Mrs. Woozley's great niece, the other found dead here in mid-town."

"Damn, Julia. Girls victimized at the same age you were. This must feel really personal. So, how're you holding up?"

Julia sighed. "I'm still standing, but I'm having a hard time controlling my anger. I can feel it rising in my throat."

"Relaxation not working?"

"Haven't been able to do it. Can't clear my head enough. It's almost like I *want* to be mad. That make sense?"

"Sure. You've kept your anger under wraps all these years. You've learned how to harness that anger, use it in positive ways—especially in physical altercations, and providing extra motivation to find the bad guys. Remember, your Aunt Louise used to call you her 'little guardian' because, even as a kid, you stuck up for other kids when they were picked on."

"Good to hear I'm not going crazy."

"No need to rush it. Be aware for times when your anger calms, when you have the energy to clear your mind. Then focus, just the way you used relaxation and imagery to overcome your PTSD from being shot. It'll come."

***

Northeast Shelby County...The only light came from a battery-powered lantern. A man unlatched the trailer's rear gate, grabbed a long roll of black plastic and pulled. Half-carrying, half-dragging, he dropped it beside a trench. He held one side of the plastic in both hands and, with one foot, shoved the remainder over the edge. The black plastic crackled as it quickly unrolled. The body of a young girl dropped into the trench with a thud—face up, green eyes unseeing.

Chapter 8

Going 'Round the Bend

Monday...Tagger and Marino left Union Station and made the short drive to Harbert Avenue, headed east.

"Ever run into Sam Merrill?" Marino asked. "Homicide cop back in the day?"

Tagger shook his head. "Name doesn't ring a bell."

"Just died last Friday. Took me under his wing my rookie year. Good cop. Super investigator. Had a real sixth sense. Hadn't seen him in a few years. Then I ran into him over the weekend at a retirement party."

"I feel a story coming."

"Yeah. I'm still trying to wrap my head around it. Sammy had a few. Said he just solved a forty year-old murder case that he didn't even know was a murder."

Tagger cocked his head. "Okay..."

"Back in the sixties, a black family had moved into a white neighborhood. There was a house fire. Their nine year-old daughter died in the fire along with the next door neighbor, a white adult male. Fire Marshal suspected arson. Sammy worked the case but never found anything. They concluded the neighbor was trying to save the little girl."

"White neighbor saving a black child in the sixties in Memphis? That's a story in itself."

Marino nodded. "It gets more...interesting. Sammy says

a young woman, twenty-something, showed up at his house wanting to talk to him about that same fire. Told him a ghost was haunting the next door neighbor's house, scaring the current residents—a mother and her nine year-old daughter. Said she believed it was the ghost of the man who died in the fire with the little girl all those years ago. Said ghosts hang around when there's unfinished business. Said the ghost wouldn't leave until folks knew what had been keeping him there for forty years. She thought it must have something to do with the house fire."

Tagger raised his eyebrows. "Sounds like Sammy's gone off the deep end."

"Yeah, that's what I was thinking. Tried to leave, but he grabbed my arm, got in real close. Said he wasn't crazy. Begged me to hear him out. So I stayed."

"It get weirder?"

"Yes and no. Says the woman didn't come on like a nutcase. Says he believed her. And since it was a case he never felt good about, he was interested. Punch line is, he agreed to help her. They found the neighbor man's wife in a retirement home. Over tea and cookies she confessed to killing her husband forty years ago and starting the fire to cover it up."

"Holy—"

"Wait for it…Sammy and the woman go to the current neighbor's house, and the homeowner claims the man's ghost is gone."

"Oooo-weee-oooo," Tagger sing-songed.

Marino nodded. "You know, the department works with a few psychics on missing persons cases. Kinda like a mystical bloodhound. One or two have actually been helpful."

"So I've heard. Probably just random luck—given all the psychic visions, one or two have to be correct totally by chance. Or, you thinking maybe there're some psychics who have a legitimate *gift*?"

"Not really so strange when you consider the lieutenant's *spidey sense*. Heck, not that different from...didn't your high school football coach say you were able to guess which way the other team was going to run their plays? And then there's that connection you and the lieutenant seem to have when one of you are in trouble."

"Yeah, but—"

"No buts about it. I think you two are not so different from these psychics. Only y'all just call it a *feeling*."

Tagger shook his head. "I'm getting a *bad feeling* about this conversation."

"I'm just saying..."

They pulled up to the stop sign at South Cox Street. Marino looked up. "Looks like we're leaving the city. No sidewalks. Harbert gets so narrow I'm not sure two cars can fit side-by-side, unless one of 'em's the lieutenant's Mini-Cooper."

Tagger drove slowly. "Check out the sports field coming up on the right. Snowden Field. Belongs to Grace St. Luke's Episcopal. The school and church both use it. Railroad tracks run right behind it and angle up to the street just as Harbert makes a ninety-degree left turn."

"How come you know all this?"

"Dated a girl from that church. I think she was after my body—just wanted me on their softball team."

"Bet you could send the ball over those bleachers."

"Maybe. But I said no. Two days later she traded me in for a shortstop—the major league owners would be impressed with her ability to recruit players. Never felt the same about Episcopalians after that."

Marino smiled. "Nobody's using the field today. Can't

imagine anybody was playing in that storm Saturday night. Just in case, think you can get over your Episcopalian *issues* long enough to find out?"

"I'll do it. But I can't promise I'll like it." Tagger pointed over the steering wheel. "Only two duplexes east of the field, before things get overgrown, and the street narrows even more."

"Apartments on the north side of the street. Doesn't look like there's a clear visual of the street or the woods over that big wall or through those trees."

Tagger stopped fifty-feet short of the yellow crime scene tape, his right tires only inches off the street, enough room for Marino to get out. Marino began an inspection of the street and the narrow strip of gravel bordering the wooded area.

Tagger smiled. "Watch out for poison oak, Tony. Maybe even a snake or two."

Marino hesitated. "Getting too old for this shit," he said to himself, keeping his hands close to his body.

Tagger studied the apartments across the street, behind a six-foot cinderblock privacy wall and a stand of large trees. He bent forward, hands on his knees, till his head was even with the top of his car. "When the wind blows I can see one or two of the upstairs apartment windows. Otherwise, I can't see through the trees."

"The ground slopes up from the street," Marino said, standing near the far edge of the woods, railroad tracks at his back. "Try that at the site where the dog found Jane."

Tagger tromped through the undergrowth, met Marino at the crime tape, about sixty-feet from the street. Marino squatted, studying the area. "Don't you worry, darlin', we're gonna find the SOB who did this."

"Now you're sounding like Sam what's-his-name,"

Tagger said.

"Merrill. Sam Merrill...Really. I think we all bond with our innocent victims, especially kids."

"Okay, I'll buy that. But, Tony...if you start hearing voices, I don't want to know." He looked back across the street at the apartments. "Depending on the tree limbs, there could be a line of sight. But then, it was dark. Have to come back at night and check out the effect of that street light over there."

***

Marino climbed back in the car. Tagger walked in front of the cruiser, but froze as a car zipped around the blind curve. Tires squealed when the driver stomped on his brakes, the nose of the car dipped, stopping only feet from him. Tagger glared, pointed at the man, arm extended. The driver shrunk in his seat, hands frozen to the wheel. Tagger watched him squirm, then waved him on. The driver inched by the cruiser, rolled down his window and said meekly, "Sorry."

Tagger watched the car pick up speed past the sports field, then slid into the driver's seat. "That car just came out of nowhere. Barely able to drive by. Maybe someone saw a car parked here Saturday night."

Marino nodded. "No way any driver could have missed seeing a vehicle parked on this curve. Wonder what the traffic's like on the weekend, especially Saturday night."

Tagger followed the street as it turned and descended. Marino glanced out his side window, down the steep hill at East Parkway Boulevard. On the left, the cruiser passed a small parking area, then a driveway to the apartments. Two large homes appeared, far behind tall cinderblock walls. Their driveways sloped down through iron security gates to Harbert which quickly intersected East Parkway's southbound lanes.

"OCU did a canvass of the apartments and these homes Sunday morning," Marino said. "Got zilch. What if we set up a roadblock Saturday night? Could get lucky, find a driver who remembers seeing a car on Harbert."

Tagger nodded. "Especially a parked car."

Chapter 9

Illegal Aliens

*Monday, Saint Michael Catholic Church...*Julia left midtown, drove east on Summer Avenue. Five minutes later she rang the side porch doorbell. A buzzer sounded, followed by a click. She stepped through the door and approached a woman seated behind a wooden desk—hair medium length, almost black, an office telephone to her ear. Julia thought her youthful face contrasted with hard and wary eyes. Her name plate read, ALEXA TORRES. She motioned to a chair.

Julia sat, read a hand lettered sign: FOR THE DRINK MACHINE leaning against a small glass bowl filled with quarters. A larger silver coin stuck up part way. She could make out the letters ELCOM along the edge. *ELCOM? ... elcom? ... Welcome! Like the Alcoholics Anonymous buttons.*

Alexa finished her telephone call. "You must be the officer who wanted to see Father K." She glanced down at the white light. "He's on the phone."

Julia nodded. "I'm Lieutenant Todd." She gestured. "You get lots of takers on the drink money?"

Alexa appeared puzzled, then brightened. "Oh. The quarters. Yeah. Almost all the kids want a soda. But I think it's more about putting the quarters in the machine, hearing the cans fall, and digging them out. Father K gets a kick out of it. He takes all the quarters out of the machine and dumps them back in the bowl."

Julia smiled. "I understand y'all have mass in Spanish."

Alexa nodded. "Father K's mother is Mexican. He's fluent in Spanish. More and more Hispanics come to church every Sunday. Everyone loves him."

"You been here long?"

Alexa's body tensed, her face went blank, eyes somewhere else. After a pause, she managed, "Not long." The phone's light went out. Alexa snatched up the receiver and buzzed him. "A police officer is here to see you, Father." She hung up. "He'll be right out," she said, then swiveled her chair, pulled a file folder.

A door opened. "Lieutenant? I'm Father Jacob Kaszewski. Please come in." He smiled, gestured. "Choose whichever plastic chair you think will be the most comfortable." He sat behind his desk.

Julia took a seat directly across from him. "Your secretary said nice things about you."

"I can say the same about her," he said.

"Funny, I couldn't tell how old she is. I'm guessing she's had a tough life. Younger than she appears."

"Right you are, Lieutenant." He paused, lowered his voice. "I've heard her speak to groups of young girls out at Youth Villages. I'm sure she wouldn't mind me sharing that information with you. Alexa has a tragic history—molested by her stepfather, ran away in her early teens, grabbed by some pimp in Little Rock and forced into prostitution. She ran away and was living on the Memphis streets when my predecessor found her. Protective Services placed her in a Youth Villages treatment program for drug addiction and counseling. She did well. A bright girl, earned a GED. The priest maintained contact, offered Alexa a part-time job assisting our school custodian. The principal took her under her wing, and the school secretary taught her clerical skills. I hired her when my secretary retired. She's just nineteen. A real success story."

"A success story, indeed, Father."

The priest smiled. "I understand you want to know more about our Spanish speaking parishioners. Anything in particular?"

"Not speaking Spanish, I'm in unfamiliar waters. I'm hoping you can help. I'm with Homicide."

"Homicide?"

Julia pulled out a photograph of little Jane Doe and handed it across the desk.

The priest's smile disappeared—first from his eyes, then his mouth. "Mother of God," he said, crossing himself. "This child is dead."

Julia nodded. "Her body was found Sunday morning in midtown. We don't know who she is. There's nothing about her that matches any missing persons list we have. There are a few things that make us think she could be from Mexico or Central America. Any chance you recognize her, or you know of a family who's missing a daughter?"

He shook his head and handed the photo back to Julia.

"We're wondering if she could be a new immigrant, someone whose paperwork hasn't caught up with her. Or maybe an illegal."

Father K's eyes narrowed. "We don't use that term. *Illegal* applies to a crime, to a criminal. Certainly, this child is not guilty of any crime."

"What term would you use?"

"How about we begin with *undocumented.* They certainly weren't illegal in the mid-1800s when American business leaders and the federal government encouraged Mexicans to cross the border and work in the United States. But all of a sudden they are illegal, because the Hispanic population in the United States has swelled. Too many whites feel threatened. And there's a growing paranoia since 9-11 that terrorists are crossing our borders, so naturally all outsiders have been painted with the same non-white fear brush."

Julia nodded. "Okay. I get it. *Undocumented*, it is." She held up the photo. "I want to find the person who killed this little girl. And we're afraid she's not the only one. Chances are she was undocumented. I need some direction, Father. Help me help her and others like her."

Father K took a deep breath, exhaled loudly. "As you probably know, this part of town has seen a major influx in Hispanics. So many of our Spanish speaking parishioners live in fear, even those with green cards and legitimate visas. They don't want to be deported. And children born in this country don't want their undocumented parents to be sent back. For many it would be a death sentence."

Julia glanced at the picture, considered the irony, but said nothing.

"We can't imagine the hardships these people have endured to get here, the pure hell they went through." His fingers tightened into fists. "Mexican cartels alone have been killing five thousand people a year. Their blood money corrupts politicians and police." He shook his head, opened his fists. "The people trust no one. They have an intense fear of anyone in a uniform, government officials, and predators—both south of the border and certainly here in Memphis." He remained quiet for several seconds. "I cannot go further unless I have your solemn promise that you will not report any undocumented immigrants to the authorities."

"I can only assure you that I am not interested in their undocumented status."

Father Kaszewski leaned forward, elbows on his desk,

spoke softly. "I do not know this girl, but you are right." His voice grew louder. "There have been others like her...and their sisters, and their mothers—kidnapped, threatened, beaten, hooked on drugs, forced into pornography and prostitution. Some, like this child, have been murdered. Others simply have not survived the physical and emotional ordeal."

"We want to put an end to that. We want the perpetrators."

He sat back in his chair. "My parishioners trust me. I cannot do anything to jeopardize that trust. If there's any way you can protect our undocumented people, I'm willing to help."

Julia took out a notepad and pen, looked up expectantly.

He sighed. "Immigrants may receive a green card for permanent residency from Homeland Security's Immigration Office. Or they can get a visa if they are sponsored by relatives or employers. They can also get a visa if they are fleeing for their personal safety, but that's almost impossible to prove."

Father K paused. "Most times Memphis receives new immigrants from Mexico and Central America by way of Texas, especially the eastern end of the border—McAllen or Brownsville. They come on Greyhound and are met at the station by immigration officials. They're taken to a shelter, then assigned to one of the agencies or religious groups who have been approved to assist in their resettlement."

"How large is the Hispanic community in Memphis?" She asked.

"I've heard estimates as high as forty-thousand."

"And the number of agencies working with them?"

"It varies. Right now there are ten or twelve agencies assisting the documented immigrants. Mostly small operations, often taking just one or two families at a time. There are several church-affiliated volunteer programs. Catholic churches work through the Catholic Diocese. Saint Michael's has by far the largest Hispanic resettlement program, by virtue of our neighborhood's changing demographics. Agencies and volunteers meet on the second Thursday of the month at the Catholic Diocese office in east Memphis."

Julia finished writing, looked up. "And the undocumented immigrants? The ones coming more recently.

"Can't say. Maybe three or four thousand. But more are coming. The border states have seen more and more undocumenteds crossing the border to escape the violence. More Central Americans, and certainly more children. Many find their way here."

"How do you learn about new undocumenteds?"

Father K blew out a breath, walked around his desk, sat beside Julia. "Most times I only know about new folks when they show up for mass. When they have visas or green cards people eagerly introduce them to me. Otherwise, they stay away, trying not to stand out. It's only later a parishioner lets me know who they are."

"How many would you say are in your church?"

"Thirty, maybe forty."

"How do they get here?"

"They're used to moving around, hiding. Some just bounce around from city to city. Typically, a friend of a friend from the same village takes them in."

"Okay. But what about children like our murder victim? Would she come a different way? Would she come alone?"

"I've already told you too much. It's time you talked to Cheryl Francis, over at the Berclair Free Legal Clinic."

Chapter 10

Roadblocks

*3:30 PM, Monday...*Julia found the Berclair Free Legal Clinic in a strip mall on Summer Avenue, a half-mile from St. Michael Church. A handmade sign on the door indicated irregular hours of operation, none of which included the present time. She tried the door anyway. It opened. A soft double-tone sounded as she pushed through the door.

"Be right there," a female voice hollered. "Ten un asíento, por favor."

The waiting area was clean but sparsely furnished—scratched and weathered wooden chairs along the walls, one small office desk facing the front door. Posters hung on the back wall describing the US Immigration Office's green card and visa requirements. A bulletin board displayed a handful of HELP WANTED notices, most handwritten. Julia flipped through a few brochures.

A woman came through a side door. Julia judged her to be in her mid to late forties, five-three, slightly overweight. She wore a colorful circle skirt. Blue-rimmed glasses matched her blouse. She carried a clipboard. "Police? Hope you have a subpoena. Otherwise we have nothing to say to one another."

"Well, good afternoon to you, too," Julia said.

The woman did not speak. Her face expressionless, eyes

penetrating.

"I'm Lieutenant Todd, Homicide. And you are…?"

"I don't have time for this," the woman said as she turned to walk away.

Julia felt her cheeks flush. "Funny. I didn't think you'd be the type to prefer an interrogation room outside the county jail."

The woman stopped in the doorway. Waited a few seconds without turning. "You know I'm an attorney."

"And we've already established that you know I'm a cop. A cop who's growing damn tired of your little song and dance. Now, what's it going to be? Here or there?"

The woman let out a huge sigh, lowered her head, then slowly turned, scowling.

"Okay. Let's start over. I'm Lieutenant Todd. And you are…?"

"Cheryl Francis."

"Ah. You're the one Father Kaszewski suggested I talk to."

Her scowl eased. "Because?"

Julia reached into her shirt pocket and pulled out the picture of Jane Doe. "Because he thought you might be able to help me find out who this little girl was, and maybe even help me find out what led to her murder."

Francis took the picture. Studied it. Handed it back. "I've never seen this girl."

"But you have seen girls like her, haven't you?"

Francis said nothing.

"Look. I have no interest in arresting or reporting undocumented immigrants. I'm only interested in finding this little girl's killer, and stopping other girls like her from getting abducted or murdered."

"We can talk in my office."

***

"So," Francis said, "the University of Memphis has a contractual relationship with this non-profit clinic. It's been a win-win-win arrangement for all parties. The university gets a placement setting for students studying foreign language, social work, and law. Students get valuable real world experience and course credit. As a law school faculty member, I provide supervision for our third-years. Similar arrangements exist for other faculty and students placed here. I also put in extra time and meet my personal pro bono service goals. The clients receive assistance in protecting their rights and in assuring them access to the services the system has to offer. And the part-time clinic staff gets needed help."

"That's quite an operation," Julia said. "Who pays for the clinic?"

"It's totally funded by donations and grants. Actually the university helps with grant writing as well. The clinic director, Cecilia Gomez, oversees the operation, assures all accountability mandates are met, and maintains the paperwork. Father K chairs the board of directors."

"Let me skip to the sticky part—undocumented immigrants."

Francis paused. "Undocumenteds have a right to legal representation like anyone else. And, of course, all such representation falls under attorney-client privilege."

"I get that. But what I need to understand is how they show up in Memphis. Like our Jane Doe. Where'd she come from? How'd she get here? Was she traveling with a group or with parents? Were there escorts? People must have known she was coming. Otherwise how would she know where to go? Are those people still looking for her?"

"You've been saving up, Lieutenant. Good questions. Not sure I can give you answers."

"Suppose you give me a hypothetical?"

"Okay…Hypothetically…You understand there are myriad ways for undocumented immigrants to come across the border." Julia nodded. "Many come by themselves or in large groups. They're betting they won't get caught, although most are. Some come with the assistance of individual guides called coyotes, and the cartels smuggle others as part of their sex trade or slave trade. Depending on where they are picked up and the time of day, these captured undocumented immigrants are processed and either escorted back across the border or taken to a shelter for food and a bed where they wait until the next step—appealing to an immigration judge, transporting them to a US city, or returning them to Mexico."

Julia made notes.

"There's little about this process that could be called typical or standard. The number of immigrants trying to escape the murderous cartels continues to grow and the US customs staff are overwhelmed. People being people, sometimes decisions are made on the fly. So, hypothetically, let's say *Louisa* and her daughter *Rosa* cross the border illegally into El Paso. The number of undocumented immigrants caught that day is great. The mother and daughter cannot be processed and are sent to a shelter, where they find themselves in a long line. And let's say one of the shelter staff decides to "help" Louisa and Rosa. One could imagine a scenario in which mother and child are given a one-way bus ticket to a US city. One could further imagine an underground network of individuals willing to take in undocumenteds. And perhaps the decisions regarding the designated city are influenced by numbers of existing undocumenteds or by the presence of people from the same Mexican village as Louisa and Rosa."

"So…hypothetically, Memphis could be one of the cities

in such an underground network."

Francis nodded slightly.

"That would require an established line of communication alerting folks that Louisa and Rosa were on their way."

"Hypothetically. And let's imagine that Louisa were to hire an American attorney in El Paso, say with her last peso. Then all communications would fall under attorney-client privilege."

"Which might mean a referral from an El Paso attorney to a Memphis attorney, maintaining the protected confidentiality for the new clients."

Francis smiled slightly.

Julia leaned forward. "There would also have to be a process for collecting Louisa and Rosa when and where they arrived. And if the clients never reached Memphis it could mean someone, like my Jane Doe's killer, had access to that confidential information."

Francis lost her smile.

***

*7:45 PM...*Tagger and Marino each took an officer and set up check points for cars entering Harbert from the southbound side of East Parkway, and for cars driving east on Harbert beyond the sports field. Blue strobe lights pierced the night.

Traffic was light. They asked the driver and any passengers of each car whether they had been on Harbert the previous Saturday evening, and whether they saw a car parked near the big turn. None had.

After two hours Tagger called Marino. "Tony, haven't had a car in fifteen minutes. I'm ready to call it a night. How about you?"

"We've had a few for the apartments. They turn off before

ever getting to you. But, yeah, it's been a while. Hey. One's coming our way now."

A late model Ford Escape, music blaring, slowed to a stop. Marino approached the car. A male driver, two young couples. He lowered his window, cigarette smoke billowed out.

"What's going on?" the driver asked.

"How about you turn off that noise and I'll tell you."

The driver fumbled with the stereo, switched it off.

"We're checking folks to see if they were on this street last Saturday evening."

"Last Saturday? You mean a few nights ago?"

Marino nodded.

A young woman in the rear seat spoke up. "Yeah. Remember? We were coming back from Sonic, you went around the corner and almost hit that pickup?"

"Oh, yeah. The guy changing a flat tire in the rain." He laughed. "That was wild."

"What time was this?" asked Marino, bending forward to make eye contact with the woman, waving the smoke away.

"Let's see. I'd say it was after eight."

"Tell me more about this pickup and the driver."

All four began talking. "It was a black. ...No, it was green. ...He was an old guy. ...What do you mean *old*? He was about my father's age, maybe forty-five. ...Like I said. Old. ...And soaking wet."

Marino let loose one of his piercing whistles. Everyone went quiet. "You need to follow me to the Union Station. We're going to go inside, sit down, and have a nice chat." He radioed Tagger. "May have something. Taking these kids back to the Station."

"Meet you there," Tagger said.

***

Marino, Tagger and the two officers each interviewed one person, then met in the conference room. Marino stood at the white board. "Now what kind of information do we have? Start with the time." They filled in the white board.

	1	2	3	4
Time	8:15 – 8:30	Just after 8:00	8:30	Probably 8:30
Vehicle	Black pickup, facing east.	Dark green pickup, facing east	Ford F-150, 2000-03, facing east	I don't know. They all said pickup
Driver	Male, white, 40's, clean shaven, 5'6", medium,	Male white, 50's, 5'8", medium	Couldn't tell. Bent over, back to me. Not fat	I wasn't really looking
Flat tire	Rear right	Rear right	Rear right	I Don't Know
Clothes	Rain poncho, hood	Rain coat, baseball cap	Rain poncho,hood, jeans, black shoes.	Wasn't paying attention

Marino stepped back and looked at the white board. "Okay. These are all Christian Brothers students. From what I heard, they left the university library at seven-thirty, walked to their car, then drove up to the Sonic on Poplar for a snack before heading to the girls' duplex on Harbert to…do more studying. After the library it doesn't seem like anyone really looked at a watch."

"Makes sense they'd be watching the clock in the library," said Tagger. "I know I did."

"Ah, to be young again," Marino said.

"And have a car," said Tagger. "And have a girl friend who has her own duplex."

Marino smiled. "So they're guessing about the time they saw the pickup, but it's a consistent guess."

"And it's within the ME's TOD estimate," Tagger said.

"They also have some agreement on the vehicle being a dark-colored pickup, maybe an F-150."

"The girl I questioned was certain it was an F-150, 2000 to

2003, with a rounded grill and sloped hood. Said her ex-boyfriend had a 2002. Said the design changed in 2004 to the more, and I quote, 'angular and in your face macho style of the Dodge Rams'."

"Now there's a girl who knows her pickups."

"Hey, Tony, I just had a thought. The kids all describe the driver as being bent over. What if they assumed he was changing a flat? What if he was getting ready to pick up Jane and take her into the trees?"

"Did any of the kids say they saw the pickup tilted because of a flat tire, or maybe saw a jack or tire tool or spare tire?"

The others shook their heads.

"Damn it," Marino said, dealing out file folders like playing cards. Call 'em. Find out why they believed he was changing a tire."

***

*Southeast Memphis...*A middle-aged black woman pulled out a sheet of freshly baked cookies, set them on the stove. She heard whimpering. She untied her apron, draped it over a chair, and walked down the hallway. She stopped at the first bedroom. "It'll be okay, sugar. No need to cry. You smell the cookies? I'll get you some, soon as they cool." Crying coming from the next bedroom. Metallic scraping. She stepped inside. "Never you mind, young-uns. I'm gonna take real good care of you. You need to settle down, take it easy. You're just gonna cut your wrists all up." More cries from the next room. She wheeled, marched down the hall. "God Damn it. I've had as much as I'm gonna take. You sniveling newbies are pissin' me off. Stop the damn crying! You ain't gettin' nothin' to eat as long as you're crying!"

She left, walked to the fourth bedroom. Quiet. Two young girls brought in minutes earlier—unconscious, one arm handcuffed to their bed. An adolescent female stood at the foot of Gabriela's bed. The woman walked up, ruffled the teen's hair. "You did good. These are top-dollar girls." One began to rouse. The woman pointed. "Get her ready. Poppa Bear will be here soon. He likes the young ones. He'll want her fully awake. Make her look good. She'll be my gift to him."

Chapter 11

The Networks

Tuesday morning, Union Station...Julia sat at her desk studying her notes. Cheryl Francis had given her the names of Berclair clinic's three part-time volunteer attorneys and their schedules. *Could one of these be the underground legal contact? Could it be a student? Who makes the pickup? How does the perp get the transportation info and beat them to the pickup site?*

She pulled up the Greyhound Bus website. Routes from El Paso to Memphis took just under twenty-four hours, depending on stops. Almost as much time coming from Brownsville to Dallas, with scheduled stops in Texarkana, North Little Rock, Forrest City and West Memphis. *It might be less conspicuous to pick up the undocumenteds at night in smaller Arkansas towns, then transport them into Memphis by car.* She heard footsteps, then a quick double knock on the doorjamb.

Marino appeared, Tagger behind him.

"Whatchagot, fellas?" Julia said, gesturing to the chairs by her desk.

"We set up roadblocks last night on Harbert, above and below the curve," said Marino, taking a seat. "Some Christian Brothers students saw a black or dark green pickup, maybe an F-150, parked on the street."

"Right time, right place?"

Marino nodded. "Within the ME's estimated time

of death."

"The kids saw a man at the rear of the pickup, bending over," said Tagger. "Same side of the street Jane was dropped. Thought he was changing a tire. But nobody remembered seeing the pickup leaning from a flat tire, or even a jack or spare tire. We're wondering if he was bending over Jane."

"So, how do we find this F-150?"

Marino pulled out his notepad. "Shelby County's registered thousands of 'em, private and commercial. More in the surrounding counties. I'll get with IT to run a search of dark-colored 2000-2003 F-150s by private owner over age thirty. Then I think we should narrow the search to the midtown area first, just because people don't drive down that street unless they know the area."

"Speaking of that," said Tagger. "Grace Saint Luke's had scheduled a soccer game that Saturday. Turns out they even play in the rain, and of course they've got those big night lights for the field. Game was over by six and the place cleared out a half-hour later. So no possible witnesses from that group."

Marino smiled. "You run into your Episcopalian girlfriend?"

"As a matter of fact, she's the one I talked to. Still wants me to join the team. Said they'll be needing a shortstop this spring."

"I'd hold out for first baseman. A lot less work."

Julia's mouth open, her eyes squinted. "Huh?"

"Johnnie has a personal history with that section of Harbert and a woman who desperately wants him to play ball."

Tagger smiled. Julia rolled her eyes.

"What about you, Lieutenant," said Marino. "You find anything?"

"I spent my time on a different street—Summer Avenue. Talked to a priest at St. Michael's, and an attorney at the nearby free legal clinic. Both are heavily involved with immigrants, mainly Hispanic. Neither recognized Jane's picture, but they weren't surprised. Pretty sure they've seen this kind of thing before."

"But they haven't reported anything to the police?" Tagger said. "I don't get it."

"Afraid of getting anyone deported. I had to convince them I had no interest in blowing the whistle on *undocumented* immigrants." She paused. "They prefer *undocumented immigrant* to *illegal alien*, even though that's what's written in the federal law. No problemo. I understand where they're coming from. Anyway, they gave me hypotheticals and partial answers which led me to conclude there's an underground network of American citizens that smuggles undocumenteds into the US. And Memphis is one of the cities in the network."

"You mean, 'I've met the enemy and it is us'?" Marino said.

Julia cocked her head. "Something like that. In this case, lawyers may be key players, affording some level of protection under attorney-client privilege. If I'm putting the pieces together correctly, our little Jane Doe may well have crossed the Texas-Mexico border, where she and probably her mother were given bus tickets to Memphis to be picked up by a member of the network. If they made it here safely, Jane was probably snatched off the street in Memphis, but her mother's not going public with it. Given the secrecy and questionable legality, nobody's going to report her as missing."

"And, if they didn't make it here safely," Tagger said, "then you're thinking somebody got hold of the secret travel itinerary? Maybe intercepted Jane and her mother, abducted them and brought them to Memphis, where Jane was killed?"

Julia nodded. "Some version of that."

Tagger continued. "And this somebody chloroformed them both, but overdid it with Jane? What about Jane's mother?"

"She'd probably be in her mid-to-late twenties," Marino said. "At the upper end of the range for sex trafficking. Maybe forced servitude? Or both?"

Julia shivered visibly and growled. "I don't know who pisses me off the most—the bastards who kidnap these women and kids, or the pigs who create the sexual demand."

Tagger and Marino waited.

Julia looked down. "Sorry…just blowing off. I hate that people, especially females, are treated like a stick of gum—mangle it till it doesn't satisfy you any more, then throw it away." Julia took a breath. Made eye contact. "Present company excluded for sure."

Marino leaned forward. "Preachin' to the choir, Lieutenant. What's next?"

"There're at least two networks here—one that smuggles undocumented immigrants to Memphis in hopes of giving them a better life, and one that kidnaps girls and enslaves them into a life of prostitution—whether American citizens or foreign born."

"And our only leads are a pickup truck that may or may not have anything to do with Jane, and a free legal clinic that may or may not be involved in the underground network," said Marino.

Julia blew out a breath. "That about covers it. But it's more than we had yesterday. Professor, follow-up on that F-150. Tag, let's check out the folks at the clinic. We'll take some eight-by-tens of Jane to post in the waiting area and hand out." She checked her watch. "The director's expecting us."

***

Marino highlighted printouts of registered F-150s. A third dark paint color had been added to the screening, something Ford called Toreador Red. The list had been narrowed to twenty-three dark colored F-150s from the years 2000 to 2003 whose owners were at least thirty years old and lived in midtown Memphis. He gave copies to officers designating five entries each. “Here’s the deal. I’m looking for a pickup that was parked on the east end of Harbert Street, just before it cuts down to the Parkway. An F-150 was seen parked at this site from about eight to eight-thirty last Saturday evening, around the time a nine year-old girl’s body was dumped there. Check alibis. Consider each owner a person of interest. Report back to me as soon as you’re done.” Marino checked his copy. The last eight entries were his.

***

*The Berclair Free Legal Clinic…*A man and woman came out of the clinic. The man smiled, held the door for Julia and Tagger. “He must be documented,” Tagger whispered. Julia rolled her eyes, shook her head.

Inside, a woman sat holding a small child on her lap. Next to her, a young woman taking notes, whom Julia took to be one of the university students. Another woman, not much older, came through a doorway. Julia judged her to be under five feet and barely ninety-pounds. Yet everything about her seemed larger than life—her self-confidence, poise, posture, the bounce in her step, and her engaging brown eyes. She stopped to speak to the woman holding the child, using what seemed to Julia to be fluent Spanish. She turned, smiled at Julia, then her eyes rolled up to see Tagger, her head tilted back. He nodded. She regained her composure and offered her hand to Julia. "I'm Cecilia Gomez."

Julia shook her hand. "We spoke on the phone. I'm Lieutenant Todd. And this is Sergeant Tagger."

Tagger raised a hand, gave a small smile.

"We have a conference room," Gomez said, talking over her shoulder as she walked. "I've asked one of our attorneys to join us, if that's okay."

The small windowless room was furnished with a long folding church table and beaten-up wooden chairs matching those in the waiting area. An older white man sat on the far side, wearing a starched white dress shirt and burgundy red silk tie, loosened at the neck. Everyone took a seat.

"This is our most dedicated attorney," Gomez said, "Gardner Frankel." Frankel acknowledged the introduction with a nod. "Mr. Frankel has been with us on a part-time basis for almost three years. His real job is with the firm of Lowden, Rhimes and Woodall, out in Clark Tower. Mr. Frankel, this is..."

"Lieutenant Todd and Sergeant Tagger," Julia said, pulling out the picture of Little Jane Doe. "We're investigating the murder of this child."

Only Frankel's eyes moved. He glanced at the picture, then looked at Julia. "And you are here because...?"

"Because we've been unable to identify her. She doesn't match up with any missing persons report—local, statewide, or national. Evidence is consistent with the child coming from Central America or Mexico. So we're checking out the possibility of an undocumented immigrant."

"And I ask again," Frankel said. "Why are you here?"

"It may seem trite, but we have to start somewhere. And given this clinic serves the largest portion of the impoverished Hispanic community in Memphis, it seemed like a good place to start. Maybe someone knows this girl. Maybe someone was expecting this girl."

"Expecting this girl? What are you implying, Lieutenant?"

"We're pretty sure undocumented immigrants are assisted in their quest to reside in the US. And we're just as sure Memphis receives some of them."

"I'd be careful about defaming this clinic."

Julia's gaze bore into Frankel's eyes. "Look, counselor, I didn't come in here to play hard-ass. But if that's your choice, I will." Julia leaned forward, forearms on the table. "Let's say, hypothetically, that there is in fact a connection between a Texas border town and Memphis that supports the smuggling of undocumented immigrants into the US."

Frankel moved to speak.

Julia pushed ahead. "And let's say, hypothetically, that the connection is with someone in this very Berclair Clinic. Now, keep in mind that neither I nor my team is interested in deporting anyone. We are only interested in finding the person or persons who killed this little girl. So, from our perspective, someone in this clinic has screwed up. They're under the mistaken belief that their communications with this Texas town are confidential, secretive. But in fact, they are not." She turned to Tagger. "What was it you said about this?"

"I said the fox has the keys to the chicken coop and knows the farmer's egg collection schedule."

"Yeah. That's it." Julia turned back to Frankel. "And that *fox* is kidnapping the undocumenteds before they can be safely delivered to Memphis. We believe the fox is selling the undocumented females into prostitution, or in this case, murdering them."

"Now just one minute—"

"No!" interrupted Julia. "I don't have one minute to waste. I suggest you get with your colleagues and talk about this. You can help us find this creep and put him or her away for a very long time."

Frankel stood quickly. "I don't have to listen to any more of this unwarranted speculation."

"You're correct, counselor. But, if I'm right, you *do* have a responsibility to find out who's involved. And you don't want another child's murder on your hands."

Frankel left. Gomez didn't move—the effervescence gone, her large brown eyes reduced to normal size.

Julia slid the picture of Jane across the table. "Ms. Gomez, please post this. Someone may know who she is."

Gomez cleared her throat. "I've never heard anyone talk to Mr. Frankel that way. You sounded as if you were accusing him of immigrant smuggling."

"Are you saying you know nothing about this?"

"Me? I've been here for ten months. I've never heard anything about smuggling undocumented immigrants."

"You do not serve undocumenteds?"

"I didn't say that. The law says undocumenteds have a right to an attorney just like anyone else."

"So you do serve undocumenteds."

"They have the right to legal counsel, a free public education, medical services, and poverty-level food supplements. We help them get those services."

"But you don't know anything about your clinic taking part in smuggling the undocumenteds to Memphis?"

"No," said Gomez. "Honest. I've never heard anything like this."

"Well, wake-up and smell the soy latté," said Julia. "I think it's happening right under your nose."

"What about your computers?" Tagger asked. "Who services them? Did anyone vet them?"

Gomez looked up. "CJ Electronics. They've been doing it

since the early days of the clinic. They've always been available and do good work. I understand the director of Catholic Charities referred them a few years ago. They service all the Catholic Charities' computers. The clinic's biggest problems are old computers, some so old we can't run the latest antivirus software on them."

"It makes sense that if someone has figured out the schedule of undocumenteds, they did it through the computers," Tagger said.

Julia nodded.

"What do you want me to do?" Gomez asked.

"See what you can learn without scaring anybody off," Julia said. "Keep your eyes and ears open. Chances are good one of your attorneys is doing this, all under attorney-client privilege. But that's not the person I'm after. I want the person who hacked into that privileged information, and used it to kidnap kids. That person needs to be locked up."

***

Tagger and Julia climbed into the squad car. He paused before starting the car, looked at her. "This case is hitting close to home, isn't it, Lieutenant?"

Julia looked straight ahead. "Ever been a throwaway kid, Tag?"

"Can't say I have."

"Thank your lucky stars."

Tagger opened his mouth to say something, but stopped... looked away, and started the car.

Chapter 12

Encryption

*Union Station...*Teresa buzzed in. "Ms. Sanchez on line one, Lieutenant. She asked for you."

Julia punched the blinking light. "Todd."

"Lieutenant Todd, this is Liz Sanchez. I'm an attorney at the Berclair Free Legal Clinic. I understand you want to talk to me—actually, to me and Randal Wallace, another attorney who volunteers at the clinic. Our private offices are on the corner of Poplar and Belvedere, across from the wine and liquor store, the one with the crazy Sputnik sign. Any chance you could meet us there?"

"Name the time."

"Say, thirty-minutes."

***

*Across from the Sputnik sign...*Julia parked behind the two-story brick building. A casually dressed man met her at the back door. She judged him to be in his thirties, six feet tall. He was thin, collar-length blonde hair parted in the middle, blue eyes, clean shaven, wire rim glasses. "I'm Randal Wallace," he said.

"That was going to be my first guess," Julia said.

He didn't smile. "Liz is in the conference room. Follow me."

A woman stood as they walked in, medium height and weight, curly dark hair, brown eyes. Julia figured her for late twenties or early thirties. "Liz Sanchez?"

She nodded, gestured for Julia to sit, then settled into her chair. Wallace sat next to Sanchez. Neither smiled.

Julia laid the poster of Jane Doe on the table. "We've seen it," Sanchez said. "Gardner called us after the two of you met this morning."

"Gardner Frankel?"

Sanchez nodded. "He suggested we meet you off-site. He also described in some detail his conversation with you."

Wallace slid Jane's picture back to Julia. "Look, we're the new kids on this block. We don't have near the experience or expertise of Gardner or Cheryl. But we share their passion for helping underserved and vulnerable people."

"My mother is still undocumented," said Sanchez. "She went through hell escaping the Mexican cartels, and has played by all the rules as they were enforced back in the day. She's living the American dream through me."

Julia picked up Jane's picture. "I hope your colleague made it clear that I have no interest in anything but finding the person or persons who killed this little girl and maybe others like her."

"Gardner told us that," Sanchez said. "And he told us you have it in your head that an attorney at Berclair clinic is part of some underground railroad. A questionable enterprise. One that, at the very least, could get an attorney disbarred, and worse, a prison sentence."

Julia nodded. "That's a fair representation. Did he also tell you I believe the existence of any such network has been compromised? And regardless of any positive intent, is resulting in the kidnapping, sex trafficking, and murder of kids?"

Sanchez reached for Wallace's hand. They shared a

glance.

"Look," Julia said. "I'm walking the same kind of questionable line as you by refusing to turn in any undocumented immigrant. So, can we agree to a dance? A careful dance which will allow us to get to the bottom of these atrocities without any of us compromising our ethics, or losing our jobs?"

"What do you have in mind, Lieutenant?" asked Wallace.

Chapter 13

The Take Down

6:20 PM, Tuesday...Julia's phone rang. "Hello."

"Julia, this is Ray Ayers. Got an offer you can't refuse."

"Fill me in."

"We're about to take down a prostitution site—our source says it has newly trafficked teenage girls, maybe younger."

"Where and when?"

"Staging area's at the Mount Moriah Station. We go at nine tonight. Y'all make sure to bring your vests."

8:15 PM...Julia drove fifteen minutes southeast to the Mount Moriah precinct. As she pulled in she saw the TACT Unit in black jumpsuits and body armor gathered around their van. There were also several small groups of men and women wearing bullet-resistant vests labeled **POLICE** or **TBI**, as well as a vested German Shepherd. Marino pulled in a minute behind her, followed closely by Tagger.

Major Ayers motioned them over. "Thought y'all would want to be a part of this. TBI tracked down a guy who kidnapped a teenager up in Union City. Rescued the girl. Got him to talk. Said he'd arranged to sell her to a Memphis gang. Admitted he's sold several girls to the same gang. TBI's been working with our Metro Gang Unit to locate the gang's place of business. Can't say this is related to what happened to the dead girl found in midtown, can't say it isn't. At her age she would've brought big bucks."

"Appreciate the invitation, Major," Julia said.

Ayers glanced at his watch. "We've got a crazy mix of folks—OCU, TBI, Metro Gang Unit, TACT Unit, Canine Unit, uniform patrol, and now of course, Homicide. Paramedics are standing by, along with Sheriff's Department vans for prisoner transport, as well as folks from Children's Services and Rape Crisis to process the girls."

"Who are we looking for?" asked Julia

"Gangster Disciples. This gang's been involved in sex trafficking for a number of years—it's more lucrative than selling drugs and, because the state hasn't beefed up its laws, they've done less time when they were caught. They buy girls, mostly ages thirteen to sixteen, who are funneled to them from across the tri-state area. A majority of these kids are runaways from physically or sexually abusive homes, either their own or foster care. They're scared, hungry, with no place to stay. Too often they fall prey to experienced pimps who offer them friendship, food, a roof over their head, and what they believe is love—before selling them. Others are simply kidnapped. The younger the girls, the higher the bounty. And virgins are always a bonus."

"When do we get our hands on these scumbags," Tagger asked.

"In about ten minutes," Ayers said. "We're going to hit two sites simultaneously. First is a strip mall at Mendenhall and Winchester where the pimps collect johns for a five-minute mini-van ride to the party house. Our spotter on site reports two pimps, a scantily dressed girl for marketing purposes, and a dirty cop standing guard in a squad car. Johns drive up, pay for a van ride, condoms, a "room" fee, and the sex. Any drinks or drugs they have while they wait in the van are extra. A van leaves the parking lot every thirty minutes or so, drops off the new johns. At the same time a second van picks up the satisfied customers and brings them back to their cars, parked behind the stores."

Ayers checked his watch again. "Second site is the party house south of Winchester, east of Clearbrook, end of a short cove. The gang bought the houses on both sides of the street, to form a buffer zone in the cove. This is where I'll be and this is where I want you. We'll take up positions around each site. On my signal everyone moves in."

They climbed into a black SUV.

***

Police vehicles remained out of sight. The two settings differed markedly—one wide open, the other secluded. The assault would come via fast-moving vehicles at the strip mall, and on foot at the party house.

A half-block from the party house, officers poured from their vehicles and double-timed to the cove. Boarded-up houses with overgrown yards lined each side of the cove. TBI agents, half the TACT Unit, the Metro Gang Unit, and the police dog approached the party house taking the left side of the street. Ayers led the organized crime contingent and rest of the TACT Unit on the right side, with Julia's team following.

As they neared the party house, Julia pulled up short, thrust her arms in front of Tagger and Marino. They stopped. A shot rang out from the last house on their right. Julia felt the bullet zip past her face. The three dropped to the ground and grabbed their Sig-Sauers.

At the sound of the gunshot, Major Ayers yelled into his hand set, "Go! Go! Go!" Officers sprinted across the front yard to the party house. Simultaneously, vehicles screamed into the strip mall, cutting off avenues of escape. Officers materialized on foot, making a semi-circle radiating from the store. They closed in, barking orders.

"I saw the flash," Marino said, pointing with his weapon to the right. "He's on the left side of that house."

The three rose to crouched positions and cautiously approached. A shadow moved away.

"There he goes," said Marino. "Into the backyard."

Tagger sprinted to the right side of the house. Julia ran to the left. Marino followed her.

The threesome focused intently for any noise or movement in their immediate area. They barely heard the more distant "BAM!" when the TACT Unit's handheld battering ram blasted open the party house front door, followed by yelling and gun shots.

Julia slowed as she came to the back corner of the house, dropped low and peeked around the corner, her eyes barely above the unattended weeds. She saw nothing. Then, from the far side, she heard the soft sound of quick movements swishing through the weeds. She came up running, Marino trailed.

BANG!

"Tag!" yelled Julia, running faster. She made a feet-first baseball slide at the corner of the house, her Sig held in both hands as her head cleared the corner. Even in the darkness she recognized the large shadowy figure.

"I knew he'd be coming 'round this way," Tagger said. "I put him down. His gun went off when it hit the ground." Marino came up behind Julia, panting.

A variety of vehicles roared into the cove, their headlights pushing away the darkness, sirens making it hard to hear, blue and red strobes making visibility almost painful. The man on the ground moaned. Tagger bent down, rolled him over and cuffed him. Marino grabbed the man's weapon and snatched one arm, as he and Tagger hoisted him to his feet. They frog-walked him to the Sheriff's paddy wagon, dropped him off.

"Better have a paramedic take a look at his jaw," said Tagger. The three approached the party house, weapons held at their sides.

The yelling continued. The front door hung askew, the smell of gunpowder strong, house lights dimmed. Two men lay motionless just inside the front door—one on his back, the other on his stomach. A half-dozen partially dressed men of different ages and races sat on the floor, clothes in front of them, pockets turned out, hands on their heads. Across from them a man and a woman knelt, hands cuffed behind their backs. The man moaned loudly, bleeding from a shoulder wound. "For Christ sakes, fool," the woman said. "Suck it up."

Barefoot girls appeared, wrapped in blankets and looking dazed. Black and white, but none with obvious Mexican features. A female officer escorted them down the hall and outside to waiting ambulances.

Ayers came up. "Ya'll okay?"

"We're good, Major," Julia said. "Sergeant Tagger caught the shooter. He's being loaded in the paddy wagon as we speak."

He shook his head. "Hell, I thought sure the gunshot had screwed up our assault. Fortunately, their music was blaring. Only the guys close to the front door were alerted. TACT took them out quick. A third man came around the corner with a gun. They put him down, too."

"Major," yelled an officer, appearing at the front door manhandling a man in handcuffs, a shirt sleeve ripped. "Jesse caught this one climbing out a back window. Would you believe his pocket was full of crack?" He dropped down and rough-housed with the dog, "Good boy, Jesse. Good boy."

Ayers waved him toward the paddy wagon. He turned back to Julia. "I didn't think it'd get to me. But I have two daughters, seven and eleven. When I saw those kids with those perverts..."

Julia nodded. "What about the girls? What shape are they in?"

"I don't have a hard tally, but most seemed to be thirteen to fifteen, one older and one a lot younger. They all had heavy make-up and wore skimpy outfits, at least the ones who had anything on. One or two looked like they'd been beaten—swollen faces, bruised arms. A few, I guess the newest ones, had one wrist handcuffed to the bed. They all have tracks on their forearms."

"Same for the real small one?" asked Tagger.

"Yeah. The little girl seemed to be drugged. The pervert in the room with her had stuffed animals. God knows what kind of sick games he had in mind. Still had ten thousand dollars cash in his pocket." He paused. "All the girls are being transported to the MED. We'll assign officers to stay with them till we can sort everything out."

"Any of these gang-bangers above the rank of foot soldier?" asked Marino. "Any cell captains or commanders?"

"Afraid not. Our source told us at least one would be here tonight. Maybe he was scheduled to come later. The woman was the ranking member of this group. Name's Terrencia James. Goes by *T.* She's the madam..." Ayers stared off.

"We've got paperwork to do on the guy who took a shot at us," Julia said. "See you at 201?"

"Be at the jail later. I wanna stop by the MED first, check on the girls."

***

At "201"...The Criminal Justice Complex is located on the northern edge of downtown at 201 Poplar Avenue, and widely known simply as 201. The complex includes the county jail for men, the general sessions courtrooms, as well as the administrative offices of the Shelby County Sheriff's Department, the Memphis Police Department, and the District Attorney General, among others.

The paperwork completed, Marino nudged Tagger. "I told you."

"Told me what?" Tagger said.

"You and the lieutenant have the psychic gift."

"What are you talking about?"

"How'd the lieutenant know that clown was about to take a shot at us? She was looking at the party house, not off to the right. She stops dead in the middle of the sidewalk and thrusts her arms out like a crossing guard, nano-seconds before a bullet screams right in front of us."

"She did, didn't she?"

"I've got the bruise on my chest to prove it."

Tagger smiled. "She probably saw movement in her peripheral vision."

Marino shook his head. "Then you, my large friend, immediately run to the right side of the house to wait on said clown to come to you. How'd you know he'd come your way?"

"Just logical. He was running away from us."

"Logic had nothing to do with it. I'm the logical one, remember. And I thought he'd just sit in the weeds and try to pick us off. Nope. You two are clearly on the psychic continuum."

"How about you having a conversation with Jane Doe in the woods?"

"A one-way conversation. Jane never said a word."

***

*Midnight...*Julia drove up her driveway. She heard yapping, and opened her door to find Parsley trying to jump into her car. She swung her legs out and scooped him up. "What in the world are you doing out at this hour? Does your mommy know where you are?"

"Julia. Julia," Mrs. Woozley said panting, as she half-stepped up the driveway with her cane. "I just couldn't wait."

Julia stood, holding Parsley. "Mrs. Woozley? What on earth?"

"She's okay. She's okay."

"Who's okay?"

"Ollie, of course. I've been waiting all evening for you to come home. The police found her tonight, here in Memphis. Called her parents. They drove to the MED immediately. Ollie had been drugged, but..." Her face reddened. She looked down, spoke through clinched teeth, her voice quivered, "Nobody laid a hand on her." She looked up at Julia. "The doctor checked."

Mrs. Woozley cried, quietly. Julia put Parsley down and hugged her. The embrace squeezed out alligator tears, and her body convulsed as she gulped air. Julia just held her. Parsley yapped and jumped against their legs.

Chapter 14

Poppa Bear

11:30 PM, Gangster Disciples headquarters, southeast Memphis..."How many dead?" Phillip Beard demanded.

"Two," Lil J said. "Wall and Lewis. Tuey got shot in the shoulder, Woody was chewed up by a police dog, and Zo got him a broken jaw."

"Where the hell was Washington? Dammit! I pay that cop to warn us when we're gonna get hit."

"He's down at 201 with all the dudes."

"T out east at the women's lockup?"

"Yeah. She wasn't hurt."

Beard began to pace. "Shit! That's a goddamn new whorehouse. I put a lot of time and money into settin' that place up—houses, vans, new young girls. I was gonna expand. Add more girls, cut the johns' time down to fifteen minutes a pop. That was fixin' to clear a million a year, maybe more if we played it right." He slammed his fist into the wall, broke through the sheet rock. "Goddamn cops." He pulled his fist back and looked at it, flexed his fingers.

Lil J waited. "Chub's the only one got away. He's waitin' on you."

"Get his ass in here."

Lil J walked across the room, open the door. "Chub! Poppa wants to see you."

A short, heavy-set teenager appeared at the door, but did not enter.

"Get your fat ass over here!" Beard roared.

Chub, eyes down, took slow short steps. He started to sit down.

"Nobody told you to sit!

Chub lost his balance trying to stand from a half-sit, grabbed the chair back and held on.

How'd those cops sneak up on the party house. Y'all was posed to be on lookout."

"I seen 'em comin' round the corner. Lots of 'em, and they had a dog. They was comin' fast. I looked across the street at Zo. He seen 'em too. He got his gun out and motioned me to get down."

"Neither one of y'all called the house?"

Chub shook his head. "Zo went 'n' shot at the cops. He missed. Bullet broke the window over my head."

"They shoulda heard the shot inside the house," said Lil J.

"Not enough time," Beard mumbled to himself. He looked up. "Best check the rest of the houses. Call our other cops. We don't wanna get caught with our pants down again. And I wanna know the name of the pig that set up this raid. He's gonna be mine."

***

12:10 AM...Lil J clicked off his phone and went to find Beard. "They hit us with everything but crossing guards, Poppa. TBI got the intel, pulled cops from the Gang Unit, Organized Crime, SWAT, a police dog, Sheriff's Department, and even Homicide."

"What homicide?" asked Beard. "They never found any of our bodies."

"I'm guessing it was that dead kid in midtown they

discovered the other day. A nine year-old girl we'd agreed to pay for."

"Where from?"

"Mexican. Snatched up in the neighborhood."

"Who killed her?"

"Accident. From what I hear, she couldn't take the chloroform."

"No way they tied that to us. So why homicide?

Chapter 15

Front Page

*Wednesday morning...*Julia planned to skip her morning exercise and grab an extra hour's sleep. But her internal alarm went off at the usual time and she couldn't get back to sleep. So she laced up her shoes for a run, just to get her blood flowing. The air was thick, misty, hard to breath. Her blood flowed, but focus and concentration eluded her. *Sure hope the whole day's not going to be like this.*

***

Julia stopped at Otherlands for her morning coffee and nutrition bar. She skipped the newspaper, and ordered another coffee for the five-minute trip to the Union Station precinct.

"Hey, Teresa."

"Good morning to you, Lieutenant. You don't look so peppy this morning. Must have had a long night, huh?"

"You could say that."

"The guys are in the conference room. Already drank most of the coffee. I just made an extra pot."

"Thanks."

"*They're* not very chatty either. Let me guess...I know. You were all part of last night's big raid. At least it looked like your pictures on the front page, standing behind Major

Ayers and the TBI dude."

"Front page?"

Teresa handed Julia the newspaper. "How come I'm the last one to know y'all were going to bust an underage sex trafficking house? I have to learn about it in the paper. Front page, no less. What's going to happen to my reputation? I've been lying all morning, telling everybody I knew all about it but was sworn to secrecy."

"This picture's from the staging area." Julia opened the paper. "And this one's when we came out of the party house. If this photographer had been a Gangster Disciple, the raid would've been a bust." Julia walked to the conference room, newspaper in hand. The men's eyes were at half-mast. Marino had his elbows on the table, Tagger slouched back in his chair.

"Good likeness, wouldn't you say, Lieutenant?" said Marino.

"Hope the major is looking into this press leak," Tagger said. "So much for surprise assaults."

Julia nodded. "But let's leave that to the major." She remained standing, feeling the need to get something done. "What do we know about the F-150?"

Marino pulled his printout. "We had twenty-three registered F-150s in the midtown area. We found nineteen of the owners—fifteen with alibis for Saturday night. One of the owners talked about taking the Harbert exit. He cuts across to a paved opening through the Parkway's median. I drove it. There are two near the Harbert entrance—one to the north, one south."

"You have to brave three lanes of oncoming traffic to make that north cut-through," said Tagger."

Marino smiled. "Yeah, but if you live, it gives easy access to northbound lanes."

"And the cut-through to the south?" Julia asked.

"Lines up perfectly with the back entrance into Christian Brothers, eliminating a traffic light. Wondered if our pickup might belong to a student or employee. Checked with CBU. There are, in fact, three older F-150s with parking tags—none from the midtown area. Then I checked with their fleet of vehicles. Bingo. They own two F-150 models of this vintage, both assigned to maintenance men who are on call 24/7. Found our man. Clive Andrews. Lives on Vinton Avenue, just one street north of Harbert. He did indeed have a flat tire Saturday night on Harbert while responding to a service call from the university. CBU records back him up."

"Nice catch, Tony," said Tagger. "The good news is our young female witness had an incredible eye for Ford pickups. The bad news is this truck had nothing to do with Jane. Back to square one."

"I'm hoping for a report from Major Ayers about the girls," said Julia. "Hoping for a description of one or more of the kidnappers."

Tagger shifted in his chair. "You remember Sergeant Willingham?"

"You mean *Diane*, your lady friend?" asked Marino. "Or does she make you call her Sergeant now?"

Tagger shot him a look.

Julia rolled her eyes. "Of course I remember her. What about her?"

"Saw our pictures in the paper. That's how she knew we were in on the raid. Told me she got called in early this morning as part of the Child Advocacy Center team to interview the girls. Said they're in pretty bad shape. Decent interviews will have to wait till the drugs run their course."

"Good to have somebody we know working the case," she said. "I'll want to talk to her."

Tagger took out one of his cards, scribbled a number on the back, slid it over to Julia.

Marino folded up his printout. "We sure could use a break."

Julia flipped open her notepad. "We may have something on the underground network. I met with the other two attorneys from the Berclair clinic—Liz Sanchez and Randal Wallace. They're a couple." She locked eyes with each man. "This is not to leave this room, but I'm pretty sure they're the Memphis legal connection in the undocumented immigrant network."

Tagger smiled broadly. "Did you give 'em the bad-ass cop routine you laid on Frankel?"

Julia shook her head. "I couldn't. Didn't have my good cop with me."

"What'd I miss?" Marino asked. "Don't tell me Johnnie played the *good* cop this time. Love to have seen that."

Julia smiled. "These two starry-eyed idealists are committed to helping folks. That's a good thing. But I think I've convinced them they're in over their heads. At least they're willing to make things right."

"They gonna give us access to their computer?" Tagger asked.

"Won't do that. No way they'll break attorney-client privilege. And no way any judge would force them to do it. But we may have found a work-around. Turns out they use encryption in all their professional computer work."

"The same thing they use on the network to keep the undocumenteds' itinerary secret?" Tagger asked.

"Right. But there are several encryption programs on the market. The network's encryption program is different from the one they use for their practice. I called IT, talked to Elwood Banks. Did you know he still has the souped-up laptop we confiscated from the twins a while back?"

"The one they used to hack ultra-secure medical files at all those hospitals and doctors' offices?" said Tagger.

"The one El promised to send down to the evidence room as soon as he was through examining it?" said Marino.

Julia nodded. "I gave him the attorneys' network encryption disc, along with the typical contents of a hypothetically encrypted email from a Texas border town. Now, if all goes well, El's going to set a cyber trap."

"How's this gonna work?" Marino asked.

"El will disguise his IP address and send an email to Wallace telling him a mother and daughter will be coming by Greyhound with stops in Dallas, Texarkana, Little Rock, Forrest City, and West Memphis."

"Where do we think the perp will intercept them?" Tagger asked.

"I'm thinking the network's pick up is West Memphis. Then they drive the undocumenteds across the bridge and drop them off at the home of one of the local Hispanic families."

"That makes Forrest City good for the perp's snatch," said Tagger.

"If they're bringing the undocumenteds back to Memphis," Marino said. "What if our perp is freelancing in Arkansas, too? Maybe selling to gangs in Little Rock or Jonesboro?"

Chapter 16

House

*Union Station...*Teresa escorted Major Ayers to the conference room to join Julia, Tagger and Marino. Ayers greeted them with a raised hand. "Sorry to keep you waiting. Got tied up."

"You look like you could use some coffee," Julia said, reaching for the pot.

Ayers nodded.

"Have a seat," Julia said as she poured him a cup. "We're anxious to hear what you found."

"I'm sure you know by now the little girl we rescued was, in fact, your neighbor's relative."

Julia smiled.

"What's this?" asked Marino. "Your neighbor? The one with the super dog. What's his name?"

"Cilantro," Tagger said.

Julia rolled her eyes. "Parsley. His name is Parsley."

Marino looked at Ayers. "This puppy has already saved the lieutenant's life twice. Once from a car bomb and once from a cartel hitman. He's golden." He turned to Julia. "Was Parsley involved in saving the girl, too?"

Julia started to shake her head, stopped. "Well, now you bring it up, I'd have to say kind of. My taking him back to his owner in the rain Saturday night led to me finding out about the girl's abduction—her name's Ollie. And since we were all involved in the take down last night...Well, it's a stretch."

"But we're going to give it to him," said Tagger. "Two Silver Stars and now a Bronze Star. I think we should put in for him to be an honorary member of the canine unit."

Julia signed a 'T'. "Time out. Let's get back to the Major's report."

"Good to know about Parsley," said Ayers. "Sounds like he deserves *some* kind of recognition." He took a large sip, burned his tongue, jerked back and splashed coffee on the table.

"Julia flipped a few napkins in his direction. "Welcome to the morning after club."

Ayers sucked on his tongue as he soaked up the coffee. "Okay. Let me try again." He took a cautious sip. "Intel was good. The girls had been trafficked—abducted within the last two weeks. We found plenty of their naked pictures online."

"Even Ollie?" Julia asked.

Ayers nodded. "They'd been drugged, and as we saw, some beaten. The girls had pretty consistent stories. Food, water and blankets were withheld unless they cooperated. They were threatened, slapped, and whipped with coat hangers, belts and such. Had guns waved in their faces. Told they'd be shot in the spine so they'd never walk again. Those with parents were told their families would be killed if they didn't do as they were told—like always smiling at the johns, no matter what. Each had a dollar figure they were told they had to *work off* before they could leave."

"Didn't get a good look last night," Julia said. "Any of the girls Hispanic?"

Ayers shook his head. "Only black and white."

"This isn't the only party house the Gangster Disciples are running, is it?" Tagger asked.

"Afraid not. And this isn't the only gang in the sex trafficking business. Our Hispanic gangs are tight with the Central American and Mexican cartels. Their MO is to transport American girls across the Mexican border. They're partial to blondes. Asian gangs are more likely to abduct any non-Asians, but they tend to move the girls through west coast ports."

Marino shook his head. "Jesus, Mary, and Joseph. Homicide is bad enough. But this crap makes me sick."

Ayers sipped his coffee. "Feel the same way, Sergeant. Didn't sleep last night. Couldn't get the girls' faces out of my head. Kept getting up to check on our daughters."

No one spoke for several seconds.

"This is no small deal," Ayers said. "The GDs are well organized, with operations in more than twenty states. Would you believe they even have a board of directors that oversees governors who control geographic regions of the country, which in turn are filled with local cells?"

"Sounds like a company on the stock exchange," Marino said.

Ayers smiled. "True, money-wise. But I see them trying to be more like Japan's Yakuza, or the Mafia. You know, they have their fingers into everything—murder, extortion, drugs, prostitution, loan sharking, and smuggling of all sorts. They consider themselves a family. They have a hierarchy for everything, including disciplining members for leaving the gang, or taking action without approval."

"What kind of discipline?" Julia asked.

"From beatings to murder," Ayers said. "They keep their troops in line."

"So, if there's a hit, the head GD must have approved it?" she said.

Ayers nodded. "Depending on how important the target

is, approval can come from a local leader or, as the value of the victim goes up, it has to be okayed by a regional governor, or maybe higher." He took another sip. "The GD in charge of the Memphis area cell is Phillip Beard, aka Poppa Bear, aka House."

"'House', because…?" asked Marino.

"Because he's pretty good size. Easily six-three, over three hundred pounds."

"And when he hits you, it's like a house fell on you?" Julia said.

Ayers smiled. "You got it."

"So how do we get to House?" Tagger asked.

"So far we haven't. He's well insulated by his bangers, and none of them has ever talked. Or at least ever lived long enough to talk. He has a reputation for taking punishment to the extreme."

Chapter 17

Volunteers

*Wednesday afternoon...*Tagger drove to the regional US Immigration Office in east Memphis, near the Wolf River. The secretary buzzed the Director. Within a few minutes, a tall, light-skin African American woman approached, dressed in a black skirt suit. Her hair was closely cropped with streaks of gray, red-rimmed glasses hung from a black neck cord. Director Jody McNeil was all business when she introduced herself and instructed her secretary to have the supervisor report to her as soon as he was free. She led Tagger to her office, gestured to a chair, then sat behind a desk piled with forms, notebooks, and a burgeoning in-basket.

"So, Sergeant, you are working a homicide case and you think the victim might be an illegal alien?"

Tagger handed her a flyer with Jane's picture. "There's nothing on file—no fingerprints, not on any missing persons list. There's still the slim chance our Jane Doe was killed by a parent who's never reported her missing. But the evidence points to her being an undocumented immigrant, probably from Mexico or Central America. We're thinking someone kidnapped and murdered her. We want to know who she is, and, of course, who killed her."

"I do not recognize her. But I am sure she would look a lot different in life."

"We've already met with Father K at Saint Michael's and a few folks at the Berclair Free Legal Clinic. They've agreed to post Jane's flyer and circulate copies to key people in the nearby Hispanic community. We're hoping you could point us in the direction of groups who work with other Hispanic immigrants coming from Texas."

"The majority of the legal immigrants we see come through other cities, where they are initially processed and given a visa or a green card. Many of those from Mexico do come by way of Texas. As with all immigrants, we make sure the paperwork is complete and assign a staff member to connect them with housing, education, health care, food supplements, potential jobs, language interpreters, and legal services. At last count, we have over fifty different languages represented among immigrants moving into the Memphis area."

Tagger whistled. "I had no idea the number was that big."

"I am told we are lucky. The west coast handles three times that number. Just generating forms in so many languages is a major problem. Maintaining a cadre of multi-lingual volunteers is a different can of worms. Without someone who speaks their language, the processing gets bogged down. The number of immigrants continues to increase, and we rely heavily on volunteers for day-to-day follow-up and advocacy. They handhold the immigrants, and let us know when they need help."

"Do you have a list of these volunteers?"

McNeil pulled a multi-page document from one of her stacks, and handed it to Tagger. "I believe you'll find all the agencies and individuals listed here, along with interpreters and attorneys who make their services available on a volunteer basis. You'll see each entry includes their preference for services offered, languages, religions, country, adults, children, gender, etc."

There was a knock on her door. "Come in," McNeil hollered.

A white man opened the door—balding, gray on the sides, black-rimmed glasses. He wore a white dress shirt, a simple military-knotted brown tie hung around an open collar, sleeves rolled to his forearms. Tagger put him in his sixties, maybe five-eight. "You want to see me, Director?"

"Sergeant Tagger, this is Jefferson Utley, my right-hand man. Jefferson, the sergeant is investigating the murder of a young child. Thinks it may be an immigrant, an illegal."

"An illegal? Haven't dealt with any illegals in four or five weeks. What country?"

"You process illegals?" Tagger asked.

"Our officers or local law enforcement occasionally find illegal aliens," said McNeil. "We confirm their status, take their information, and make arrangements for deportation."

"It's not like we don't have enough to do just keeping track of the green cards and visas," said Utley.

Tagger gave him a flyer. "We think this girl's from Mexico or one of the South American countries. Ever see her before?"

"Believe I saw this very picture on the news." He handed it back. "But I've never seen her."

"Jefferson, I've given the sergeant a list of our volunteers. You work with these folks every day. Could you go through the names with him, and answer his questions?"

"The line's pretty long today, but I'll do my best. Come with me, Sergeant."

Tagger thanked McNeil and followed Utley to his office.

"Whatcha need, Sergeant?" Utley asked.

"I'm looking for somebody who knows how undocumented immigrants get to Memphis. Somebody who then abducts them and sells them to local gangs as part of their sex trafficking rings."

"Judas priest! I don't know anyone like that. Look, I don't have any sympathy for the illegals. They're overburdening our agencies, taking jobs, using up our tax dollars, and ruining our language. But selling kids for sex. Even I draw the line on crap like that."

"Glad to hear that, Jefferson. Now I can cross you off my list."

Utley's eyes opened wide. He dropped into his chair.

Tagger waived McNeil's handout in Utley's face. "This is most likely a multi-step process. Someone has to let the undocumenteds into the US. Someone has to help get them to Memphis. Someone has to hide them once they're here. And someone completely different has to know they're arriving in Memphis, kidnap them, and sell them to the gangs. Anyone on these pages you suspect of being a sympathizer of undocumenteds? Someone who'd help them once they're in Memphis?"

Utley gulped. His voice cracked. "Everyone on this list has been vetted and trained by me. They all know we do not condone or assist illegal aliens. They know the federal Immigration and Nationality Act says such harboring of illegal aliens is a felony and could result in up to five years in prison. No, Sergeant. I don't suspect anyone on this list."

"How about anyone on this list who might know something about them being kidnapped?"

"I just told you. None of my people would be involved."

Chapter 18

Sam's Funeral

*Noon, Wednesday, Berston Funeral Home...*Marino signed Sam Merrill's guest book and entered Chapel B. Halfway down the center isle he joined the viewing line, nodded to a small group of MPD officers gathered in the pews. Sam's only son stood near a closed casket, receiving visitors. His family sat in the first pew.

"I'm so sorry," Marino said, extending his hand. "I'm Tony Marino."

Sam Merrill, Jr. stepped forward and hugged him. "Good to finally meet you. You know you were always Dad's favorite. He followed your career closely. Bragged on you all the time. Said you had great cop instincts. And, when we'd watch *Jeopardy*, he always said you should be on the show because you knew more stuff than anyone. It was like you were a *second* son." He smiled.

"Wow. I didn't know. I certainly held him in high regard. He taught me so much. Hadn't seen him in quite a while, till I ran into him at a retirement party."

"And he told you about his ghostly experience."

"Yeah. How'd you—"

Sam Junior interrupted. "And you had a hard time believing him."

Marino nodded.

"We can't explain it. All I can say is that he and his young friend did in fact solve a forty year-old murder, and his final days were some of the happiest I'd seen him."

The minister walked up. "We will begin shortly. Please be seated."

***

The Cross On The Hill Cemetery...Berston Funeral Home sat on a rise overlooking the cemetery. Funeral guests had an impressive view of the cemetery as they began their short winding drive down the hill. Marino waited until all cars had joined the procession. *Oh, what the hell. Might as well go to the graveside service. I owe Sam that much.*

The procession snaked to a stop near a green tent-covered burial site, parked alongside the road. The sound of closing car doors was muted by the open space. People slowly approached the tent. Funeral attendants called for the pallbearers to join them at the hearse. They carried the casket up a slight rise. Family members fell in behind. Following the attendant's instructions, pallbearers set the casket onto a lowering device, above the grave. The minister stood at the head of the casket, Bible in hand, as family members were seated.

Marino had the longest walk, but didn't hurry. The minister was well into the service by the time he arrived and stood in the back, just outside the tent. He heard a woman crying, looked around but could not spot her in the group. The minister read another passage. Marino heard the crying again, but the sound came from behind him. He scanned the cemetery, found a woman across the road, alone, on her knees in the wet grass. *Oh, God. I don't do crying women.* Marino turned back to the service, another reading. Her crying became louder. He searched the group, but no-one else seemed to hear her. *What the hell's that about? It's like she's calling to me, just to me.*

Once the service concluded he waited his turn to pay his respects. Mourners left in small groups, got in their cars, and began driving away. The woman continued to cry. Marino zigzagged through gravesites, crossed the road, climbed the slope and stood beside her. She startled, looked up, a small white handkerchief in one hand, rosary beads laced between the fingers of the other. She struggled to stand. Marino helped her.

"Oh, officer. I've been praying for God to send someone, and you came."

"Ma'am?"

"Look at my Daddy's grave. It's just terrible. The rows of sod are separated and the grass is popped up like a muffin top. The director says his casket is leaking gases."

"Gases?"

"That's why his grave is bulging." She pointed. "See? Momma's grave is level with the ground."

"Are they going to fix it?"

"He said the casket seal has failed. There's nothing he can do. We just have to wait until all the gases work their way out." She began to cry, and leaned into Marino.

"Did the director say whether or not this kind of thing happens often?"

"Yes, and I've looked. I found a few graves that have pushed the grass up."

Chapter 19

Pecking Order

*Thursday, Catholic Diocese, East Memphis...*Tagger and Marino arrived late for the monthly meeting of agencies that assist Hispanic immigrants. An attractive young black woman sat behind a desk. "May I help you?"

"We're looking for the meeting of folks who work with Hispanic immigrants," said Tagger.

"They're in the large conference room, just down this hall," she said, pointing.

Marino said quietly to Tagger. "I'll go to the meeting. Why don't you see what you can find out from her?"

Tagger gave an upward nod, turned to the woman. "I'm Sergeant Tagger. Maybe you can help me. I don't know anything about this group. Any chance you have a list of the people who attend these meetings?"

"Of course. I'm Bree. You sure are tall. How about you sit down so I won't hurt my neck?"

Tagger smiled, pulled up a chair.

"Oh, that's *so* much better." The woman pulled a file from a desk drawer, fished out a membership roster, handed it to Tagger. "Now what did you want to know?"

"Pretty much everything. Who are they? How long they been doing this? Any juicy gossip?"

Bree smiled. "Well, let's start with the basics. They'd

already been meeting regularly when I came here two-and-a-half years ago, just a lot fewer of them. Used to meet in the director's office."

Tagger checked the roster. "This is quite a list—agencies, churches, and I guess, volunteers."

"Lots of volunteers, and two are what they call *consumers.* You know, actual Mexican immigrants. Although these two," she said, pointing, "speak pretty good English."

"And the gossip?"

Bree leaned forward, lowered her voice. "We host several of these meetings, each serving immigrants from different countries. But there's always a pecking order. Maybe it's a culture thing or a racial thing, or maybe it's just a money thing...but within each country there always seems to be folks who are on top and folks who are on the bottom." She smiled. "My grandparents live on a farm, raise chickens. You only have to watch them for a little while before their pecking order is clear. That's what I see here. Pecking orders. The ones on top I call the *peckers.*" She smiled, winked.

Tagger grinned.

Yup, they're real peckers to me. I call the ones on the down the line, *peckees.* Of course, the *peckers* are first in line for all services. It's always me, me, me."

"That's quite an observation," He said. "Do people just fall in line, or do they have to be reminded of their place?"

"From what I've seen, the women clearly fall in line. In fact I've yet to see a female consumer member last longer than a few meetings. We have a Spanish-speaking social worker who organizes small groups of Hispanic immigrants, kinda like focus groups. She likes my classifying of peckers and peckees. She tells me she has a hard time getting the women and other peckees to speak up. Either they're afraid to do so, or they get shot down quickly by the *peckers.*"

"Ever hear anything about undocumented immigrants?" Tagger asked.

"You mean the illegals?"

He nodded.

"Actually, yes. I've heard the agency folks and volunteers talking in the hall. They've got pretty strong feelings—some for, some against. But either way, I'd think illegals would be the super *peckees*."

Tagger handed his roster back to Bree. "Could you mark folks who've been the most outspoken? A zero beside those who are pro-undocumenteds, and an X beside those who are against?"

Bree went through the list, returned it to Tagger. "Speaking of *peckers*, the same applies to the natural born US citizens." She pointed. "This volunteer, Fred Dancer, is a real piece of work."

"There someone he especially likes to peck on?"

Bree smiled. "Yeah. This other volunteer, Leonard Owen, is his favorite *peckee*. What a pair."

"Tell me more."

"One loves giving orders and the other seems to be perfectly fine taking them. Like last month, after the meeting the two were talking quietly when Dancer yells out, 'I told you. It's going to work. You just do your job'."

"Any idea what they were talking about?"

She shook her head. "As soon as Dancer realized everyone was looking at him, he hurried outside. Owen followed like a puppy dog, right on his heels."

Tagger cocked his head.

"Like I said. A real *pecker*."

Tagger smiled tight-lipped, moved his finger down the list. "What's this plus mark?"

"That's for Eve, a super nice sister—nice about everything

except illegals. She was opposed to any services to illegals and didn't care who knew it. She used to be a regular."

"Used to be?"

"About two months ago she stopped coming."

"How come?"

Bree shook her head. "I heard she left town. Never told her husband, her family. Nobody. There was talk of an affair." She shrugged.

***

Father Kaszewski stood as Marino entered the room. "Here is the reason I asked y'all to wear name tags today. I've been contacted by police Lieutenant Todd. She requested to meet with us." He looked at Marino. "This is obviously not her. This is…?"

"Sergeant Marino, Father. The lieutenant is unable to make it."

Father K nodded. "It's all yours, Sergeant."

Marino walked around the room passing out Jane Doe's flyer. "This child's body was found last Saturday. Evidence at the scene indicated she's from Mexico or Central America. We have reason to believe she's an undocumented immigrant."

"This is certainly horrible," Fred Dancer said. "But what does it have to do with us? We're not serving illegals."

Marino locked eyes with Dancer, paused before speaking to the group. "I want to be clear. My job is finding justice for this little girl. So my focus is on finding who killed her. I have no interest in her undocumented status, other than to help me find the murderer. You folks know far more about the Hispanic community than I do. It would be logical to assume that if there were any word out there about our little Jane Doe, you'd be the first to hear it."

"That makes perfect sense," said Leonard Owen, glancing at Dancer. "But I've heard no mention of this from the families I serve."

Other group members shook their heads.

"You mean the Hispanic community is not upset by these murders?" Marino said.

"I don't think we can overemphasize the power of fear in this community," Father K said. "They come from a country plagued with the evil of the cartels—tens of thousands have been murdered, people routinely snatched up and beaten, government officials and police bought and paid for. Then they come to the US, where they are discriminated against and set upon by *our* gangs. That's on top of the long reach of the cartels tracking down immigrants here in the states to squeeze more money out of them. And, of course, there's always the threat of deportation. Honestly, faced with all that, I wonder how I'd cope. I marvel at how well they are doing." He paused. "Sorry. I didn't mean to deliver a sermon."

"Not to worry, Father," Marino said. "Good background. Makes it even more important we find the murderer."

A man looked down, fidgeted.

"Something you wanted to say Mr.…er…Hendricks, is it?"

Marshall Hendricks looked up, appeared surprised to see everyone looking at him. "Me?"

"You seemed to be in deep thought," Marino said. "Wondered if there's something you'd like to say."

Red blotches appeared on his neck. "It's just…the Father's comments made me feel guilty. I mean, I've just been going through the motions." He paused. "Sure, I go down my checklist to make sure my assigned family has enough to eat, has access to all the services. But I've never really opened myself up to consider their feelings, what they must have experienced, and the challenges they still face."

"I don't think that's our job," said Sara Hanks. "I think we all work hard just monitoring the checklist. And, Lord save us from the illegal aliens. We're stretching our tax dollars beyond limits as it is. I'm sorry about this child, but we don't need to be giving *anything* to the illegals."

Chapter 20

The Girls

Thursday, the MED...Julia found Ayers in the hospital break room. "I'm just checking on the girls, Major."

"A lot slower going than I'd hoped," Ayers said. "Lots of dehydration, and some malnutrition, as well as heroin withdrawal. Ran a boatload of tests looking at all the things you'd expect—infections, STDs, contagious diseases, and drugs. So far heroin and sleeping pills appear to be the drugs of choice at this operation. Except for the eighteen year-old. She had signs of marijuana in her system and old tracks on her arms, but no current heroin or sleeping pills."

"Anyone looking at their emotional state?"

"The Child Advocacy Center sent over a team of police and therapists. They're way better than us at talking to kids."

"Any preliminary stuff?"

Ayers cleared his throat. "They're throwing a lot of ten-dollar words around, but the essence is they've all got some degree of PTSD."

"No surprise there."

"Child Advocacy works directly with an assistant DA, and is trained to gather objective court-ready statements from kids. They've got plenty of eyewitness accounts of threats, beatings, drug injections, and withholding food. Two teenage girls claim a week ago they saw two younger girls being carried in, unconscious. They were put in the next room. Said at least one was Mexican. Said the girls were maybe fourth or fifth graders. They heard yelling. The woman called T said one girl was dead. A man passed by their door. Described him as very big, black, wore lots of gold. Never saw those girls again. They think they're both dead."

"T's the woman we arrested Tuesday, right?" Julia said.

"Most likely. And the big black dude makes me think of Beard."

"Any bodies to back this up?"

"None we know of, but I'd love to rattle Beard's cage," Ayers said. "Tell him we got a witness. See what he does."

"Let's thumbtack that idea—at least for now. See if we can get more information before we show our hand."

Ayers nodded.

"Any descriptions of the creeps who kidnapped the girls?" Julia asked.

"These kids all come from West Tennessee. None appear to be Mexican. A few of the runaways were scammed by con artists who befriended them, promised them the moon, then sold them to the GDs."

"Nice guys."

Ayers closed his note pad. "We have names but they're probably aliases. The kids are working with our sketch artist. The others said they never knew who grabbed them—hood over their head or they were drugged. The little one, your Ollie, is pretty sharp. She got a good look at her assailant's SUV, a ring he wore on his thumb, and a tattoo of a naked doll on the back of his right hand."

Julia smiled. "Great work, Ollie." She turned serious. "I assume the parents have shown up by now."

"Three of the girls lived with their parents. They're all here. The advocacy center folks are keeping an eye on one of the fathers, watching his interactions with his daughter. The girl physically tenses up whenever he comes around, won't speak, reaches for her mother. He looks nervous, can't take his eyes off his daughter, especially when she's talking to an adult. His behavior is a match for either a physical abuser or a molester. That would explain why she ran away from home in the first place."

Julia's fists clenched. She remembered how her mother acted whenever protective services came to their home—hovering around her and Wayne, kept hugging them, glaring at them whenever the investigator asked questions. How she and her brother were too scared to speak to any adult.

"Julia?"

She looked up, embarrassed. "Just thinking how scared these kids must have been." She relaxed her shoulders. "How long they gonna be hospitalized?"

"Doctor said at least three days," Ayers said, "maybe a week for the girls having the biggest problems with heroin withdrawal. We've pulled all the kids together, moved them to the security wing so we can keep a close eye on them."

"You expecting trouble?"

Ayers shrugged. "Just want to play it safe. The nurses have picked up on bad vibes between a few of the girls and the oldest one. Said they call her 'Little T'. She was undressed when we raided the place, but there wasn't any man with her. She just fell in line with the other girls when we wrapped blankets around them. She's the one with no heroin in her blood. One of the officers interviewed her. A hard case. Uncooperative, mouthy, spouted jailhouse law. Has a rap sheet going back a few years."

"You think she's part of the GD's operation?" asked Julia.

"Good chance. Her record matches T's—prostitution, drugs, simple assault. Maybe T's training her to be a madam."

"I don't suppose T is talking?"

"None of 'em are," he said. "All lawyered up. The one that took a shot at you claims he's gonna sue for police brutality. Except he has to write everything 'cause his broken jaw is wired shut."

Julia smiled.

Chapter 21

Crime Scene

Friday morning...Tagger drove the squad car into *The Cross On The Hill Cemetery*. "Okay, Tony. We're here. Now will you tell me what's got you so worked up?"

Marino pointed. "Go around this curve, and pull up behind those cars."

Once he'd parked behind a Sheriff's squad car, Tagger turned to his partner. "We're not getting out of the car till you talk to me."

Marino fidgeted. "Okay, here goes. We've known each other a long time, been partners for almost eight years."

"Yeah..."

"You know I'm not crazy, right?"

"No crazier than the rest of us."

"This all started with that retirement party I told you about. The one for Sam Merrill?"

Tagger nodded. "So?"

"I've always been a skeptic—logical, scientific."

"Yeah, the doubting Thomas of the department."

"Last Wednesday I went to Sam's visitation, then to the graveside service at the cemetery. A woman was crying."

"That supposed to be unusual?"

"The unusual part is I heard her from some seventy-five yards away." Marino paused. "Nobody else seemed to hear her…and I was drawn to her. I had to go to her."

Tagger remained silent.

"Turns out the woman was crying because her father's gravesite had expanded, the top had risen above the surrounding grass. The cemetery director told her gases from her father's deteriorating body had escaped through the casket's seal."

Tagger gestured to get to the point.

"I thought leaking gases must be a freaky one-off thing, with all the embalming and such. But the woman said she'd found other graves like that in the cemetery. I got this horrible sense that bodies might be buried…on top of caskets. Honest to God, Johnnie. I couldn't shake the feeling."

"Any mental illness in your family?"

Marino punched him in the arm. "Come on, damn it. I'm doing my best to tell you what happened. Believe me. I know how crazy it sounds. But I'm lasered in on this thing. I can't stop thinking about it."

Tagger rubbed his arm. "Okay, partner. Keep going."

Anyway, I played it cool. Talked to the woman about getting an attorney to force the director to dig up the grave, check things out. She got all juiced about the idea. Apparently, so did her attorney. They didn't let any grass grow under their feet on this one." Marino pointed to a small group of people, including a sheriff's deputy. "The funeral director got served this morning."

"Jesus, Tony. What'd you do? What's going to happen when they don't find anything?"

"I didn't tell anybody about any buried bodies, Johnnie. I promise. The woman and her attorney are only investigating the escaping gas thing, and hoping to fix the gravesite." Marino opened his door. "Come on. I have to be there for this."

Marino walked quickly. Tagger caught up.

A workman used a flat square-point shovel to remove the top layer of sod, which he piled to one side, then switched to a rounded point-tip shovel, and drove it into the newly exposed soil.

"Hold up," Marino said as he neared the gravesite. "Let's take it easy. We don't know what you might find."

"Huh?" said the workman, looking up to see Marino and Tagger in uniform. "Okay, you're the boss. Easy does it."

He deposited half-shovels of soil on a thick plastic tarp laid beside the grave. The soil was loose, and within minutes he had cleared about two feet of soil evenly throughout the grave. His next shovel thrust yielded a sudden *thud.*

Tagger glanced at Marino.

"Stop," Marino ordered. "The dirt's pretty loose. Dig around that place with your hands."

"Hell, it's just a stick," the workman said.

"Maybe so. But humor me. Use your hands."

The workman glared at Marino, swore under his breath, dropped to his knees. He stuck his hands into the soil and, like a dog, clawed away dirt. He stopped. Lowered his face closer to the dirt, slowly scraped away more.

"What is it?" the woman asked. "What have you found in my father's grave?"

The workman continued to brush away the dirt. He looked up, wide-eyed. "It's a shoe, ma'am. A small shoe."

"Stop digging," Marino directed. "This is a crime scene."

***

Marino and Tagger stared at the shoe emerging from the grave. Ten feet away, the woman knelt in the grass, then sat on her heels and rocked, her arms wrapped around her chest. "Oh, sweet Jesus. What have they done?"

Marino looked up. "I'll have a chat with this groundskeeper while we wait on the crime scene unit."

Tagger gestured toward the rise. "Good time to meet the funeral home director."

***

Couples and small groups gathered in the parking lot began to funnel into the entrance. Tagger followed them. Sunlight streamed through the floor-to-ceiling windows, highlighting floating dust specks. The dark carpet was worn but serviceable. Shiny upholstered side chairs and highly polished wood lamp tables bordered the foyer. A young woman rose to join the group, clearly headed for the chapel on the left.

Tagger winced at the heavily scented air—a mix of flowers, perfumes, and colognes. He pressed a finger under his nose to stop a sneeze. It didn't work. He pulled out his handkerchief just in time.

A middle-aged white woman in a muted paisley dress approached. "May I help you, officer?"

"Yes, ma'am. Sergeant Tagger to see the director."

"I'm Colette Berston Robbins. Marcus Robbins is my husband. He's not here at the moment."

"I need a list of your employees, with addresses and phone numbers."

"Does this have anything to do with the subpoena?"

"It does indeed. Apparently you haven't heard—we found a body buried on top of one of your caskets."

Robbins stiffened. "Impossible. I'm sure there is some kind of misunderstanding, some mix-up. I have never heard of such a thing. This is a family business." She gestured to two large black-and-white portraits, gray haired men in pinstriped suits. "My grandfather Berston started this full-service funeral home in 1958. His son, my father, followed him. And now it's mine."

"And Mr. Robbins?"

"Well, it's my business. But Marcus and I run it together. He handles preparation of the deceased and administrative duties like security, drivers, groundskeepers, and hiring and firing."

"Is there a lot of firing?"

"We maintain a loyal group of employees, including a few family members. So there's very little firing. I handle more of the people end of the business—meeting with the family, marketing, sales, making sure the churches and our chapel are prepared with flowers, guest logs, and such."

"Nevertheless," said Tagger. "There is a body. So, I need that list. And please call your husband. I really need to talk to him."

"My office is just over here," Robbins pointed and began walking. Once inside, she picked up the phone, punched two numbers. "Sweetie. Please make a copy of our list of employees with addresses and phone numbers. And, do it now and bring it to me as soon as you finish."...She listened..."The police are here. I'll explain later." She depressed the cradle button, dialed a number, listened. "His cell went to voicemail."

"Do you have another number?"

"Only our home number, but he wouldn't be there."

"Please. Try it anyway."

Robbins made a face before she punched in the numbers. She listened, then held the phone out so Tagger could hear their home voicemail message.

Mrs. Robbins looked at the door. "This is my granddaughter coming now." A young woman walked toward them carrying two sheets of paper. "Thank you, sweetie." She took the papers and looked them over. "Yes. These are up-to-date." She handed them to Tagger.

"Are all these people here now?"

"My goodness, no. We employ over thirty people, from those who work in the mortuary preparing the remains for viewing or cremation, to those who maintain the grounds. You will see from the list that we have sales, marketing, funeral attendants, security, bookkeepers, and custodians. Some work evening hours, some only weekends. Many frequently work off-site."

"And your husband? When will he be back?"

"Honestly, I don't know. He left shortly after we received the subpoena. Told me not to worry, that it was just a hysterical woman. Said he'd be back after lunch."

***

Tagger drove down the hill to Marino, still at the gravesite. They studied the employee list. "The ones with check marks are supposed to be on-site today," Tagger said. "The ones with an *E* are evening staff. Still nothing from the director. Have to wonder if he's avoiding us."

Marino pointed at the list. "I talked to this guy, the one who dug up the grave this morning. Says there's five more groundskeepers who work under him. Only two know how to handle the backhoe. I talked to four of them. They claimed not to know anything. The fifth guy is the other backhoe operator. He left early this morning claiming a personal emergency. No answer on his cell. The woman who answered the home phone said he was at work. I put out an all points."

"Have to wonder where the security guards were when someone fired up the backhoe and buried that kid. They're in on it, or somebody assigned them to be elsewhere. Speaking of which, I'm headed to Robbins's home."

Marino nodded. "I'll work on a warrant for the company books and Robbins's personal accounts. Then I'll follow-up on these security folks."

"Be back to pick you up, Tony."

***

Tagger drove away as a caravan of cars rounded a curve in the cemetery, headlights on and emergency lights flashing. A motorcyclist left his rear guard position and passed the cars as they began to park alongside the road. He stopped beside the lead motorcyclist. Marino dodged mourners as he walked down the hill to them.

The men remained seated on their motorcycles, helmets off and cigarettes lit. They watched Marino approach.

"Morning, gentlemen. I'm Sergeant Marino. Like to ask you a few questions."

The men's facial expressions remained unchanged.

He unfolded the employee list. "You are?"

"Whatcha doin' coming up on us like that?" said the lead motorcyclist.

"Just investigating a murder. No need to get all pissy. That is, unless you did it."

The two men exchanged looks. The lead rider flicked away his cigarette. "I'm Watkins," he said, then nodded. "He's Barnes."

Marino checked the list. "According to this, you both double as security guards and traffic control for the funeral processions."

They didn't answer.

"Either of you pull night security duty?"

"Yeah..." Watkins said. "Monday through Thursday."

"Y'all got some interesting tattoos. They prison tats?"

"What if they are?" said Watkins. "Ain't no law against it."

"No trouble getting jobs here as security guards?" Marino asked.

"Part of the early release program," said Barnes, smiling.

"Don't suppose either of you know anything about extra bodies being buried here?"

"It's a cemetery, man," Barnes said, fist bumping a smiling Watkins. "Lotsa bodies."

***

Tagger turned a corner and began checking street numbers. He found the house, a car in the driveway, trunk open. He pulled in behind it as a middle-age white man hurried out the front door, a suitcase in each hand.

Tagger unfolded from the squad car and waited. "Marcus Robbins? I need to talk to you."

"Can't do it now. Have a plane to catch," the man said.

"I don't think you're going anywhere, except with me."

Chapter 22

A Red Diary

Friday, The Cross on the Hill Cemetery...Julia walked between gravesites. It seemed surreal to see the Medical Examiner's head repeatedly pop up from the ground and disappear again. Getting closer, she could see Dr. Evelyn Sales on her knees in the grave, nose to the ground, carefully removing dirt from around and under the body.

"What are y'all doing to me?" Sales asked. "It's not enough that you drag me out to look at bodies all hours of the day and night. Now you got me digging in the cemetery, where they have an unlimited supply."

"Good to see you, too, Doc," Julia said.

"What's the back story?"

"We flat out stumbled on this, following a citizen's complaint on the state of her father's grave. Now we're hoping we haven't discovered the gang banger's body disposal site."

"Really? Gang bangers?" said Sales. "Well if that's true, they're picking on kids. This one's a pre-pubescent female. Can't tell for sure, but it looks as if her neck was broken, the result of a blow to the side of the face."

"Any idea how long ago she was killed?"

"Bloating and skin discoloration make me think she's been dead about seven to ten days. And, Lieutenant?"

"Yes."

Sales held up a clear plastic evidence bag. A small red book showed through. "It has a name in it, and handwriting on the beginning pages. A foreign language. I'm guessing Spanish. Looks like a diary. Most likely this little girl's diary."

***

Julia found Tagger and Marino standing over another bloated gravesite. "Anyone want to explain to me why we're here, way out in the county?"

Tagger glanced at Marino, then spoke. "Short version… Tony attended Sam Merrill's funeral here last Wednesday, and ran into a woman who was upset about her husband's grave sticking up above ground." He looked at Marino. "Right, Tony?"

"Yeah. Except it was her father's grave. Said the cemetery director told her it was just gas escaping from the body, that sometimes the casket seals leak and there was nothing he could do about it. I told her she could always get an attorney to force him to do something. I had no idea she'd actually do it."

"Okay. I get that. But how'd you two get involved?"

"In a weak moment, I gave her my card and promised to be with her when her father's grave was being dug up." He looked at Tagger. "Johnnie just came along for the ride. What are the odds there'd be an extra body in the grave."

"Apparently the odds were pretty good," Tagger said. "We've been looking around. There are several bloated gravesites in this place. If it ain't gas from the caskets, then it's gas from newly buried bodies."

Marino spoke up. "Or maybe the second grave digger didn't have the finishing skills of the first grave digger—didn't know how to level out the pieces of sod, especially if he was working in the dark."

Julia shook her head. "Well the shit's rolling downhill. Turns out the Sheriff and our Director have been talking. And since you two were already on site, we've been assigned to investigate any and all *extra* bodies found in this place."

"Us?" they said in unison.

"But wait. There's more. Seems the Director has waved the white flag and asked TBI to come in. They in turn, have seen fit to invite DMORG to help organize, identify, and classify any and all such bodies. And the National Sex Crimes Network is on standby in case y'all have stumbled upon a sex trafficking ring."

"Holy shit," Tagger said.

"That goes for me, too," said Marino.

"And finally," Julia said, "you must promise me that one day soon, over a margarita and chips, you'll tell me how you two really got mixed up in this."

Chapter 23

Crime Board

*Friday, early evening, Union Station conference room...*Tagger and Marino walked in, found Julia writing on the crime board. "This won't take long," she said, over her shoulder. "I just want to make sure we're on the same page." She stepped back. "So far we have at least two murder cases, and maybe a third, according to the girls rescued from the party house, not to mention the possibility of more at the cemetery...and Phillip Beard is a person of interest."

Jane Doe

Gabriela Delgado

More bodies in the cemetery

Julia pointed to the list. "Ollie and two young teens were discharged earlier today, back home with their parents. They were all newly abducted. Last Tuesday was their first day being sold to the public. One told the social worker she ran away from home because her father had been sexually molesting her. They confronted the father. He confessed."

"The only decent thing the jerk did," said Marino.

Julia nodded. "Hospital also discharged the older girl, who's likely a member of the Gangster Disciples. The three remaining girls are foster care runaways. Unfortunately, this was not their first experience being prostituted, and they've spent the longest time on heroin. Still dealing with withdrawal, but their recovery seems to be on schedule. Hospital may keep them another three or four days."

She moved down the list. "I'm thinking the hacker has the option of abducting the undocumenteds and selling the girls to the GDs, or simply selling the information itself to the GDs."

"The GDs probably pay more if the hacker does all the legwork," Tagger said. "Reduces the risk of the gang getting caught." He passed papers to Julia. "I picked up a list of agencies and volunteers working with Hispanics from the regional immigration office. A supervisor said he personally vets all such persons and instructs them on the law. Says he vouches for every one of them."

"Johnnie and I went out to lay eyes on some of these folks at their monthly meeting," Marino said. "This group is devoted to helping immigrants. I kinda expected them all to be like Father K. Funny how some members are so opposed to helping when the immigrant is undocumented."

"Opposed enough to abduct kids and sell them?" Julia said.

Marino shrugged. "We'll follow up with those members. See what we find."

Julia shook her head. "Nothing to report on Elwood hacking the hackers."

Marino jumped in. "Nothing on any other vehicle seen on Harbert last Saturday night. Our best shot was the guy with the F-150 who worked for Christian Brothers. Since tomorrow's Saturday, we can set up another road block, see if we find anything from regular Saturday night traffic."

Julia nodded. "As for Gabriela, we have two drugged-out girls who put a man answering Beard's description at the scene. They talked about two younger kids being in the next room, and they heard T say one was dead. But they did not witness any murder. At this point, I'm assuming one of the younger girls was Gabriela. The timeline is right. If that's true, I'm afraid we're going to find the second girl is dead, too. Speaking of which, anything on the cemetery?"

Tagger spoke up. "I found the funeral home director, Marcus Robbins, at home, all packed with a one-way ticket to Edinburgh, Scotland. He's cooling his heels down at 201."

"The groundskeeper," Marino said, "the one who probably buried Gabriela, flew the coop. Got an all-points out. But I did get a real good hit on the security guards. Talked to two of them—covered with GD tattoos, prison quality. Probably the same for the rest of the security team. Someone had to approve their hire. My money's on Robbins."

"So what's our plan?" Julia asked.

"We need somebody to talk," Tagger said. "I want to get up close and personal with Robbins and that brother in blue who stood guard for the GDs at the strip mall."

"I'll go back and talk to some of the funeral home staff," Marino said. "Then Johnnie and I'll start questioning the volunteers who are so opposed to undocumenteds."

"Sounds good," Julia said. "I'm going to put a burr under Elwood's saddle. See if I can't get him moving faster on setting up a fake delivery of undocumenteds. When he's ready, we'll need to travel to Forrest City, maybe even Little Rock—on very short notice."

Chapter 24

The Star of David

*Friday, Shelby County Morgue...*Julia stuck her head inside the room. "Hey, Doc. You wanted to show me something?"

"Yes, Lieutenant," said Dr. Evelyn Sales. "Come look at this."

Julia took in the latest Jane Doe, laid out on the metal exam table—so innocent. *We're going to find out who thought they could throw you away, sweetie.*

"Over here, the side of her head." Sales moved the overhead lamp. "Had to shave her. See it?"

"What the...is that a Star of David?"

"Sure looked like it to me. Someone slugged this little girl hard, just above the temple. Hard enough to break her neck. See the bruises outlining knuckles on either side of the star? My best guess is the assailant's ring left this indentation. I'd say he backhanded her, used his right hand." She turned to Julia. "Thought you said you were looking at gang bangers."

"We are."

"You after a Jewish gang?"

Julia rolled her eyes. "You're pulling my chain, Doc. You've seen more of these tattoos on your table than most of us will ever see. This six-pointed star's a symbol for our very own Gangster Disciples. You know, putting two triangles together is a much easier way to draw a star. Took me years to get the hang of the five pointed star. Shortcuts like this helped me get through second grade."

Sales smiled and thrust a magnifying glass at her. "Use this. Look carefully...See anything?"

Julia examined the mark. "There's something in the middle of the star." She straightened up. "What is that?" Then bent down again to look closer.

"I'm thinking a letter, maybe an initial," Sales said. "Looks like a vertical line, with one horizontal bar extending from the middle. So, maybe an F, or an E?"

Julia looked again. "My money's on an H. I'm betting it belongs to a guy with the nickname House."

***

Southeast Memphis...Julia, Tagger and Marino pulled up in front of a two-story house, circa 1950. Young men and women congregated on the large front porch, some in chairs, two on the railing. Each wearing something blue or black.

"Hey, Tony," Tagger said as they started up the walkway. "Ever see so much underwear in public?"

Marino smiled. "Only in TV commercials."

"Don't you have some old suspenders you could donate to the cause?"

"Yeah. But they are all some shade of red," Marino said. "You know—Vice Lord colors."

A woman hurried inside the house. Soon, a large black man filled the doorway, paused, then swaggered onto the porch. He stopped at the steps and took his time studying each officer, sneering. His gang bangers smiled, their bodies moving, as if driven by some internal rhythmic music. One wolf-whistled, grabbed his crotch, pointed at Julia. The others laughed.

Julia walked to the bottom of the steps, looked up.

"Phillip Beard?"

"That's me, tasty cheeks," said Beard. "Say, ain't you the one I saw in the paper the other day? The bitch from Homicide?"

Julia narrowed her eyes. "Me and some friends paid a visit to your party house Tuesday night. We were hoping to see you there."

"*My* house? Who says it's my house?"

"According to the tattoos and colors, all the guys were *representing* the Folk Nation, more specifically, Gangster Disciples. That's you, isn't it?"

Beard turned to his gang members. "The bitch cop's been studying up." They all laughed. Beard turned back to Julia. "Ain't you gonna ask where I was that night? I'm sure I was right here. That's my poker night. Every night's my poker night." He smiled broadly, jabbed his thumb over his shoulder. "Just ask 'em."

Julia pointed to Beard's right hand. "Looks as if you lost your fancy ring."

He looked at his hand, lost his smile, then recovered. "Had shit for luck. Had to throw it in the pot." He looked back at his 'Greek chorus'. "Easy come, easy go. Right?"

The gang bangers smiled, threw gang signs, and made comments:

"Right, Poppa."

"You know that's right."

"It is what it is."

Julia asked, "You know where your ring is?"

"Had a bunch of dudes from out of town. One of 'em's got it." He smiled. "Why you askin'?"

"Cause a little girl was killed about ten days ago."

Beard lost his smile, again. "What's that got to do with me?"

"We've got a witness who can put you at the scene. And

there's an impression of your ring on the girl's head."

"What kind a game you runnin'? You don't got shit. I got witnesses that I was here, whatever day that was. And I ain't got no ring, haven't had it for a month."

Marino nudged Tagger, and nodded with his chin at a heavy set teenager standing by himself, on the left side of the porch. They walked past Julia and continued up the steps to Beard, one on each side. Beard reached out, put his massive hand on Marino's arm. Marino stopped, slowly looked at Beard's hand, then locked eyes with him. Gang members moved toward them. Tagger stopped in front of Lil J and stared him down. Lil J took two steps back, but did not break eye contact. Tagger moved past him, held the grip of his holstered Sig Sauer, and stuck his left hand out in front. "Y'all be nice, now." The group backed up. Beard removed his hand.

Marino walked behind Tagger and carved the kid out from the group. He led him down the steps, tight grip on his bicep. Tagger followed.

"Where the hell you goin' with Chub?" Beard roared. "You can't come in here on *my* turf and snatch up one of *my* boys. You got no cause."

"We're not arresting him," Julia said. "We just want to have a little chat. We'll bring him back, real soon." She backed away to the car, climbed in the passenger seat. Tagger drove, Marino sat in back beside Chub. Beard remained motionless as they pulled away, then threw a universally-recognized sign, using both hands.

***

"Somebody talk to me," bellowed Beard. "Why'd they take Chub?"

The bangers shrugged, shook their heads and as a group, melted away. Lil-J moved next to Beard. "Maybe they got video of him being at the party house last Tuesday. Recognized him."

Beard lowered his voice, stared into Lil-J's eyes, spoke softly. "You got rid of my ring like I told you, right?"

"Of course, Poppa. It's long gone. No sweat."

"Some fool been talkin'. Only one I know was with me was T. Now, I got to worry about, Chub. We need to clean this up."

"You want me to run this by the bosses? I think they kinda like T. Not sure they'd want to see her get hit."

"Do I look like I give a shit what they think? I told you—clean this up!"

Lil-J nodded. "No problem."

***

Julia turned in her seat. "Hope you two know what you're doing. Almost started World War III back there. We were out-manned and sure as hell out-gunned. You two have been acting awfully strange the last few days."

Marino leaned forward from the backseat. "Thanks for backing us up, Lieutenant." He stretched an arm over the front seat, the edges of a white handkerchief hanging down from his fist. "We grabbed this kid because he was wearing this..." He opened his fingers, unfolded the handkerchief.

Julia looked at a huge gold ring—shaped like the Star of David, an H in the center.

***

Tagger pulled into the Union Station parking lot.

Julia got out quickly. "You two have a nice long talk with this young man."

"You're not coming with us?" Marino asked.

"Got to get this ring to the lab. But first I'll need a little extra reinforcement."

"You making a chocolate éclair run, right?" Tagger said.

***

Julia drove to La Baguette bakery and made her purchase. Ten minutes later she walked into the crime lab with a box of éclairs. Technicians quickly gathered around. Julia pulled the box to the side and held up the handkerchief wrapped ring. "This ring may have been used in the killing of a little girl. I need the results as soon as possible. Call me and I'll come get it, carry it to the Medical Examiner. We need to see how well it matches the indentations on the little girl's head." The techs all nodded, then descended on the bakery box.

***

*The Union Station...*Julia handed a picture of Gabriela to Teresa.

Teresa winced. "Poor baby. This just sickens me. And this is number two?"

Julia nodded. "I don't think this'll make a good picture for the newspapers or flyers. Get this over to the sketch artist, tell him we need a drawing of how Gabriela actually looked before getting her face smashed."

Teresa nodded. "Will do."

"And, Teresa. I need it as soon as possible."

"I'll lean on him."

***

Julia sat in her office, pulled a business card and punched in the numbers.

"Sergeant Willingham," she answered.

"Diane, this is Julia Todd."

"Oh, hey, Lieutenant. Johnnie said you might be calling."

"I'm concerned about the girls. In fact, Ollie, the youngest one, is related to my next door neighbor."

"I'm not a therapist, but I can say the girls all show signs of trauma. They've been threatened, beaten, frightened, drugged, and forced to do things they're way too young to know anything about. Little Ollie is one together kid. But even she showed behavior changes, directed her fear and anger at her parents when they came to pick her up. I see it all the time—it's not unusual for the child to blame her parents for not protecting her. We've lined up a therapist at one of the state's child advocacy centers near their hometown, for both her and her parents."

"And the others?"

"Each girl is different—their maturity, their life experiences, their adult support systems, even their sense of hope. All have been getting therapy at the hospital and seemed to be responding. They're scheduled to be followed after discharge. You've probably heard about the girl who'd been molested by her father."

"Yeah. At least he did the right thing and confessed, took the pressure off the girl."

"Turns out he didn't do it willingly. I had to push him pretty hard. And even after he admitted to the molestation, he was all about blaming his daughter. Claimed *she* seduced *him.* Then he spouted some bullshit about his not being as bad as those terrible parents who beat their kids. Some of these guys just trigger your gag reflex."

***

Tagger knocked on the door jam. Julia looked up from her desk and waved him in.

"Tony's staying with the kid. Goes by the name Chub. He's

scared to death—of House, not us. He keeps telling us he's no snitch and he ain't sayin' nothin'. But then he can't keep his mouth shut. Says a week or so ago Beard ordered one of his lieutenants to get rid of the ring, a guy called Lil-J."

"Probably the guy we saw standing close by Beard, not hanging with the bangers."

Tagger nodded. "According to Chub, Lil-J didn't do as he was told, hid the ring underneath some kind of Kung Fu trophy. Chub saw him. The ring mystically called to Chub. Said he just had to look at it, had to hold it. Then he pocketed it. Guess our showing up got him to want to feel the ring's special powers, because Tony saw him pull it out and slide it on his finger, before sticking his hand back in his pocket. That's when he moved to cut him from the herd."

"Good eye. Smart move."

"That's not all. Chub told us he was on lookout for the party house when he saw us move in. He was on the north side of the street. Said the bullet that almost hit you, almost hit him, too."

"He still talking?"

"No. Got hungry. Tony took him to McDonald's. Told him he could have whatever he wanted. Judging by his girth, that may have been a mistake."

Chapter 25

A New Perspective

Saturday...Julia jogged home from the gym, cooled down and showered. She couldn't get Gabriela's distorted face out of her head, and now she had a sketch of what Gabriela would have looked like—a young, vibrant bright-eyed girl, full of promise. She toweled off, stood in front of the mirror, and shook her hair into place. *What if Aunt Louise hadn't taken Wayne and me in when I was Gabriela's age?* She touched her face. *What if I'd been thrown away permanently, how would I look? Would a sketch artist have to recreate my face?*

***

Tagger sat outside the interrogation rooms at 201 Poplar.

"Hey, Sarge," the sheriff's deputy said. "Just put Robbins in number three. He's all yours."

Tagger nodded thanks and walked to the one-way glass for a look. The once confident, well-dressed mortician had been reduced to jelly—a rounded defensive posture, his eyes fearful, widening at the slightest noise.

Robbins startled as the door opened. He began to relax when he saw a familiar face, but slumped again as Tagger sat across from him, flinched when he spoke.

"Hello, Marcus. You don't look so good. Prison life not agreeing with you?"

"You. You did this. You put me in here with all these... these..." He looked around.

"All these...*prisoners*? That's what you were going to say, wasn't it, Marcus?" Tagger paused. "First of all, you too are a prisoner, because you've done some bad things, some very bad things. And second, a helpful tip, don't even think about calling people names. Cause, you know, it could make some prisoners feel disrespected."

"You've got to get me out of here."

"Can't do that, Marcus. But I'm pretty sure we can get you better accommodations. That is, *if* you tell us about your little business arrangement. You know, the one where you agreed to hide bodies in your cemetery."

"I can't do that. They'll kill me."

"Don't look now, Marcus, but t*hey* are already well represented here at 201, and *they* probably want to eliminate the possibility that you'd talk. Pretty sure *they* can find you."

Robbins put his head in his hands. "Oh, God. Oh, God."

"Had a peek at your bank statements, Marcus. You seem to have periodic deposits from a consulting firm named "Cleaners, LLC." Big checks—ten to twenty thousand dollars. The most recent check was just last week. We found one body this morning, buried on top of an existing casket. Medical examiner said the little girl had been murdered about that same time. Odd coincidence, don't you think?"

Chains clinked as Robbins put his hands on the table. He looked at Tagger, said nothing.

"The Cleaners is not listed on your funeral home books. Have to wonder what personal services were involved. What 'personal service' did you provide, Marcus?" Tagger sat back.

Marcus remained mute.

"You'll be happy to know the TBI will be checking your entire cemetery. I'm thinking when they find more bodies—and they will—the medical examiner's determination of dates of death will coincide with the deposit dates from the Cleaners. That's gonna be conspiracy after the fact—one count for each body. That's hard time. That's why the judge set your bail so high."

Robbins trembled, whimpered.

"Come on, Marcus. What's it gonna be?

***

*The Berston Funeral Home...*People filled the vestibule and hallway. Organ music in the background. Marino spotted a woman assisting mourners, giving directions. She wore a black dress, her eyes red and puffy. She saw him, turned and walked away. Marino followed, got close. "Mrs. Robbins?"

She stopped. Dabbed her eyes with a tissue, did not turn around.

Marino walked around her. "Mrs. Robbins? I'm Sergeant Marino. I believe you spoke with my partner, Sergeant Tagger?"

She barely nodded.

"There some place we can talk?"

She regained her composure and led him to her office, lowered herself into the chair behind a desk, posture erect, face fixed.

Marino took a seat across from her. "I'm sorry for what you must be going through."

"You have no idea." Her hands tightened into fists. "A body found in our cemetery. A young girl...murdered. Marcus arrested. Our cemetery on the front page. Police and Sheriff's Deputies everywhere. Non-stop calls from people demanding proof no other body will be buried on top of their loved one." She blew her nose, gestured toward the door. "And still, I'm expected to carry on as if nothing's happened—to comfort the bereaved." Tears rolled down her cheeks.

Marino waited. *Another crying woman.*

Robbins pulled more tissues, dabbed at her eyes. She grabbed a mirror from the drawer and took a quick look, tossed the mirror back. "I knew something was wrong. I knew it when Marcus terminated our security firm contract, and hired those scary men with their ugly tattoos, nasty attitudes and foul language. He refused to explain himself. Just said it was for the best and I shouldn't be concerned."

"Did you know they are gang members, with prison records?"

"Prison records? My, God. What was Marcus thinking?"

"Did Marcus have any problems with drugs or gambling?"

"Not drugs. ...But he's always been a gambler. There was a time when he got into really bad debt. Then he started winning again, and everything has been okay."

"Any chance that was about the time he hired the new security guards?"

***

Outside the interrogation rooms at 201..."Busy day, huh, Sarge?" the sheriff's deputy said. "LaDarius Washington's in number two. Thought you'd appreciate a fresh interrogation room."

Tagger stopped outside the one-way mirror. Washington was nothing like Robbins—black, short, muscular, several tattoos, slumped posture, lips tight, stare defiant, a swollen eye. Tagger walked around the corner and into the room, stood beside the table.

Washington looked out the corner of his eye, managed a grin, snorted a puff of air from his nose. "I know the drill. Don't be blowin' smoke up my ass."

"That's funny, LaDarius," Tagger said. "Given your situation, I bet having a little smoke would be a blessing, given what you're about to have shoved up there."

Washington lost the grin, looked down at the table.

Tagger walked around to the front, put ten fingertips on the table. "What the hell were you thinking?"

Washington looked at Tagger. "You say that like you expect me to give a damn. I get disrespected every day by folks on the street, even been shot at twice. And for what? I don't make shit. Have to get extra money where I can."

"Guess you won't have to worry about the low cop salary anymore." Tagger leaned in, hands flat on the table—face to face. "And it takes one sorry-ass sick-in-the-head man to make money off pimping little girls."

Washington sat up. "I didn't have nothin' to do with that. I just sat in a squad car. Most the time smokin' weed."

"You remember the topics at the Academy? Specifically the one that says if you are a party to a crime, you're definitely going to do the time. Seems you also missed the lecture about what happens to cops who are part of the crime. They get the book thrown at 'em. You've got plenty of *time* coming your way."

"So what's the deal? You want names. I want outta here."

"You've been watching too much TV, LaDarius. How can you even think of getting out of here?"

"You want Phillip Beard, don't you? I can give him to you."

"On what charge?"

"I saw him at the new party house."

"As a john?"

"Hell, no. He was giving orders, talking shit to that whorehouse madam."

"The one called T?"

"Yeah. That's the one. She'll confirm my story. Now, what

can you give me?"

"That's old news, LaDarius. We'll need something much bigger than that."

Chapter 26

Checkpoints

*7:50 PM, Saturday, Harbert Avenue...*Marino set up at the intersection of East Parkway for those cars travelling up the incline on Harbert. Tagger intercepted those driving east on Harbert, a hundred feet from where Jane Doe's body was found. The first car approached Tagger—a white female driver, middle age. He stopped her. "Evening, ma'am. Just talking to folks who might have been driving this way last Saturday night about this time. Any chance you were here?"

"Yeah. I work Tuesday through Saturday at the Easy Way, just two blocks back," she said throwing her thumb over her shoulder. Then she gestured to her left. "I live in these apartments here. Driveway's just around the curve."

"Any chance you saw a vehicle parked right about here last Saturday?"

"Sure did. You know, there's not much room on this pitiful little street anyway. A pickup pretty much blocked the street. No lights, no flashers. Had to squeeze around it. Real dangerous in that rain storm. The nerve of the guy."

"The guy?" Tagger asked. "A man was in the truck?"

"No. Not in the truck. In the trees."

"The trees?"

"Made me mad to see him coming out of those trees. But you know how you men are. Can't hold your beer, don't care where you relieve yourselves. And this one didn't care if he blocked the street while he was doing it. I know his momma didn't raise him like that. I'd have given him a piece of my mind, but the rain was coming sideways. I couldn't even roll down my window without getting drenched."

"You mind stepping out of the car and showing me where you saw him?"

She led Tagger passed his cruiser. She gestured. "The pickup was parked here. Dark color, maybe black." She walked to the edge of the street and pointed. "Here. He came out right about here."

"You get a good look at him?"

"It was dark, raining, hard to see. I'd say he was white, but I'm not sure. Baseball cap and knee-length raincoat. Not real tall. He was moving fast, like he didn't want anyone to know he was peeing in the woods. But he didn't walk like a young man. You know, no spring in his step, even when he was trying to hurry."

"One last question, ma'am. Did the pickup have a flat tire?

"Not that I saw."

Tagger switched on his two-way. "Tony. Got something."

Marino drove up the incline and parked in front of Tagger's cruiser. They met in the street.

"The woman says a dark-colored pickup was parked right about here," Tagger said.

"Same as what the CBU students told us," Marino said.

"Except this woman said she saw a man coming out of the woods, and she points directly at the place were little Jane was found. She thought the guy was taking a piss. Probably only minutes before the students drive by and see a man and a pickup. Has to be the same pickup and the same guy. What are the odds he's hanging around in the woods in the exact same place Jane was found? He musta just dumped

Jane's body."

"She describe him?"

"Said it was too dark and rainy. But her description wasn't much different from what we got from that one girl, the one who knew all about F-150s. And the woman was pretty certain there was no flat tire."

"So the man dumps Jane, hurries back, and pretends to be changing a flat tire?"

Tagger nodded. "It works."

Marino shook his head. "I got confirmation from CBU maintenance that he'd had a flat tire."

"Could have punctured it himself. Makes a real good alibi."

Marino bent down and flipped through his note pad in front of a headlight. "Okay," he said. "Let's find Mr. Clive Andrews."

"Can't wait to see the inside of his house. Think we can swing a search warrant tonight?"

Chapter 27

The Room

*10:45 PM Saturday, midtown...*Three squad cars pulled up in front of a one-story house with attached garage—white with green trim, red brick framed the front door. Marino and Tagger were first up the sidewalk.

"You two go around back," Marino said. "Stick a light in the garage windows on your way. You two stay here till we need you. Marino pounded on the door with his flashlight. "Police! Open up!" He banged again. An inside light came on, then the porch light. "Police, Mr. Andrews. Open up!"

The door opened as far as the latch chain allowed. A middle-aged white man cautiously peeked through, glasses cockeyed, thinning hair mussed.

Marino held up tri-folded papers. "We've got warrants for your arrest and a search of the premises. Open up!"

Andrews closed the door, unlatched the lock, opened the door and stepped back. "What the hell's goin' on?" he demanded, standing taller.

Marino moved in quickly and cuffed Andrews. "You're under arrest for the murder of a ten year-old girl."

"I didn't kill nobody," Andrews said loudly. "I want my lawyer."

"Perfect, Mr. Andrews, because, just like the undocumented

girl you killed, you have a right to one." Marino stuffed the warrants in the pocket of Andrews's pajama top. "Johnnie, please read this man his entire list of rights, and have his ass bussed down to 201."

Tagger took Andrews by the arm. "My pleasure." He turned Andrews over to the two officers. Then found the officers in the backyard. "Come on, we need to clear the house for the crime scene team."

"Bring the bolt cutters!" Marino yelled from the front door.

Tagger dug into the trunk and jogged to the front steps. "Find something?"

"Got a padlocked door," Marino said. "Have to see what's behind it." He grabbed the bolt cutters and led the way to what looked like a bedroom door. He cut through the padlock's thick shackle on the second try. He handed the cutters to one of the officers, snatched off the lock, opened the door, and coughed. "Smells like a damn outhouse in here." He searched the wall for the light switch and flipped it.

"Jesus," Tagger said.

Two girls laid on separate air mattresses, handcuffed to the same metal post. Marino was already moving to them. "Bring those bolt cutters back," he yelled, still looking at the girls.

The girls pulled their sheets up, shielded their eyes.

Everything's okay now," Marino said. "We're police officers." He touched one on the shoulder.

She screamed and rolled to the other girl. They grabbed each other, held tightly, fear in their speech. Marino stepped back.

"You sure they speak English, Tony?" Tagger asked. "Sounds like Spanish."

"Either of you speak Spanish," Marino asked the officers.

"A little," said the shorter one.

"Well get yourself over here and calm these kids down," Marino directed.

The officer handed Marino the bolt cutters, dropped to one knee beside the girls, and in broken Spanish said, "We do not hurt you. We are to help you."

The girls stopped crying and looked at him. Marino came closer with the bolt cutters. The girls began screaming. He backed up.

"Keep talking to them," Tagger said to the officer. "Tony, go ahead. Cut the damn cuffs. "They'll stop screaming when they're freed up."

In Spanish, the officer said, pointing to one handcuff, "It is okay. We want take off." He took one girl's hand gently, held her forearm steady while Marino cut her cuff. The girl pulled her hand back, rubbed her wrist and sat up. She spoke to the other girl in rapid Spanish. The second girl held out her shackled hand. Marino cut her cuff. The two girls sat hugging one another, talking excitedly.

For the first time, Tagger looked around. "The room's soundproof—egg crate foam on the walls and ceiling, cork-board flooring."

Marino spoke into his two-way. "Need an ambulance. Two Spanish-speaking girls, possibly drugged, probably molested." Then he pulled his cell. "Lieutenant. … Marino. Got something you'll want to see."

***

Julia arrived as the paramedics took vitals, the girls wrapped in blankets, sitting in the living room. She checked on the Crime Scene techs who were working the hostage room. She grimaced at the smell.

Tagger walked up, gestured. "Hey, Lieutenant. We can

talk at the kitchen table."

All three scooted their chairs close to the small table. Julia leaned in. "Great find, you two." She turned to Marino. "This is the CBU repairman, right? The one you thought had an alibi?"

Marino made a face. "Yeah. That SOB. Lucky we found a witness who saw him coming out of the woods exactly where little Jane Doe was dumped."

"We had enough to interrupt a judge during the ballet at the Orpheum," Tagger said. "Got a search warrant."

They looked up as the girls were being walked to the ambulance. One broke away and slammed into Marino, buried her face in his chest. He held her close, his eyes welled up. He no sooner let go when the second girl plunged in.

"They may not speak English," Tagger said, "but that's universal language for *thank you.*" He glanced at Julia. "Tony was the first one in the room, and the one who freed them from their handcuffs."

Julia smiled. "Nice moment." She paused. "Now, we need to know if Andrews acted alone, and whether this has something to do with the network."

Chapter 28

T

*Sunday morning, midtown Memphis...*The mist felt good on Julia's face on her run to the InsideOut Gym. Her workout began with stretches. She headed for the side room and heard the "tap...tap" of the heavy bag being hit softly.

"Whoa, Girty," Julia said. "You can hurt yourself hitting the bag like that."

Girty stopped. "I was just trying to do what you do."

Julia smiled. "What are you...four-ten, four-eleven? Ninety pounds?"

Girty put her gloved hands on her hips and stuck out her chest. "I'm five feet and ninety-two pounds."

"Okay. I stand corrected. Here, let me show you." She took Girty's arm. "Keep your knuckles, wrist, and forearm in a straight line. Square your body. Feet shoulder width, toes straight ahead...Yes. Bend your knees a bit. Slowly, punch straight ahead with your right hand. That's it. Now this time, step forward with your left foot when you punch."

Girty threw a punch. "Oooh. That feels funny."

"You just have to get used to the technique. Then you can build up your strength, without breaking or spraining anything. Now try the left hand."

Girty threw punches, barley moving the bag. She stepped back, blew out a huge breath. "I need a break. I'll watch you for a while."

Julia put on her gloves and made a few punches in slow-motion. "See how I keep that straight line? How I drive from my shoulder?"

Girty nodded, and threw a few air punches.

Julia hit the heavy bag slowly at first, then moved to the balls of her feet and began to bob and weave. She attacked with single punches and combinations, waited for the bag to swing back then let loose a few sidekicks. After five minutes she was soaked. She grabbed a bottle of water and dropped down on a nearby bench.

Girty threw her a towel. "I'll never be able to do that."

Julia stood. "Don't see why not. Just take it slow, get your technique down. It'll come." She tossed the towel in the hamper. "I'm outta here. See ya."

Julia jogged home. As she put the key in the lock, the phone rang. She snatched it up. "Hello."

"Julia. ...Ray Ayers."

"Hey, Major. What's up?"

"Thought you needed to know. Guards went to bring T to the interrogation room to meet her attorney. Found her dead in the mess hall. Anaphylaxis."

"What? She allergic to peanuts?

"Shellfish. Apparently a serious one. Had a special diet. Cook swears she made her breakfast as per medical restrictions. Of course, nobody saw anything. Lab's working on it."

"Think this has anything to do with our visit to Phillip Beard yesterday?"

"Can't rule it out. Gang Unit says the word's out that Beard was really pissed. I think you and your team should keep a sharp eye out."

Julia hung up, then called Marino. "Guards found Terrencia James dead. Anaphylaxis. Allergic to shell fish. Looks like someone doctored her food."

"You shittin' me? You thinking it's Beard?"

"That's what Ayers believes. Said the word's out that Beard had a major meltdown when we left. He's tying up loose ends. Speaking of which, where's Chub?"

"Safe house."

"Good. Ayers also thinks we're on his list."

"You call, Johnnie?"

"He's next. Watch yourself. Remember, these guys are known for their drive-bys. And they probably have everything set on automatic."

"Just like the Mexican cartel, except those guys rode motorcycles. Might want to cut out the running for a while, Lieutenant. You're too predictable. Makes you an easy target. Jog in place in your living room."

"I'll think about it, Professor."

Chapter 29

Dem Bones

Sunday morning, The Cross On The Hill Cemetery...Sunlight broke through the clouds, reflecting off the wet lawn and tree branches. The previous day's rain left leaves scattered on the acres of trimmed grass. An SUV sat on the gravel-covered shoulder alongside a narrow paved road, tailgate up. TBI Special Agent Rafael Dawkins leaned in, a lit cigarette hanging from his mouth, began unrolling a large map. A female agent made a big show of waving away the smoke, and moved beside him, extended the map, secured the corners. Dawkins backed out, took a deep drag, exhaled through his mouth. He smashed the cigarette's lit end against the sole of one shoe, field stripped it, and slipped the remaining paper in his pocket. He ducked back under the tailgate.

"We're here," he said, making a small black **X** on the map, then pointed. "We'll start here, on the west end, where all the graves are marked with in-ground plaques, and stake out sections for the radar units. Let's hope the damned weather forecast is right and we'll have a few dry days."

A convoy of four black SUVs crept in and parked behind them, single file. Doors clicked open. Men and women slowly climbed out, most with coffee cups in hand, all wearing dark blue wind breakers, large yellow letters on the back—TBI.

***

Tagger pulled in behind the SUVs, hiked over to a small rise where Marino watched the activity. "Hey, Tony."

Marino nodded.

Tagger looked around. "We're sitting ducks on this hilltop."

"Suppose so," Marino said. "But here in the cemetery, my money's on the security guards. So hit the ground if you hear a motorcycle."

"Cute."

Marino put his hands in his pockets. "Can't say I was surprised by the Lieutenant's call this morning. Beard didn't strike me as the thoughtful, calm kinda guy. Knee-jerk and violent would be more like him."

Tagger nodded. "The GDs have made some major inroads. Takes a lotta influence to pull off a hit in the jail. Guards and cameras everywhere. Can't do anything that can't be seen by somebody."

"You thinking one or more guards were in on it?"

"Don't you?"

Marino nodded. "I'm worried about the lieutenant. She's got to be high on Beard's hit list. And she's way too casual in her exercise routine. An easy target."

"Remember, that car bomber waited for her to finish her run before he tried to blow her up. Hadn't been for that dog—"

"Parsley," Marino interrupted.

"Yeah, Parsley." Tagger flipped a stone away with his toe. He looked up. "I tried to talk her into carrying her Sig when she runs. Said it'd just bounce around, leave bruises."

"She's probably right. But her backup piece might work. She could strap that little Kimber Solo to her calf."

"Don't count on it." Tagger watched the TBI agents.

"We need to do something. If Beard went after T in a well-guarded prison, he's sure as hell going to take a crack at the lieutenant out in the open."

"What about us? You doing anything different?"

"I've had my head on a swivel—checking for a tail, scoping out places for an ambush."

"Me, too," Marino said. "But like she told me. It'll probably come from a drive-by."

Tagger took a deep breath, nodded toward the TBI agents. "So, how's *this* stuff going?"

"TBI certainly knows what they're doing," Marino said, taking his hands from his pockets, pointing. "They've cordoned off sections. When they finish analyzing one section, they take their stakes and twine and outline the next one."

"You must be in hog heaven with all this organization. Heck, I bet you'd come out here on a Sunday morning just to soak up the structure."

Marino ignored him. "See? It looks like they're mowing the grass with a push mower, a push mower with oversize tires."

"You're going to tell me they're not really push mowers, right?"

"Really," Marino said. "This is cool stuff. Those gizmos they're pushing around are ground-penetrating radar units—*GPRs*. They send a signal to a computer screen at the top of the handle bar. Generates an image of whatever's lying as far as three feet under the surface."

"And these GPRs can find a skeleton, right?"

"So they say."

Tagger became serious. "Had any more intense feelings about what's in those graves?"

Marino gave him a look. "Dammit, Johnnie. I can't explain this...You haven't told anyone, have you?"

"Me?" Tagger touched his chest. "I haven't told a soul. Don't want you carted off to Lakeside Hospital in a straight jacket."

"Look. I'm doing everything I can not to freak out."

"Sam Merrill probably went through the same shit."

Marino sighed.

"Keep in mind, there really was a child's skeleton in that first grave, and it looks like there could be more. Sounds like we're back to the Sherlock Holmes rule. You've eliminated all the logical options, so the mystical option must be correct, no matter how crazy."

"I don't think Arthur Conan Doyle ever wrote those words, but I get your meaning. Still scares the hell outta me."

Tagger brightened. "Even the TBI's been convinced enough to dump a lot of money into finding more skeletons."

Marino shook his head. "Speaking of the TBI, let's check out the command center."

Marino led Tagger to a tent just off the road. All four sides were rolled up revealing two long church tables holding laptops, lamps, and a coffee pot. Agents sat in folding chairs. A thick yellow electrical cord stretched some fifty feet to a low-humming generator. "Their laptops have synchronized the GPR imaging screens with a cemetery map showing all the gravesites, allowing for a complete analysis of every burial plot."

Tagger whistled. "If there's more kids buried here, looks like the TBI's going to find them."

A TBI agent motioned them into the tent. "Come on in, guys," he said, pointing at his screen. "Looky here. GPR 2 has located another body, just under the surface." Marino and Tagger bent down for a better look. "That makes four. So far each one has been in a grave with raised sod. Like the one you found, Sergeant."

"When you gonna dig 'em up?" asked Marino.

"We're waiting on the folks from DMORT. The team leader is already on site. Most of the team should be here tomorrow, the rest by Tuesday."

Tagger turned to Marino. "D what?"

"The Disaster Mortuary Operational Response Team. A group of professionals who come together as a team to assist locals on cases when there's an ungodly number of bodies. Organized out of the National Disaster Medical System. Has volunteer funeral directors, medical examiners, pathologists, morticians, and other forensics specialists."

"Yeah. That's them," said the agent. "They make sure everything is handled by the book. Worked with them in East Tennessee a few years ago. They know their shit—take care of everything from forensics, to chain-of-custody, to identification, to storage, to counseling next of kin."

"I was going to say it sounds like overkill," Tagger said. "But I won't say anything."

The agent shook his head. "That's what we need—more cemetery humor."

"What's the deal with the three-foot limit?" Tagger asked.

"That's pretty much the range of the agency's GPR models," said the agent. "But it's a non-issue, since that ought to be about the top of the casket liners."

"I thought caskets were all buried six feet deep."

"There's some variability, but most graves are dug out to a depth of six feet. The caskets are about two feet high. And most of those buried around here, within the last fifty years or so, will have some kind of heavy duty liner or burial vault that covers the casket. That'll be another foot." He shrugged. "Leaves three feet of dirt on top."

"Back up," said Tagger. "What's the deal with a liner?"

"In the old days it was to prevent body snatching. Since then it's more to protect against the weight of the heavy machinery—lawnmowers, trucks, backhoes and such."

"What's your timeline for checking all the gravesites?" Marino asked.

"This cemetery has about eight hundred fifty plots, seven hundred of which have in-ground grave markers. The others have tombstones. Special Agent Dawkins says we're working all day as long as we have daylight and good weather. He's shooting to have the first seven hundred done by the end of Tuesday. We're looking at another day or so to finish those with tombstones. So, depending on the rain, it'll be Wednesday at the earliest."

"Meantime, DMORT should be digging up the first scanned skeletons beginning tomorrow." Marino said, more loudly than he intended. He looked around.

Tagger looked around, too.

***

*Sunday afternoon...*Julia drove into the Saint Michael's Church parking lot, and spotted Father K on one knee in the flower bed beside the church, pulling weeds. She walked over to him.

"Don't just stand there," he said. "Give me a hand."

"Need help getting up?" Julia asked.

"No. I need help getting rid of these weeds."

Julia rolled her eyes, tucked her flyer in her pocket and stepped into the flower bed. She squatted, began pulling weeds and wayward grass.

"That's more like it." Father K looked up from under his wide-brimmed straw hat. "Together we can clean this whole bed before I leave to distribute communion to our hospitalized parishioners."

Julia dropped more grass in the small pile she'd created. "I really came because we found another girl."

Father K straightened. "Is this the one from the cemetery? The one I read about in yesterday's paper? There was no name."

Julia nodded. "We didn't release the name. She was about the same age as our little Jane Doe. This one had a diary with her. Says she's from the mountains, northeast of Mexico City. Undocumented, as far as we know. Killed last week." She pulled the flyer, unfolded it and handed it to him.

He looked puzzled. "This is a sketch?"

"Thought we'd try to give a more accurate representation of her face."

"Sweet Jesus." He read aloud quietly, "Gabriela Delgado…"

Chapter 30

Sunday Dinner

*afternoon...*A bright red Mini-Cooper convertible sat in the driveway, top down, a French baguette and a bottle of Benton Lane Pinot Noir on the backseat. Mark Sanders slid in. "Okay, we're good to go." He stretched his arms upward. "Perfect top-down weather."

Julia drove to the Haven for Seniors Retirement Community. "God, it's beautiful," she said. "Huge trees everywhere. No cars on the street. We should be in a commercial." Soon, she turned into a long driveway bounded by trimmed azaleas, verdant lawn on either side, sprinkled with crepe myrtles, large oaks and colorful sweet gums. "This is how it is when you drive to work here every day, right?"

Mark smiled, his head back, eyes half-closed. "It's so much better with you."

Julia stifled a laugh. "You pick up that line in Scottsdale?"

"Too much?" he said, opening his eyes. "Well, let's just say it's good to be home. It's good to be with you." He reached over and squeezed her hand.

She parked in the shade. They crossed the parking lot and triggered the automatic doors. The scent of spices greeted them. A display dominated the lobby's center—a big pumpkin sat on a wooden picnic table ringed by pies and cookies, and on a second picnic table, a large black cauldron surrounded by mugs, each holding a cinnamon stick, and different varieties of apples scattered about.

Julia signed the guest register, and the couple climbed the stairs to the second floor. Before Julia could knock, her Aunt Louise opened the apartment door and greeted them with hugs and kisses. "Right on time. Come in, come in. I want to hear all about whatever it was you did to get your picture in the paper, dear. And I want to hear all about your trip, Mark."

Louise steered them to the loveseat, then sat in her winged lounge chair. "So? What about the picture, dear? I saw your two sergeants. The ones who came here to stop that horrible man who tried to kill you, Mark."

Mark looked at Julia. "You guys had your pictures in the paper?"

Julia nodded, turned back to Aunt Louise. "It was a last second thing. We were asked to join a raid on a newly opened house of prostitution. It was supposed to be a surprise raid. That picture should never have been taken."

"Oh, my," Aunt Louise said. "So much for the surprise."

"Could have been bad if they'd known we were coming," Julia said.

Aunt Louise nodded. "I don't recall you being involved in this kind of raid before."

Julia shook her head. "No. Prostitution's not usually our beat. But in this case we've been investigating the murder of a ten year-old girl."

"Ten year-old? What's that got to do with prostitution?"

"These so-called prostitutes were all young girls, ages ten to sixteen."

Aunt Louise's hand went to her mouth. "My word. This sounds like a foreign country—one that treats its women and girls like possessions...and worse."

Julia stared at the carpet, her fingers dug into the loveseat cushion. "Like trash…just chew-em-up-and-spit-em-out throwaways."

Aunt Louise leaned forward. Mark monitored Julia from the corner of his eye, but said nothing.

No one spoke.

Julia sensed their eyes on her. "Sorry," she said quietly.

"You have nothing to apologize for, dear," Aunt Louise said. "I used to have the same feelings about you and your brother, Wayne." Her eyes welled up. "Two beautiful children, beaten at your mother's whim, my brother not there to protect you. Unloved. Uncared for. Unwanted." She moved to Julia. Mark rose. Louise took his place. She wrapped her arms around Julia and cocooned her. Julia felt the tension leave her body, and her emotions calm.

Aunt Louise laid her cheek on Julia's head. "This reminds me of the early days, after you and little Wayne came to live with me, when there was a nighttime thunderstorm. You'd come to my room, slowly turn the knob and just stand there. But at the next clash of thunder, you'd run to my bed and dive in, one on my right and one on my left." She pulled back, locked eyes with Julia. "It was pretty clear something very bad had happened during a thunderstorm."

"I watched you conquer those fears and harness your anger. You stuck up for children who were being teased or bullied."

Julia hugged Aunt Louise. "You saved our lives. We weren't throwaways anymore."

Mark smiled, raised his glass. "Best therapy session ever," he said. "What's for dinner?"

Chapter 31

Next of Kin

Sunday...After celebrating the day's last mass, Father K knelt in prayer, his face pained. He pulled a sheet of paper from his pocket and unfolded it. He touched Gabriela Delgado's reconstructed face, traced her features. He took a deep breath, made the sign of the cross, genuflected at the end of the pew. He walked slowly to his car. He drove the short distance from Saint Michael's Church and parked in front of an apartment complex, across the street from a playground. He opened his door to the squeals and laughter of young children. Two women sat on a bench, strollers nearby. He walked to the apartment and knocked.

A young teenage boy opened the door a few inches. His eyes grew large. "Oh. Father K."

The priest greeted him in Spanish. "Hello, Jorge. May I come in?"

"Si, Padre." Jorge smiled, yelled over his shoulder in Spanish, opened the door wide and waved him inside. His parents, Ricardo and Leticia Delgado, came quickly into the small living room, grasped the priest's hands. "Father. Welcome to our home. We are so blessed to have you," Ricardo said in Spanish. "Please, sit." He turned to his wife. "Something to drink for the Padre."

Leticia returned with a glass of lemonade. Father K

smiled, thanked her, took a few sips, put his glass down. His face turned serious. He leaned forward. "I have very sad news." He pulled out the MPD flyer with the sketch of Gabriela, unfolded it and handed it to Ricardo. Leticia pressed close to see the flyer, written in both English and Spanish.

Father K watched them, eyes glistening. "You have just been reunited with your niece Gabriela. This is such horrible news." He placed his hand on Ricardo's shoulder. "I was shocked when the police gave me this flyer. …She was found in a grave with her diary. That's how they know her name."

Chapter 32

Who's in Charge?

*Monday morning, MPD conference room, 201 Poplar...*Julia strode down the hall wondering why this last-minute meeting was called. She entered to find a mix of MPD officers and Sheriff's deputies, some standing, some seated.

Ayers walked up. "Just got word, Robbins was knifed this morning. Looks bad. He's in surgery at the MED."

"Don't suppose we know who did it?" Julia said.

Ayers shook his head. "Doctor says if he survives, he won't be able to talk to anyone for days."

Tagger and Marino entered. "Any idea why we're meeting?" Marino asked.

"It's the official, *we're all going to work together* meeting," Ayers said.

They turned as TBI Special Agent Dawkins came in, followed immediately by the Director of the Memphis Police Department and the Shelby County Sheriff.

"Let's grab a seat," Julia said. Once seated she motioned Marino and Tagger in tight. "Robbins was knifed this morning. In surgery. May not make it."

"Damn it," Tagger hissed.

The seats filled up. The Director and Sheriff pulled up chairs side-by-side at the head of the conference table, Dawkins on their right.

Julia listened as the Sheriff and the Director kicked off the meeting in a political show of solidarity, clarified that the cemetery investigation was under the jurisdiction of the Tennessee Bureau of Investigation and had their full support, then left.

Dawkins moved to the head of the table. Julia remembered Dawkins from the Tuesday night raid on the GDs' party house. She thought he looked older in the light—graying hair, laugh lines, weathered skin, nicotine-stained fingers, and circles under his gray eyes. She pegged him to be in his late forties, trim and muscular—the body of a thirty-year-old.

Dawkins cleared his throat. "It's always important to have the bosses' blessing." He smiled. "I hope from here on we're just a group of professionals working together on behalf of these victims. I understand we need to thank Sergeant... Marino, is it?"

Marino lifted his hand off the table.

Dawkins nodded. "Sergeant Marino's the one who opened this Pandora's Box when he found the first body. As of last night, we've scanned some two hundred of the cemetery's eight hundred-plus graves. So far, we've found images of four more bodies, all buried two or three feet below the surface. We hope to complete our scanning by Wednesday afternoon."

Dawkins waited for the side conversation to die down. "I talked to your county medical examiner, Dr. Sales. She said she could use some help, especially if there'll be more bodies. The Disaster Mortuary Operational Response Team will assist us in identifying the remains. The size of the team will depend on the number of bodies we uncover. Regardless, the team will have at least one medical examiner to help Dr. Sales collect forensic evidence. He arrived yesterday. We expect DMORT to have all its members on site by Tuesday.

They'll start digging up remains as soon as they're ready. We appreciate the Sheriff's Deputies who have been providing security at the cemetery, 24/7."

Dawkins looked at the only female in the room. "Lieutenant Todd?"

Julia nodded.

"I understand you've begun an investigation into the death of the first recovered victim. I'll need to be briefed. We want to make sure this is a coordinated investigation. Let's talk after the meeting."

Julia tensed. *Here it comes. My new dance partner is stepping on my toes and second guessing my moves.*

***

The room cleared except for Dawkins, Julia, Marino, and Tagger.

"I'm Raphael Dawkins. Folks just call me Rafe. I remember you three from the raid on the party house last week. Major Williams tells me you're his best homicide team. I know Lieutenant Todd and Sergeant Marino, but I don't think we've been introduced, Sergeant...?"

"Tagger. Johnnie Tagger."

"Good. First things first. I'm not out to interfere with anything you'll be doing. At the same time, it's vital that we stay in sync. And for the time being, I'd like all media interviews to come through me. That work for you?"

Julia nodded.

"I've been briefed on the young girl found last week. Looks like there's a good chance that both she and the child in this first grave came across the Texas-Mexican border. You're working both those cases, right?"

All three nodded.

"My experience in other jurisdictions is that folks can get

riled up about illegal aliens. So much so they do a piss-poor job of investigating. On the other side, the immigrant group doesn't trust law enforcement, and they're scared to death of the gangs that run the trafficking. Hostile law enforcement and scared immigrants make a successful investigation almost impossible. Now, just between us chickens, I don't give a rat's ass about legal or illegal aliens. My job's to solve these murders, and if I'm lucky, keep any more from happening."

Julia smiled. "Preaching to the choir, Rafe."

"Out-friggin'-standing. Now, bring me up to speed. What have you done? What do you know? What do you need to know? And how can I help?"

Chapter 33

Update

MPD conference room, 201 Poplar...Julia stepped back, reviewed her writing on the white board, then looked at Dawkins.

Victim	Perp	Details
Ollie (9 yrs)	Abducted in Savannah, TN by freelancer. Sold to GDs.	Cupie doll tattoo. Gold thumb ring. In party house last week.
Jane Doe (9-10 yrs). Two girls—early teens.	Clive Andrews	Dead. Chloroform. Two girls found in his home, chained to floor.
Gabriela Delgado (9-10 yrs)	UK	Cemetery. Diary. Killer wore large star-shaped ring.
T	GD hit?	Madam at party house. Dead.
Marcus Robbins	GD hit?	Funeral home director. Surgery at MED.

"Okay," she said. "Here goes. We have five girls: three age nine or ten, two early teens, all found within a ten-day time-frame—two dead, three alive. My neighbor's grand niece, Ollie, was abducted Friday before last from Savannah in West Tennessee, and sold to the GDs here in Memphis. She was the little one of the group we rescued last week." Dawkins nodded. "We're thinking the kidnapper's in business for himself. She said her perpetrator had a tattoo, possibly a cupie doll, on the back of his right hand. Wore a plain gold band on his right thumb."

Julia pointed. "Number two is a Jane Doe, found dead the very next day in midtown. Indications are she could be from Mexico. Died of chloroform poisoning. We have a witness who saw Clive Andrews come out of the woods where Jane was found, consistent with the medical examiners TOD. We arrested him two days ago."

Marino jumped in. "We searched Andrews's home. Found two girls alive, early teens, locked in a soundproof room and chained to the floor. They're recently documented immigrants, kidnapped as they walked home from school in a rainstorm. Andrews offered them a ride. We see him as a pedophile. Young teen girls are his preferred targets. We think he grabbed the younger Jane Doe primarily to sell her. The teens are undergoing tests at the MED."

Julia tapped the white board. "And just five days later, we dug up the remains of a third girl in the Cross On The Hill Cemetery. According to a diary found in the grave, she's from Mexico. Name's Gabriela Delgado. Murdered about a week ago. Girls rescued from the party house reported having been with two young girls the week before. Never saw either girl again. They heard the house madam T say one was dead. We think that girl was Gabriela. The girls also said they saw a man matching Phillip Beard's description. He's the head of the local GD cell. Makes Beard our top suspect for Gabriela's murder."

"The next victim on the board is the party house madam, T, found dead in the women's county jail. Name's Terrencia James. She may have been an eye witness to Gabriela's murder. We suspect Phillip Beard ordered a hit to keep her quiet. And finally, we arrested Marcus Robbins, director of the funeral home and the Cross On The Hill Cemetery, for his role in burying Gabriela's body. He was knifed this morning." Julia pointed. "Next door in the men's jail. He's in bad shape. Nobody knows if he'll pull through. No update on his condition."

Julia returned to her seat. "Now we're waiting on the results of your effort at the cemetery, Rafe. I'm betting it's a GD burial ground."

Dawkins nodded. "What's with the Mexican connection?"

Julia took a deep breath. "We've been working on that. So far, we're dealing with smoke and mirrors. Looks like there's a network dedicated to protecting undocumented immigrants who've been smuggled into the US."

"I've heard the same thing in other parts of the state," Dawkins said. "But what's that got to do with illegals getting murdered?"

"This is the part that adds to the smoke," she said. "Or maybe the mirrors. We're working on the possibility that someone has hacked into the network's computer system and is kidnapping the kids before they arrive in Memphis, then selling them to the GDs. Clive Andrews could be involved."

"First I've heard of anything like that," said Dawkins.

"Going back to T," Marino said. "We visited Phillip Beard's stronghold last Friday. Set off some fireworks. We questioned him about the party house and any involvement in the death of Gabriela. We told him we had a witness who could place him at the scene of Gabriela's murder."

"Those girls from the party house?" Dawkins asked.

"Yeah," said Julia.

"Anyway," said Marino. "Caught him off guard. If someone witnessed him killing Gabriela, good chance it was T. Think he panicked. May be trying to clear the decks. T was dead the next day. I think a kid named Chub, one of his teenage gangbangers on lookout at the party house, is on that hit list. And we can't rule out the oldest girl caught in the sweep last Tuesday night. Word is she might not have been 'one of the girls'. It's looking more like she worked her way up the ranks and that T may have been grooming her for a promotion to madam. She's been discharged. Only three girls still at the MED. Major Ayers has doubled security there. And Chub is stashed away in a safe house."

"We collected a ring at Beard's place that may be linked to Gabriela's murder," Julia said.

"How so?"

"Has a big six-pointed star." Julia pointed to the side of her head. "Gabriela has an indentation in her skull that looks like something this ring would make. We think the ring belonged to Beard. It's at the lab now."

"Great update," Dawkins said. "Anyone else on Beard's hit list?"

"Yeah," said Tagger. "The three of us."

Chapter 34

Ana Sofia

201 MPD conference room...Julia, Tagger and Marino stayed behind after Dawkins left.

"As long as we're down here, I want to talk to Clive Andrews," Julia said. How 'bout you come with me, Professor?"

"Love to," Marino said. "Johnnie and I need to go over the list of volunteers we want to follow-up on. I'll meet you at interrogation."

Julia nodded and left.

Marino flipped through his notepad as he scanned Bree's list. "Folks I thought were opposed to undocumenteds match the ones the secretary marked—Fred Dancer, Sara Hanks, Marshall Henderson, Leonard Owen.

Tagger pointed. "According to Bree, Eve Lowell would be on that list as well, but she's been gone for a couple of months. Says nobody knows why."

"I'll take the first two," Marino said.

They pulled out their phones.

***

Interrogation, 201...Julia put in a request to have Andrews brought over for questioning, then grabbed her phone.

"Hello, Lieutenant," Diane Willingham answered. "What

can I do for you?"

"Down at 201 in interrogation, waiting on Clive Andrews. Wondered how the girls are doing."

"Great timing, Lieutenant. We just wrapped up a staffing at the Child Advocacy Center. Had the ADA, a bilingual trauma therapist, a nurse, my supervisor and me discussing the two girls y'all found in Andrews's house. All in all, the girls are looking good physically. Amazing what a shower, good meals, and thirty hours-worth of IVs will do. Hard to get more intense than what they've been through. The girls have developed an incredible bond. That's a good thing."

"And drugs?" Julia asked.

"Found GHB in their system."

"The date-rape drug?"

"Correct. The crime scene team found liquid GHB in the kitchen."

"Andrews offered them a ride in the rain, right?"

"Right. Parents reported the kids missing Wednesday before last. Never made it home from school. From what we've understood, he hit 'em both with chloroform as soon as they got in his pickup."

"They say anything about our Jane Doe?"

"Yeah, they knew her from the neighborhood. New—maybe an illegal. Said her name was Ana Sofia Herrera. Said she was already chained up, lying beside them when they regained consciousness. As far as the therapist could piece together, the girls refused to eat or drink anything that first night, and all three started screaming. Andrews chloroformed them again."

"Then switched to the GHB?"

"We think so. It's pretty much tasteless. Probably put it in their water. So the girls would have been in and out of consciousness. Therapist says they lost track of the days, especially with the windows blacked out. Both girls said they saw Andrews put a cloth of what they described as *smelly stuff* on Ana Sofia's mouth and nose. She passed out, he dressed her and carried her off. They never saw her again."

***

Marino joined Julia in interrogation.

"Just called Diane Willingham," Julia said. "Your two girls have been talking. Jane Doe was already there when Andrews locked them up, in the same room. They knew her from the neighborhood. Our little Jane Doe's got a name: Ana Sofia Herrera."

"Ana Sofia," Marino said softly, staring somewhere above the table top. "I can still see the place her body was dumped. I promised her we'd find the asshole who did this." He looked up. "But now that we have him, I don't feel any better."

"It's never enough," Julia said. "We can't bring 'em back. ...But don't forget the two girls y'all pulled out of that hell hole. I'm sure they won't forget you."

A sheriff's deputy approached. "Lieutenant, your prisoner's here. Room two. Got his public defender with him. She'll let us know when they're ready."

***

The deputy waved. They scooted their chairs back and walked to the one-way window. Julia thought Clive Andrews looked nondescript, average height and weight. A man who could blend into the background, come and go without being noticed. They entered the interrogation room. Andrews leaned back, appeared relaxed, confident. A young black woman sat near him, writing. She looked up.

"I'm Nadine Henning. I represent Mr. Anderson. And you are...?"

Andrews rolled his eyes, shook his head slightly and mumbled something.

"I'm Lieutenant Todd, this is Sergeant Marino, and," gesturing across the table, "I'm pretty sure that's Clive *Andrews.*"

Henning straightened, confidently flipped through her papers. Stopped. Her shoulders slumped. She sighed, returned to the top page, scratched off *Anderson* and wrote *Andrews.* She briefly met Julia's eyes, neatly squared her papers, took a deep breath and made eye contact, her demeanor now tentative.

Marino smiled. "Hey there, Clive. Long time no see."

"I haven't had the pleasure, Mr. Andrews," Julia said. "But I've seen your handiwork, even carry her picture." Julia unfolded Jane Doe's flyer, held it up. "Did you know her name?"

"Don't answer that," Henning said.

Andrews glanced at the picture, but showed no recognition, no emotion, no interest.

"Her name's Ana Sofia," Julia said. "How'd you find her?"

"Don't answer that," Henning said. "Lieutenant, what are you doing? You have no proof my client knows her, let alone had anything to do with her murder."

Julia pointed to the papers in front of Henning. "Apparently, your information's not as current as mine. We have telephone and computer records of Clive contacting known Gangster Disciples for the sale of girls. We have two witnesses who can place Ana Sofia in Clive's home on the day she was murdered. We have Clive's thumbprint on the brass button of her jeans. And we have witnesses who can place Clive at the scene where Ana Sofia's body was found."

Henning's mouth opened. She recovered her poise. "None of that means my client murdered her."

Julia looked at Andrews. "I want to know how many girls

you've abducted and sold to the Gangster Disciples. And I want to know how you found them."

"What do I get out—?"Andrews asked.

"This meeting is over," Henning interrupted. She turned to Andrews. "We've got a lot more to talk about."

Without another word, Marino and Julia walked out. "That true?" he asked in the hall. "We really have all that evidence?"

Julia shrugged. "Most of it. The lab lifted a partial from her button, matched it to Andrews. And we do have his telephone and computer. No idea if they've found anything. I just threw in the GDs to see if I'd get a rise out of him."

"From Clive's reaction, it looked like you guessed right."

Julia managed a tight smile.

"You think Andrews is involved in the network business?"

"Can't rule him out," she said. "Of course, Ana Sofia was already in Memphis, had been for a while. So she couldn't have been part of the network hack. But as a sadistic pedophile, Andrews would be open to any opportunity to violate kids."

"Been thinking about the two girls," Marino said. "That soundproof room's been there for a while. So what happened to all the other girls he held captive?"

Chapter 35

Digging Deeper

High school students emptied from Apollo Academy, a new charter school in south Memphis. Tagger stopped one and asked how he might find Marshal Hendricks. The student willingly walked him into the school and pointed. Hendricks stood in the hallway, talking to a male student. The student saw Tagger, turned, walked away. Hendricks looked back to see what made him leave.

"Mr. Hendricks?"

"Yes?"

'I'm Sergeant Tagger. Is there some place we can talk?"

"Certainly. My classroom is right here." He led him inside, walking slowly, with a slight limp. "Didn't I see you at the Diocesan office last week? In the hall, after the Hispanic immigrant meeting?"

"Good memory."

Hendricks took a step back and looked up. "Well, you're pretty tall. Hard to forget." He grabbed a gallon jug, poured a glass of water. "Doctor tells me to drink at least eight glasses a day."

Tagger gestured toward the hall. "It looked as if I interrupted your conversation with that student. He didn't seem too happy."

Hendricks swallowed some water. "He's in my Spanish

class. I was getting on him about a late assignment. Kids learn early to put on that pouty face when they don't get their way. They have it down to a science." He smiled. "You even see some professional basketball players use it when the ref calls a foul."

Tagger smiled. "My partner's the one who met with your immigrant volunteer group. I'm following up."

"About the murdered child? He showed us a picture. How horrible." Hendricks took another drink.

"We found the murderer."

Hendricks swallowed faster than intended. Choked. "Ah…that's terrific."

"Yes. A man who lives in midtown."

"And the dead girl? She was an illegal? You're certain?"

"Looks that way," Tagger said. "You aware we've found another dead girl? It made the front page."

"Oh, yes. The one from the cemetery."

"Turns out we have the little girl's diary. Another undocumented immigrant. This one's from the mountains, not far from Mexico City. Name's Gabriela Delgado. Ring any bells?"

"Well, Delgado is a pretty common Mexican name. But I can't recall hearing it recently. You have any leads on her killer?"

"Let's say we have a person of interest we're tracking. Don't worry. We'll get him."

Hendricks drained the glass.

"Were you aware of people helping undocumenteds get settled in Memphis?"

"Helping? You mean smuggling them here? That's big trouble, federal law and all."

"But you've not heard anything about such activities?" Tagger asked.

"No. How could I?"

"You're involved with the Hispanic community, you speak the language...you hear things."

"True," Hendricks said. "Of course. But I've heard nothing about any human smuggling."

"I noticed one member of your group is no longer with you—Eve Lowell."

"Eve," Hendricks stared off. "I always liked Eve," he said softly. He looked up. "We're both Spanish teachers. We hit it off right from the beginning. Then she stopped coming. We never heard why she left. Do you know?"

Tagger shook his head. Smiled. "We'll find her."

***

Marino pulled into the parking lot of the Midsouth Depository in southeast Memphis. Three spaces over sat a black SUV with the rap music's bass so loud it vibrated Marino's lips. The assaultive rhythm stopped. A young black man climbed out, dressed in an oversized football jersey, neatly pressed oversized shorts, and a baseball cap—all some shade of blue. He leaned back into the SUV, retrieved a bulging brown leather briefcase, and swaggered into the bank. Marino jotted down his license number, and followed him in.

The young man stood before a teller, hoisted the briefcase onto the ledge and opened it. Marino could see twenties and hundreds. The teller smiled. Marino thought he heard her say, "Good morning Mr. Benny." Marino took a few steps in the man's direction when, in his peripheral vision, he saw Fred Dancer hurry across the lobby. He was surprised when Dancer slapped him on the shoulder, like he was greeting an old fraternity brother.

Dancer attempted to guide Marino away, but he was immovable, eyes still on Mr. Benny. Dancer moved around him, stood in his line of sight. "Good to see you again,

Sergeant. We can talk in my office."

Mr. Benny's transaction ended. Marino watched him strut out, carrying a much lighter briefcase. Marino looked at Dancer. "Your office?"

Dancer led the way. Once inside, he pointed to a small conference table. "Have a seat." Dancer opened a closet door, hung his suit coat on a wooden hanger, and took a seat.

"Appreciate your seeing me, Mr. Dancer."

"I take it you haven't found your murderer. The person who killed the girl in midtown."

"Actually, we found the creep."

"Really? That's good work, Sergeant. I understand from the papers that a second Mexican child was found buried in the cemetery."

Marino nodded. "Name's Gabriela. Crossed the Texas border a few weeks ago. No record of her having been documented. Not sure how she got to Memphis."

"I certainly hope this is not a trend—more illegal children being murdered."

"TBI's checking each grave site at the Cross On The Hill Cemetery. They could find more."

"Surely not," Dancer said.

"Be helpful if we had a pipeline into the Hispanic community."

"It's kind of like Father K said the other day," Dancer said. "Everyone is so scared, so untrusting. Even if there were illegals coming into Memphis, they wouldn't dare tell anyone."

"But you *know* undocumenteds are here," Marino said. "They get jobs, right? Menial jobs, low-paying jobs. Private citizens and businesses are employing them. Right?"

"I'm certain you are correct. But I don't know of any specific cases. And you won't find any of them working here at the bank."

"How'd you get involved in this volunteer work with the immigrants?"

Dancer sat back. "Community participation is part of the Depository's culture, a requirement for administrators. Given the growing Hispanic population I thought I could kill two birds with one stone—fulfill my volunteer requirements *and* market the Depository to this growing population."

"And how has that worked out for you?"

"Quite well, actually. I've met many committed, hardworking people. People who are contributing to the tax base, and who are now banking here."

"What do you know about locals helping to smuggle undocumenteds into Memphis?"

"It'd be naïve to think they're not being helped by somebody."

"But you don't know of anyone associated with this?"

"Certainly not. And if I did, I would report them." Dancer stood. "If there is nothing else? I need to get back to our customers."

Marino closed his notepad.

Mr. Benny, the loud bass, and the black SUV were gone by the time he reached the parking lot.

***

Tagger sat across from Leonard Owen in the Union Station conference room. "Thanks for coming in, Mr. Owen."

"Not a problem, Sergeant," Owen said. "It's easy for me to come to the station. It's on my way home from one of my volunteer sites."

"I'm following up on my partner's visit with your volunteer group last Thursday. He talked to you about a murdered little girl, an undocumented Mexican child. We found the killer."

"That's good news. It means you've wrapped up your

investigation? So what do you need from me?"

"A second little girl was discovered buried in the Cross On The Hill Cemetery. TBI's convinced there will be more bodies coming from that cemetery. Looks like a big enterprise, and we believe a local gang is involved—the Gangster Disciples."

Owens shifted in his seat. "Gangster Disciples? What do they have to do with it?"

"It's part of their sex trafficking operation. Big money involved. We'll know more when we find out who's smuggling the undocumenteds."

Owen sat back. "The other officer didn't say anything about sex trafficking or gangs last week." He looked down. "I don't know anything about that."

Tagger leaned in. "Really? Not even a whisper?"

"I don't like your tone. Are you accusing me of something?"

"No, sir. Just seems odd to me that given your contacts, you'd be so much in the dark."

"So your partner said last Thursday. But far less accusingly." Owen looked at the door. "Are we finished?"

Tagger fixed him with a hard stare.

Owen squirmed.

Tagger sat back. "You're free to go, Mr. Owen. Thanks again for coming in."

***

Marino drove to the Evergreen neighborhood in midtown. He turned into the driveway of a one-and-a-half-story house with yellow siding and white trim. A long wooden ramp, extending from the driveway, dominated the front yard. Marino walked beside the ramp, took the steps, and rang the bell.

Sara Hanks opened the door and waved him in, closed

the door behind him. "I suppose this is about the meeting last Thursday, Sergeant...?"

"Marino, ma'am. I just wanted to follow up. Thank you for making time for me."

She gestured to a chair, and sat. "No problem. I almost never go anywhere." Her eyes drifted to a brown motorized lift recliner, still tipped forward in the raised position, the buckle end of a seatbelt lying across one arm. She noticed Marino had followed her gaze. When she spoke, her words were measured, angry. "My husband was in a bad auto accident...the other driver was *un*insured, *un*licensed, *un*der-the-influence, and *un*documented."

"Sorry to hear that," Marino said softly.

"I suppose I should apologize. I was a bit snippy in the meeting. Actually, I'm snippy pretty much all the time, now. That illegal alien stole my husband's life...stole my life. I have no sympathy for any of them. They get more government services than my American-born disabled husband, and don't have near the restrictions or the ungodly amount of paperwork and bureaucratic hoops to jump through."

Marino paused not sure how to respond. "We've been investigating the abduction and murder of two ten year-old girls—both immigrants."

"Two? I thought there was only one."

"We found a second child buried in a cemetery."

Recall registered in her eyes. "Actually, I did see the newspaper article." Hanks looked away.

Marino waited.

She looked at a photo of her husband and her, hung on the wall. "I give my time helping the legal immigrants through my church—First United Methodist, downtown. The congregation has a long history of service to the community. One of our members spent some time in Texas and worked with immigrants down there. He set up a similar program here. I volunteer as part of our church's commitment to help those in need. But I'm not the person to come to for support of the illegals."

"Just a few questions," Marino said. "We've been hearing about a kind of underground railroad, a network of citizens who smuggle undocumenteds into the country, and transport them to cities like Memphis. That ring any bells for you?"

"Given the increasing numbers of illegals in our country, it stands to reason *somebody's* helping them. A friend of mine talked about it all the time."

"Anything specific?"

"No. But she was determined to find the people responsible. She used to volunteer with the Hispanic immigrants."

"Any chance you're talking about Eve Lowell?"

Hanks made eye contact. "Yes. Do you know Eve? Have you heard from her?"

Marino shook his head. "Her name's on the list of folks who meet at the Catholic Diocese."

"Eve was a godsend after my husband's accident. We became close friends. I miss her. We agreed on everything, especially the illegals. She was a fierce law and order person. If she'd known about this underground railroad, I'm sure she'd have called in the immigration authorities." She stared somewhere in the near distance. "Then one day we didn't hear from her. I called, talked to her husband, even her son Doran." She paused, looked at Marino. "Nobody knew where she went. Police can't find her either. It's not like her to leave without saying anything. I'm afraid something bad happened. Maybe she got too close and these smugglers kidnapped her. ...Or worse."

***

Most of the rush hour traffic had cleared. Tagger followed his GPS into east Memphis, south of Walnut Grove. He found the address in an affluent neighborhood and was soon ringing the doorbell of a large two-story brick home. A short black man opened the door.

"Mr. Lowell?"

"Sergeant…Tagger, is it?" Bernard Lowell said, looking up. "Please, come in. Have a seat." He sat across from him, leaned forward. "This is about Eve, isn't it? Have you found her?"

Tagger put his hands out. "Whoa. I've just learned about your wife's disappearance. I'm afraid I have no news."

Lowell sat back, shoulders slumped, eyes vacant, glistening.

"We're investigating the murders of two children."

Lowell looked up.

"Both appear to be Hispanic, undocumented immigrants. We've been in touch with people who serve Hispanic immigrants to see if anyone might know these children. I know your wife worked with this group."

Lowell stretched and grabbed a photo of his wife, handed it to Tagger—attractive, hair cut short, light brown skin, wide smile, green eyes. "Dedication is one of Eve's strong suits. She speaks fluent Spanish and puts in hours and hours. The people love her."

"Did you ever hear her talk about anyone helping to smuggle undocumented Hispanic families into Memphis?"

Lowell exhaled loudly. "Matter of fact, yes. She was incensed. Wanted to contact the immigration authorities."

"Did she?"

"What? Oh. No. Said she wanted to have proof in hand first."

"What kind of proof?"

"I think it had something to do with computers."

Tagger gestured for him to go on.

"I'm a jeweler. Don't know much about computers. Eve did all that stuff. Eve and Doran."

"Doran?"

"Our son." He brightened. "His teachers have told us for years that Doran is gifted. The high school even arranged special community service credit for him in return for fixing their computers. He's at Duke University for the week, attending some special workshop for gifted kids. He didn't want to go because of Eve. I insisted he go, thought it'd take his mind off his mother. At least for a little while."

"So, Doran and Eve were trying to gather information about smuggling undocumenteds?"

The light was gone from his eyes. "What? ...Oh. ...Don't know. But..."

"But...?"

"But then she was gone. Someone must've kidnapped her. Nothing else makes sense. She'd never leave us...certainly never leave Doran. Her car's gone. No telephone calls. Police tried, but couldn't find her cell phone. Eve's mother in Knoxville says she hasn't heard from her. No charges on her credit cards. No contact for ransom money. The police did their missing person thing. But we've heard nothing."

"And how long ago was this?" Tagger asked.

"Seven weeks and three days."

"I'm very sorry."

"You don't think she's alive, do you? None of the other police officers think so."

"I can't say, Mr. Lowell. But it doesn't sound good."

Lowell began to sob.

Chapter 36

Lab Results

Afternoon, Monday...Julia walked into the Union Station. "Hey, Lieutenant," Teresa said. "The guys haven't made it back yet. They must've stopped at a donut shop."

Julia rolled her eyes. "They're on their way to interview some volunteers who work with Hispanic immigrants."

Teresa nodded, then brightened. "I've got good news and not so good news. Which do you want first?"

"The good news."

"Received the lab report on the gangster's ring and the little girl's diary. Got blood and prints respectively. Copy's on your desk."

"And the not so good news?"

"Elwood called. Sounded upset. More than usual."

"You know why?"

Teresa pouted. "He wouldn't tell me. Kept saying it was highly confidential, could only talk to you. I'm guessing it has something to do with attorneys."

"Where do you come up with this stuff?"

"I just keep my eyes and ears open. Be surprised what tidbits you can pick up around here and how those tiny pieces of information, when put together correctly, can tell you what's going on."

"You sure you weren't a detective in another life?"

Teresa smiled. "I do have a flare for figuring stuff out, don't I?" Her smile faded. "You haven't given me one of those special assignments in weeks. I'm ready when you are."

"Got you on speed dial," Julia said, walking to her office.

Julia grabbed the telephone message, punched in Elwood's office number, got an answering machine. She called his cell. It went to voicemail. Julia dialed IT's general office and asked to speak to Special Agent Elwood Banks. The person who answered said he'd left the office, but didn't know where he'd gone. Julia shifted gears, read the lab report and wondered how many months it would be before they had DNA results.

***

Julia swung by the lab, picked up the ring and diary, and drove to the Coroner's office, just northeast of the medical center. She worked her way through the old building. The smells got stronger. She pushed through wide metal doors to find a gowned figure leaning over a corpse.

"You busy, Doc?"

"You have to get a new line, Lieutenant. Yours is old and tiresome. How about something like, *Sure wish I could give you a hand, Doc.* Or, *I thought I was busy, but seeing you up to your elbows in stomach content analysis makes me embarrassed to even interrupt you.* Whatcha think?"

"The stomach content analysis would be my personal choice, if I could remember that many words. So? You busy?"

Sales poured the stomach contents into a bowl and put it on the scales. "Not sure where you got your manners, but I have to say you're persistent." She stretched off her gloves like a rubber band, and shot them across the room into the waste container. "I suppose you want to talk about the cemetery girl."

"Bingo. Just came from the lab. She held up the star-shaped ring. Thought we could see how well its size and shape match with the indentations on our little girl's head. By the way, the small red book you found in the grave is in fact a diary. One of our Spanish interpreters read it. Said it was written by a ten year-old girl named Gabriela. Gabriela Delgado. An undocumented immigrant from the Sierra Madre Oriental Mountains of Mexico. Looks like the girl in the shallow grave is Gabriela."

"Welcome to the United States of America," Sales said, then paused. "Gabriela, huh? Such a lovely name." Sales walked to the row of drawers and pulled out Gabriela's body. She stuck out her hand.

Julia dropped the ring in it.

"Whoa. This baby weighs a ton." Sales checked the wound, rotated the ring, and lowered it till it hovered just above Gabriela's head. "You wanna get in here? See what ya think?"

Julia moved in closely. "Looks like a match to me." She stepped back. "What could you testify to?"

"I'd say in court that a ring shaped like this one, including the H in the middle, made the indentation on Gabriela's head." She looked at Julia. "Any chance we also have a match?"

"We'll know in due time. The lab pulled blood. So they can match DNA on the ring against the DNA taken from the body."

"It'll take months to get the results, but at least she's in the queue."

Julia gave Sales one of Gabriela's flyers. "I started handing these out. Had our sketch artist reconstruct her face. Nothing yet."

Sales didn't look up. Her eyes moistened as she studied the sketch. "Such a beautiful child...My objectivity allows me to do my job—no attachments, no emotional entanglements, no nightmares. But kids are tough. Even tougher if I let myself think about them as they were in life. Then you bring me a drawing of sweet Gabriela—alive." She looked up. "Find the animal who did this. Nail his ass to the wall. Hell. Nail his balls to the wall, too."

Julia barely moved her lips. "Count on it."

Chapter 37

Wheat from the Chaff

The Union Station conference room...Marino finished scribbling on the white board, stepped back. "That about it, Johnnie?"

"Good enough," Tagger said.

Dancer	Banker	GD deposit
Owen	CPA retired	tied to Dancer ?
Hendricks	Spanish Tchr	
Hanks	Unempl	Disabled husb, undoc driver
Lowell	Spanish Tchr	Missing 2 mths

Marino remained standing, turned to Julia. "I met with the Hispanic immigrant volunteers last Wednesday. Found four who weren't afraid to speak out against undocumented immigrants, even with Father K chairing the group. We got a list of all members as well as a secretary's observations as to which ones were most opposed to undocumenteds. Got a perfect match."

He pointed. "Fred Dancer is the director of a regional bank. I pulled into that bank's lot, a few spots down from a big ole black SUV with tinted windows and shiny spinning chrome rims. This dude, flying GD colors, drops to the asphalt with a bulging leather briefcase. You shoulda been there—one hand holding up his pants, the other carrying the briefcase, marching like a drum major. I followed him inside, didn't know if he was dropping off or picking up. Saw him open the briefcase and make a *cash* deposit. A big one. I'd have learned more, but Dancer hustled over, clearly intent on keeping me from seeing the entire transaction."

"Dancer's laundering money for the GDs?" Julia said.

"Maybe just under the federal banking law's ten thousand dollar reporting limit," Marino said, sitting down. "I'll touch base with our friendly bank examiner at the Treasury.

Julia nodded. "What about...Owen?"

"A retired accountant," Tagger said. "He's scared about something. Feels dirty. According to the secretary, he and Dancer are joined at the hip, with Dancer calling the shots. I told him we suspected the GDs of being involved in sex trafficking, including our two dead Mexican girls. Owen reacted at the mention of the Gangster Disciples. Seemed surprised, worried. I challenged him. But he got up and left. He's mixed up in something. Just don't know what."

"And, Hendricks?" Julia asked.

"I talked to Marshal Hendricks," Tagger said. "He's a high school Spanish teacher. Found him at his school, talking to a student outside his classroom. The student saw me come in and took off."

Julia cocked her head. "Like he'd seen you before?"

"Or just because you're a cop?" asked Marino.

"Sounds as if y'all were in my head," Tagger said. "Had the same questions. Couldn't answer either of 'em. Hendricks said he was getting on the kid for not turning in an assignment. He denied any knowledge of a network. He *was* interested in what I knew about Eve Lowell. Said they were close."

Marino jumped in. "Speaking of Eve Lowell, I talked to Sara Hanks. Turns out her husband was permanently disabled in a car accident caused by an undocumented driver. She's royally pissed about that. Said Eve Lowell was a friend. A pair of friends with no love lost for undocumenteds. She's angry enough, but my gut says she's not involved in any kidnappings."

"And Lowell?" Julia asked.

"Eve Lowell's been missing almost two months," Tagger said. "Like Hendricks, she's a Spanish teacher. Missing persons has no clue where she is. I talked to her husband. He told me Eve was opposed to undocumenteds purely on legal grounds. Said she got wind of the local smuggling operation. Became obsessed with finding proof of the network's activities and taking the evidence to INS. Their teenage son Doran is a computer genius. The husband didn't know if Eve had found what she was looking for, or if she'd asked Doran for help. Doran's out of town. He'll be back Friday."

"We need to talk to that boy," Julia said.

Chapter 38

A Busy Tuesday

Tuesday, 5:19 AM...Julia woke before the alarm. Her brain had been firing all night. *What if Elwood sets up a phony travel itinerary but can't identify the smuggler's IP address? The perp will assume the email is legit and drive to who knows where to abduct a child. Not finding that child, he'll take anyone who's handy. We'd be no better than Sanchez and Wallace. We need backup plans.*

Julia put on her running clothes, double-knotted her shoe laces, and went outside for her morning run. The high humidity made breathing and thinking difficult. She never gave a second thought to the car parked across the street from the InsideOut Gym, despite an almost empty parking lot, and a driver inside.

***

Tuesday 5:55 AM, the MED...The police officer had pulled hospital security duty for the past four days. Till now, things had been quiet. Only three girls remained hospitalized, still dealing with heroin withdrawal. He watched a black man in pale blue scrubs push a work cart past the nurses' station, head down. Not the usual time. Thirty feet away, the officer stepped into the middle of the hallway. "I need to see some ID."

The man looked up, smiled, kept coming.

The officer loosed the security strap and grabbed the grip of his Sig Sauer. "Stop right there," he ordered, left hand extended in front, palm out.

The man continued walking, but released his right hand from the push bar.

***

*Tuesday, 6:10AM...*Tagger's cell buzzed. "Tony. What's up?"

"You left for the station yet?" Marino asked.

"Just heading for the door. Why?"

"Had a tail since I left the subdivision. Dark blue SUV, tinted windows. Made a few turns. He stayed with me. I'm on Walnut Grove coming into town, just crossed I-240. Called for help. Should be seeing flashing blues shortly. But you need to stay put. I've got cars headed your way—the Lieutenant's as well, just to be sure. Haven't been able to reach her."

***

*6:14 AM, the InsideOut Gym...*Julia slid her card under the scanner and headed for a back room to stretch before punching and kicking the heavy bag. She sat on a mat, legs straight, stretched forward, fingers wrapped around her insteps, chin on her shins. She heard metallic clicking and turned slightly to see a thin black man looming over her, flipping a butterfly knife in his left hand—open, closed, open...

Girty came in, gloved-up for the heavy bag, saw the man, stifled scream, and sneaked up behind him. She positioned her feet to shoulder width, bent her knees, stepped forward with her left foot, and sent a hard straight jab into his kidney. The man arched his back and yelled, turned to face Girty. He sneered, started clicking his butterfly knife—blade in, blade out...Girty froze.

Julia rocked back on her shoulders, knees touching her chin, like a compressed spring, then kipped up to her feet. She took one step and kicked the back of the man's knee, causing him to lose his balance. From behind, she seized the wrist of his knife hand. Girty again stepped forward and landed a straight jab to his jaw, stunning him. Holding his wrist and grabbing the side of his neck, Julia forced him to the floor, drove her knee into his back, and twisted his arm till he dropped the knife.

"Take his shoes off, Girty," Julia directed. "Give me the laces."

Girty yanked off one tennis shoe, then the other, and hurriedly pulled the laces out.

The man struggled. "Don't move!" Julia ordered, twisting his arm again, hard. He yelled, then stopped struggling. Julia took the shoelaces and tied the man's hands behind his back.

Julia looked up. Girty's eyes were open wide, her face red. Julia smiled. "You've been practicing."

Girty nodded, managed a little smile. "You saved my life..."

"And you saved mine," Julia said, touching her arm. "And together we took this SOB out."

***

5:58 AM the MED...The custodian's right hand came up from behind the pushcart, holding an MP9 machine pistol. The officer drew his Sig and squared off, both hands on his weapon. The two men squeezed their triggers. Both lurched back. The impact of the bullet spun the officer, falling on his left side. He struggled up to one knee, pressed his gun hand against his bleeding left shoulder.

A door burst open, banged against the wall. A female officer squatted, her weapon out. Her eyes moved quickly from the wounded officer to the custodian's cart. A foot stretched out from behind the cart, not moving. She flattened on the floor, eyes sighting down the top of her weapon, looking under the cart. She saw the machine pistol on the floor, inches from the custodian's hand. She jumped to her feet, ran to the far side of the cart, kicked the pistol away. She reached down. No pulse. A red circle covered the man's breast pocket, a hole in the upper left corner. She ran back to her partner and yelled, her voice echoing off the hospital walls. "I need a doctor! Shots fired! Officer down! I need a doctor, now!"

***

6:12 AM...Marino keyed his two-way. "I'm driving a silver Yukon, heading west on Walnut Grove, about to cross Highland. A dark blue SUV behind me." Blue flashers came into view, two squad cars coming toward him, no sirens. Marino pulled his steering wheel left, slammed on his brakes, causing him to skid sideways, blocking both lanes of traffic behind him. He powered down his window and aimed his Sig Sauer at the trailing SUV. The driver screeched to a stop, almost hitting the Yukon. He shoved the gearshift into reverse, squealed back. One squad car passed the SUV and blocked its escape. The second pulled in front, pinning the SUV in. Marino was out the door and striding up the street, weapon drawn. More squad cars made the scene.

***

6:12 AM...Tagger squinted through the front door peephole. Nothing. Carefully, he lifted the end of a single windowblind slat. He didn't recognize the black car parked across the street, two houses down. *How many cars? How many shooters?*

His phone rang. He snatched it up. "Hello."

"Mr. Johnnie, this is Agnes across the street. I'm not being nosey, really I'm not. But there are three men in your driveway, hanging around your car. If they're friends of yours, I apologize."

"Thank you so much, Agnes. As it turns out, they are not friends. Don't let them see you looking out your window. Police are on their way."

"But *you* are the police, aren't you?"

"I am, indeed. Sometimes even the police need help."

Tagger saw squad cars roll up from both ends of the street. The driver in the parked car laid on the horn. The three men ran from the driveway, started toward their car, stopped when they saw the squad cars. Tagger bolted out the back door, weapon in hand, and blocked their retreat. "Freeze!" he ordered. "Drop the guns! Get over here! Hands against the side of the house."

One man started to bring up his MP9 machine pistol. Tagger sent two rounds center mass. The man collapsed. His buddies quickly dropped their weapons and stretched their hands against the house.

Two officers ran, weapons drawn. One to Tagger, the other to the parked car, barking commands to the driver, "Hands on the wheel." He walked to the driver's door and opened it. "Come on out! Hands first!" The driver complied. The officer spun him around, kicked his feet apart, shoved him forward, his hands on the car.

***

*201 Poplar...*Julia's team met in booking, all three wide-eyed, keyed up, Julia still in her running gear. Ayers strode in. "You all okay?"

The three nodded.

"Perps at all sites are Gangster Disciples, Ayers said. "Found extra weapons and ammo in each of the cars, even the one at the gym."

"Guess he wanted to try out his new butterfly toy," Julia said. "Thank goodness. Don't think my body would take another MP9 round."

Nobody laughed.

Ayers paused. "A SWAT unit is prepping to descend on Beard. I assume you'll want to be in on it."

"Damn right," Tagger said.

"I'm sure he's alibied up," said Marino. "A late night poker game, no doubt. Lots of witnesses."

"We heard about the MED," Julia said. "The officer going to make it?"

"Hit in the shoulder," Ayers said. "But he took out the shooter. He's in surgery now. Never got to the girls, but did scare the bejesus out of 'em."

"Any word on Chub?" Julia asked.

Marino spoke up. "All's been quiet at the safe house."

"Finish your paperwork," Ayers said. "We need to pay Mr. Beard a visit, let him know who's running this city. I'll find a judge, get the paperwork, and contact Dawkins. Let's meet at the Mount Moriah Station. Say…oh-nine-hundred?"

Chapter 39

Remains

*Tuesday, the Berston Funeral Home...*A section of the mortuary had been set aside as a staging area for examining and identifying human remains discovered just below the surface of existing graves.

Dawkins stood in front of a dozen or so people—DMORT volunteers and crime scene investigators. "We should complete our scanning operation today. So far, scans indicate nine bodies."

Dr. Evelyn Sales stood. "As Medical Examiner, I want to thank you for coming." She looked at a man sitting far left. "Dr. John Largent, ME from Johnson City, came in yesterday. I put him to work before he could unpack his bags. We worked together a few years back in his stomping grounds, dealing with a large commuter plane crash near the Tri-Cities airport."

Largent nodded. "Perhaps the biggest difference in our situation is the plane had a passenger manifest. We don't know who these people are. A missing person's list is the closest we can come."

Sales spoke up. "We know from our first recovery here that at least one body is an undocumented immigrant, a person with no records whatever. To date we have examined four of the nine bodies—one adult male, three adolescent females, one prepubescent female. I have a team of crime scene investigators who've been sifting through the soil for evidence. We'll depend on others to reconstruct facial features, track down dental records, etc."

"If there are no questions," said Dawkins, "let's get to work."

Chapter 40

The Arrest

*8:45 AM, Tuesday, GD compound...*Beard sat at the dining room table, cussing under his breath. Empty *Burger King* bags and cups littered the table. He reached out with a big swing of his arm spilling coffee and knocked the trash to the floor.

Lil J opened the door and leaned in. "There're all waiting outside, Poppa."

"So get them in here!" he bellowed.

Lil J motioned, stood beside the door. Three men stood but did not approach. Lil J stepped toward them, motioned angrily. "Now!" he whispered loudly. The men fell in line, passed through the door, and walked up on Beard's left. Nobody sat. Lil J followed, walked to the other side of the table and took a seat on Beard's right.

Beard slammed his fist on the table. "Dammit ta hell! Was there, or was there *not*, kill orders given?"

Heads nodded.

"Then why's every damn target, 'cep' T, still standing?" He pulled a Glock and laid it on the table. "I have enough rounds in this magazine to take all y'all out, and still get those cops and kids. Who wants to be first?"

Bam! Bam!

Front and rear doors splintered open. A police SWAT unit poured inside, going from room to room, yelling. Julia followed Ayers through the front door, Tagger and Marino through the back. Ayers turned the door knob to the dining room and Julia went through first, gun pointed. Beard stood, Glock in hand. The other gang members reached for theirs.

"Drop it!" Julia ordered, aiming directly at Beard. "I won't miss. Drop it. Now!"

Ayers and three SWAT members squeezed in behind her and quickly fanned out, establishing overlapping fire zones.

Beard broke into a broad smile, placed his Glock on the table. His crew did the same.

"Hands on your heads," Ayers demanded. Turned to the SWAT team, "make sure we can match the weapon to each man."

Tagger and Marino came in. "Let me do the big man," said Tagger, moving behind Beard. "He'll take more than one cuff." He linked two flexicuffs, pulled Beard's left hand behind his back, slipped the threaded nylon cuff over his hand and pulled, then secured the right hand. Julia kept her Sig pointed at him.

"Surprised to see us?" Julia said.

"No, momma. I kinda expected it. Getting used to seeing you just show up. By the way, what's the charge?"

"Let's start with illegal possession of firearms" she said.

"Sheeit," said Beard. "We'll be walking by supper time."

"Don't count on it," said Marino. "There're so many GDs to process. Could take all night."

Beard looked at Marino. "Hey, little man. You gonna stare me down again?"

Marino smiled. "Not worth my time. Besides, my gang's bigger than yours."

"Yeah, but mine don't play by no rules."

They marched the GDs out the front door and down the steps, where five other gang bangers lay face down in the front yard, hands behind their heads. Two paddy wagons waited outside.

Chapter 41

Crossed Wires

Julia's cell buzzed as she left the coroner's office, Elwood's name on the screen. "I've been trying to get you, El. What's going on?"

"Can't talk on the phone. Come to the Sputnik." He clicked off.

Sputnik? What the hell?…Oh. Sanchez and Wallace…across the street from that liquor store's crazy sign. Julia drove the six minutes to Poplar and Evergreen to the two-story brick building, painted white. A 'closed' sign hung inside the heavy glass door. She banged on the glass. Wallace opened it, but did not speak. "Is Elwood Banks here?" Wallace gestured with his head. Julia moved past him, strode to their conference room. Wallace followed.

Elwood and Sanchez sat facing one another. As soon as Julia appeared in the doorway, Elwood blurted out, "Sorry, Lieutenant. I didn't know what to do. These two have threatened me and my family with lawsuits. This is way over my pay grade."

Julia dropped in next to Elwood. Wallace sat beside Sanchez. Julia looked at the couple, then back at Elwood. "Somebody talk to me."

"I was doing what you asked me to do," Elwood said.

"Load a copy of their encryption software into my laptop."

"But that's not all," Sanchez said, pointing a quivering finger at Elwood. "You said you wanted to see how it tied in with other systems in our computer. You promised you wouldn't pull up any confidential information. Not so much as a name."

Elwood turned to Julia. "I set up a communication, like we talked about, saying an immigrant would be arriving in Memphis on Sunday afternoon. But I didn't get a single nibble. Nobody tapped into the encrypted email. I asked the attorneys to let me check their computer. Turned out they gave me the wrong encryption disc. They gave me the one they use in their general practice."

"And you saw our client list," Wallace said, slapping the table. "No one is allowed to see that list."

"We could be disbarred," Sanchez said.

Julia raised her hands, palms out. "Certainly y'all have IT people check your computers, fix them, and upgrade them all the time."

"Of course," Wallace said. "But they've all been vetted. We've never had a policeman break into our files, let alone without a subpoena."

Julia signed a timeout. "This makes no sense. We already agreed to maintain your confidentiality. Something else is going on."

The two attorneys fidgeted, shared long looks. Sanchez cleared her throat. "Do we still have our agreement? The one in which we protect one another...as we do what you called a *dance*?"

"Absolutely," Julia said. "How about a nice slow waltz?"

"Hypothetically, let's say that last Saturday morning Elwood set up a fake travel itinerary—"

"I just said I did," Elwood interrupted.

Julia put a hand on his arm. "Hypothetically speaking. A fake itinerary on your general encryption software..."

"Yes. For a Sunday arrival." Sanchez took a breath. "And let's say that a legitimate itinerary was received that same Saturday on the *other* encryption software, also for a Sunday arrival."

Julia's eyes opened wide. "What?"

"Remember?" Sanchez said. "*Hypothetically.* Assumptions were made that the police had sent the travel itinerary, and would be there to grab the kidnapper. But it turns out the police did *not* send this encrypted email...because they had the *wrong* encryption software."

"In this scenario, are you suggesting that somebody abducted a family?"

Sanchez stared at the table, spoke softly. "A mother and child. ...It would be a logical assumption." She looked up, then at Wallace. "We feel...terrible."

"Jesus." Julia slammed her fist on the table. Everyone jumped. "More throwaways." She leveled her gaze. "I just drove here from the Coroner's Office. They have another dead Mexican girl. The second in four days."

No one spoke for a long time. Sanchez and Wallace's fingers intertwined. Elwood fidgeted. Julia focused on controlling her breathing, eyes staring somewhere beyond the room. Julia broke the silence, pointed to Elwood's laptop. "El, you remember how we got that?"

"Of course. Got it from the twins who'd hacked into medical records in hospitals and medical practices. One powerful machine."

"That's why you kept it instead of turning it in, right?"

Elwood nodded slowly.

"I think it's time to get back on the bike and take it for a spin. Can you track down who's been hijacking the travel itineraries?"

"Oh, that shouldn't be hard, Lieutenant." He looked at the two attorneys. "But we're going to have to have permission to take over their computer for a while."

Julia looked across the table. "How about it? I'm here to vouch for this IT guy. Consider him vetted, just like any IT person you hire."

"I don't know…" said Sanchez.

"Remember the issue here. We're all in agreement. We all want to help these kids and families. We want them to be safe. We want them to be free from abuse. And from what I've seen, you two do not want to be responsible for even one more immigrant being kidnapped or murdered."

Sanchez and Wallace exchanged looks, then nodded. "I'll get my laptop," Wallace said.

Chapter 42

FLIR

*Tuesday evening, men's restroom, Visitor Center, Shelby Farms Park...*Seven year-old Brandon Vick washed his hands. A man took the adjacent sink, turned the water on.

"Hey, there," the man said. "You been having a good time today?"

"Yeah," Brandon said. "But my mom says it's getting dark, time to go home."

The man grabbed a length of brown paper from the dispenser. "Your mother is waiting for you?

"Yeah."

The man balled up the wet paper, dropped it in the waste container. "Here in the visitor center?"

"Down by the lake."

The man reached in his pocket, retrieved a small brown spray bottle. "Want to smell something really gross?" He dug out a handkerchief.

Brandon stepped forward.

"Come on. Get your nose closer."

When Brandon leaned in, the man sprayed chloroform on the handkerchief, shoved it against the boy's face, and held it tightly till Brandon's body went limp. He scooped the boy up and walked through the lobby and outside. Brandon's head on the man's shoulder, looked like a father carrying his sleeping seven year-old, exhausted from a long day at the park.

***

Marino drove north on Germantown Parkway, heading home after a demanding day. The sun had already set. His speaker keyed on, "Possible child abduction at Shelby Farms," the dispatcher said. "Seven year-old white male, medium build, brown hair. Yellow jacket, blue jeans. Available units set checkpoints for cars leaving park. Acknowledge."

"This is three-four-seven," Marino said. "I can cover Pine Lake Drive, on the north exit at Mullins Station."

"Roger, three-four-seven," the dispatcher said.

Marino, driving in the right lane, forced his big Yukon across three lanes of traffic and made a U-turn.

***

*Memphis Police Department helipad...*The radio keyed on. "Captain. This is Sergeant Wilson. Got a missing seven year-old boy at Shelby Farms. You available?"

"We are," said Captain Alton Yazou. "Fill me in while I get my FLIR tech."

"Great," said Wilson. "White male. Last seen going into the visitor center. Yellow jacket, blue jeans, Nikes. Medium build, brown hair. Mother Called 911 six minutes ago. Said she started looking for him when he didn't return promptly. Don't know if he just wandered off, or if he's with someone."

"You have a search team on the ground?" Yazou asked.

"Organizing as we speak. Mother and a handful of parents have already hit the bathrooms and run around Patriot Lake to the south. Nothing. Of course there's a lot of park to cover."

"Five times as big as Central Park—I've seen the ads. So

we've got a seven year-old with maybe a fifteen-minute head start if he's on his own. He could be a ways out. No idea where he'd be if he's been abducted."

"We began setting up checkpoints on all roads exiting the park as soon as we got the call," Wilson said. "But if it's an abduction he may have already been driven out...anyway, looks like we got thirty or so volunteers, a couple of four-wheelers, and a search-and-rescue dog. The ranger's going over a map with them now. We'll give 'em a quick orientation, form a circle around the center, and walk out. Sure could use y'all's eye in the sky."

"See you in less than five." Yazou said as he climbed into the MPD Bell JetRanger helicopter. FLIR Technician Jennifer Toos was already buckling in. She had a reputation for working magic with the Spectrolab-SX-16 forward looking infrared camera—FLIR for short. Yazou piloted the chopper and, when needed, operated the Nightsun XP searchlight. The FLIR was calibrated to enhance heat, while the searchlight had 50 million candlepower and could light up the ground as if it were high noon in Death Valley.

***

Shelby Farms gate nine...Marino pulled into the one-way exit for Pine Lake Drive, not far from the Horse Cross Country stables to the east and the large playground west. Four cars sat in the parking area nearest the exit. He parked his Yukon in the middle of the road, facing the wrong direction, headlights and flashers on. Two cars approached. Marino stopped each one, checked driver's licenses and trunks. Nothing.

***

The airborne Bell Jet Ranger...Yazou settled over the darkened Shelby Farms Park, and began a spiraling search pattern, extending from the visitor center where the boy was last seen. The FLIR peppered the screen with ghostly white images of radiating heat—raccoons, dear, frogs, and any other animal. Images of adult searchers were visible as was the search-and-rescue dog. Each leaving a heat signature with every step taken.

The first two concentric aerial search circles revealed nothing unusual. On the third pass, Toos yelled out, "Hold up. I want to check these heat patterns. Looks like footprints, off the trail, in and out of these trees. Not too old. Probably adult."

She pointed to the screen, overlaid on a map of Shelby Farms. "Slide off northeast. …Damn, lost them under the canopy. Stay on the same heading, Cap. We've got a clearing coming up. …Something happened here. Lots of foot prints, leaves turned over. Keep going. …Nope. Lost him. Give me a small circle. …Whoa!" She pointed to the screen. "See 'em? *Small* tracks."

"You thinking what I'm thinking?" Yazou said.

"Yup," said Toos. "Those little tracks didn't just come out of thin air. Like a kid was being carried, then got away. Keep the tight circle. …Still no sign of the adult footprints. … Whoa! The ground's lit up in the shape of a body. Throw the LED down there."

Captain Yazou aimed the spotlight on the coordinates. "I'm not seeing anything, Toos."

"Me neither. Turn it off. I'm betting someone was lying on the ground. It's still warm. Maybe he fell, then took off running. Let's find those tracks again."

Yazou keyed his mike, "We may have something, about a half-mile northeast of the visitor center. Found tracks of an adult. Certainly, now a person of interest. We're following what looks like a child's footprints, heading east. Look for the spotlight."

"We'll give the closest searchers a heads-up," Wilson said. "Keep me posted."

"Roger that," said Yazou.

"Small footprints," said Toos, pointing. "No sign of the adult. Keep on this heading."

They followed the tracks in and out of the canopy. ..."Wow!" Toos pointed to a small heat-generated image on the screen, stretched out on the ground. "Hit the spotlight, sir."

Yazou aimed the searchlight at the target. A yellow jacket glowed. "That's him!"

Yazou hovered, keyed his mike, "Found him. On the ground. Not moving. Track my light."

A half-dozen figures broke from the circle of searchers and converged on the lighted area. "That's him," radioed Wilson. "Unconscious, but breathing. Great find, Captain."

Yazou fist-bumped Toos. "Do we need to transport?"

"We can handle it by ambulance. Much obliged."

"We'll go back and try to pick up the adult's footprints," Yazou said.

***

*Shelby Farms exit nine...*Another set of headlights took the curve, then slowed to a crawl as it approached the Yukon's headlights. Marino waved the male driver forward. The late model Ford Explorer stopped. "What's going on, officer?" the man asked.

"Driver's license please," Marino said, his hand out. The driver complied. Marino shined his flashlight on the license. "You still live at this address, Mr. Kerr?"

"Yes, sir."

"Please step out of the car and open the back," Marino said.

Leonard Kerr complied, raised the hatch. The internal light revealed only a few small boxes and a blanket in the SUV. He looked at Marino. "Who are you trying to find?"

Marino did not respond, held out the license. Kerr's forefinger and thumb grasped it. Marino squeezed it, not letting it go. Kerr looked up, confused. Marino grabbed his wrist, snapped a cuff on it. He spun Kerr around, cuffed the other hand.

"How long you had a tattoo on your hand, Mr. Kerr?"

"What? My tattoo?"

"Yeah. The cupie doll."

Chapter 43

The Day After

Wednesday morning...Marino and Tagger entered the Union Station conference room, coffee cups in hand. Julia finished writing on the crime board. "Morning, guys. Got things to talk about today. First, I'm glad we all made it through yesterday's craziness unscathed. Thanks for sending the cavalry, Professor."

"A little late," Marino said.

Julia smiled. "It's the thought that counts."

"Amen to that," Tagger said, raising his cup.

The two men *clinked* styrofoam cups.

"Beard and most of his bangers are still in jail," Julia said. "Slow going on the bail-out process. Seems felons are not supposed to be carrying guns, especially unregistered, stolen, and automatic guns. They've matched each creep to the gun they were carrying. But can't do the same for the guns we found in the house. The lab is processing all the weapons—lifting fingerprints, firing rounds, magnifying and photographing striations. Now, what about your big-time collar last night, Professor?"

Marino smiled. "Just dumb luck. On my way home last night, when a call came in on a missing kid out at Shelby Farms. The short version is they found the kid—some scratches, a bump on his head, and a chloroform hangover.

Otherwise, he's fine. I set up a checkpoint at a north exit. First two cars that came by were clean. The third seemed clean as well until the dome light shined on his little cupie doll tattoo."

Julia made a fist pump. "Good eye, Ollie. Can't wait to tell my neighbor."

Marino nodded. "She nailed it, all right."

"The TBI and Organized Crime folks are interrogating him," Julia said. "It seems he's an equal opportunity peddler, and has lots of regular customers. They've already got names, phone numbers, and email addresses that will help shut down a few sex trafficking operations."

Tagger set his cup down. "Great catch, Tony."

"We've made good progress," Julia said. "But I've got some bad news. Our plan to have Elwood get into the attorney's laptop went haywire. Turns out the network sent out a new itinerary. A mother and daughter being bussed from San Antonio to Memphis last Sunday. But Elwood had the wrong software. So it looks like the kidnappers got another girl, right under our noses."

Tagger slammed his hand on the table.

Jesus, Mary, and Joseph," Marino said.

Julia's phone rang. "It's Elwood." She swiped the icon. "El. Whatchagot?"

"Lieutenant," Elwood said. "I've got good news and bad news."

"Give me the bad news."

"I got into the laptop. I promise, I didn't read any names… not even the one that looked like my brother-in-law's."

"Elwood!"

"Yeah. Right. I could see that the hacker got in using a phishing email. Looked totally official and all, but it was bogus. I wasn't able to find the IP address. This guy's good, used a boatload of virtual private networks. Sent me to a half-dozen servers, in countries I never heard of."

"Shit."

Elwood paused. "The good news is that I sent a phony itinerary for immigrants coming into Memphis. I could see that the hacker received it. Then I scrubbed the laptop—deleted the network encryption program and all related emails."

Oh God, no. "What's the itinerary, El?"

"Our mother and child are supposedly coming from Harlingen, Texas, through San Antonio. They'll transfer to Dallas, then arrive in North Little Rock at 7:15 tonight, Forrest City at 10:05, West Memphis at 11:55, and finally Memphis at 1:10 tomorrow morning."

Julia clicked off, turned to Marino and Tagger, looking serious. "The good news is that Elwood arranged a phony trip for a mother and her little girl from the Texas border. The Greyhound just left San Antonio."

"The bad news?" Marino asked.

"Elwood was unable to find the hacker's IP address. That means we don't know who he or she is. We can't pick them up. That means they'll go to one of the scheduled stops expecting to abduct a girl or her mother. But Elwood's fantasy immigrants won't be there. The creeps would probably make off with *any* child so as not to come home empty-handed."

"I think the best strategy would be for us to meet the bus at North Little Rock," Marino said. "If the kidnappers are there, we pick 'em up."

"And if they're not...?" Julia said.

"We pass the bus and meet it in Forrest City," Tagger said. "Right, Tony?"

Marino nodded. "And the same for the West Memphis and Memphis stops. We make sure no one gets jacked by these assholes."

Julia sighed. "That's not making me feel better. Even if we guess the right terminal, we have no idea what they look like."

"The odds are with us, Lieutenant," Tagger said. "Tony and I have seen most of the agency folks and you've seen most of the Berclair folks. We'll spot 'em."

"I need to run our trip by Major Williams, get him to clear the way with the Arkansas State Police," Julia said. She looked at her watch. "Let's plan on meeting back here at five o'clock for our drive to North Little Rock. In the meantime, we've got things to do."

Chapter 44

Coming Clean

*The MED, the midsouth's premier trauma hospital...*Tagger passed the nurses' station and walked up to the police officer.

The officer stood. "Morning, Sergeant. He's awake. His wife's with him."

Tagger nodded. "Thanks for the call. The doctor's given us the okay to talk to him, right?"

"Doc cleared him just before I called you. But she did say no more than fifteen minutes. And warned me, don't upset him."

Tagger knocked. Mrs. Robbins opened the door, looked up, glared, stepped forward. "You're the one who arrested my husband, aren't you? And you're the one who took him to that terrible place. You can't take him back there."

"I just want to talk, ma'am, find out who did this to him. May I come in?"

"It's all right, Colette," said Robbins softly. "I want to talk to him."

Mrs. Robbins looked at Tagger disapprovingly, stepped back. "He's still a little dopey. Doctor said he can't talk long." She followed him. "And I'm staying right here."

Tagger walked over to the bed. "How are you feeling, Marcus?"

"Like a truck ran over me." He turned to his wife. "Can you sit me up a little?"

Mrs. Robbins depressed a button, held it.

Robbins winced. "That's enough." He repositioned himself with difficulty, turned to Tagger, gestured for him to sit. "You were right, Sergeant. They sure found me." His wife brought a cup and a flexible straw. He took a sip. "I should have told you everything when you asked me. Well, I'll tell you now." He looked at his wife. "I want you to hear this, too."

Tagger pulled out a notepad.

"I had a bad gambling problem. Couldn't stop. …Guess I didn't really want to. Got in way over my head. Arranged a loan on the street to pay off the debt. But their interest rate on the loan was off the chart. Within a few weeks I pretty much doubled my debt." He motioned for another drink, took several sips, and laid his head back on the pillow.

"Who'd you get the loan from?"

"Some guy named Benji. I was told I could find him hanging around the Summerset apartments off Hickory Hills, working out of a black SUV. Had a couple of very big guys standing behind him. Pulled out a wad of hundreds. Guess that's where he got his name." He looked as his wife. "Benjamin Franklin's picture is on the hundred dollar bill. On the street, the bill's called a *Benjamin—benji* for short."

"How much?" asked Mrs. Robbins.

Robbins hesitated, looked down. "Twenty thousand," he said quietly.

His wife sat back, eyes wide, hand covering her open mouth.

"Who was Benji working for?" Tagger asked.

"I didn't know at the time, but Benji's a Gangster Disciple." He caught his wife's eye, brought his finger and thumb to his lips. She brought his water. He took a few pulls on the straw, then squirmed to get comfortable. "One day I was in the mortuary, getting ready for an afternoon burial. Three black men I'd never seen before came in, two of them struggling with a body bag. The one man said he came to get payment on my loan. I said I didn't have the money, and I pleaded with him for extra time. He said he didn't believe I'd be able to come up with the money."

Mrs. Robbins muffled a cry.

Robbins kept his eyes on Tagger. "The guy pulled out a gun. Showed me the long-stem rose on the side. Said he and the 'black rose' had a one-time deal for me. Said either he'd shoot me *and* my wife, or I could do him this tiny favor." Robbins paused. "I asked what kind of favor."

"Oh, Marcus. What did you do?" Mrs. Robbins asked.

"He had his pals unzip the body bag, revealing a muscular black policeman with a head wound. He pointed to the casket I'd been working on. He said 'we're going to stick this bitch on top of that body, and you're going to close the casket and bury the both of them like nothing ever happened'."

"You sure you'd never seen any of them before?" Tagger asked.

Robbins shook his head and reached for another drink.

"Can you describe the guy with the gun?"

He sipped the water. "Kinda medium height, muscular, light brown skin. Hair closely cropped. Had a teardrop tattoo under his left eye, and a long-stem rose on his right forearm, just like the one on the gun."

"Did he say who sent them?"

Robbins took several sips. "Same folks I got the loan from—the Gangster Disciples."

"When was this?"

"Almost a year ago. Just before Thanksgiving."

"Anything else he ask you to do?"

"He wanted me to hire their men as security guards, and one as a groundskeeper. Said they might be burying other bodies, and, as long as I kept my mouth shut, my wife would stay alive. Then he smiled this horrible smile and said they'd send me a check for each one." He looked at his wife. "Honest, Colette. I didn't know how to get out of it. I was afraid of what they'd do to you. *And* to me."

Mrs. Robbins hurried to him, buried her face in his neck, and cried.

Tagger waited until she pulled back, still holding her husband's hand. "Do you know how many of these bodies were buried?"

"I was never notified, but I received deposits to my checking account at least ten times, counting that first body they put inside the casket."

"If you add the police officer, that number's in the ballpark with what the TBI has found using their radar machines."

"I freaked out when that hysterical woman went on and on about her father's grave. I knew there had to be another body buried there. I tried to calm her down, told her it was a faulty casket liner letting gasses escape. Nothing satisfied her. Next thing I know, a Sheriff's Deputy is serving me a subpoena. I panicked." He turned to his wife. "I was so scared I couldn't think straight. I convinced myself that if I disappeared, nothing would happen to you." Tears formed, slid down his cheeks. "I'm so sorry, Colette. Please forgive me."

She hugged him again, kissed him. She stood. Face wet, eyes puffy. She grabbed some tissues.

Tagger waited. "Tell me about the stabbing."

Robbins gently touched his sides, away from the site of the wounds and the surgery. "I was walking back from the chow hall. Black guy I'd never seen walked toward me. Out of the blue, he stabbed me, twice, hard. Shoved the homemade knife in as far as it would go, broke off the handle. …Seemed like I laid there a long time before anyone came to check on me. Doc said the guy leaving the blade inside me probably saved my life because it helped slow the bleeding."

Mrs. Robbins stood, faced Tagger. Her voice quavered. "Marcus can't go back there. You can't make him go back there."

Tagger closed his notepad. "I agree, Mrs. Robbins. We'll check with the District Attorney's office to see what kind of arrangements can be made. Meantime, we'll keep an officer outside your door." He stood. "I'm sorry this happened, Marcus. Appreciate your telling me."

Chapter 45

Money Laundering

Marino drove west on Poplar, past the Criminal Justice Complex to a square, white stone, low-rise structure built in the seventies—the Memphis Branch of the Federal Reserve Bank of Saint Louis. He found the office of Max Lamb.

Lamb stood, extended his hand. "Long time no see, Sergeant. Not since, what...the Morgan Keegan fraud days? Ponzi schemes ripping off the elderly, and a money laundering game through a car dealership."

"Good memory," Marino said. "Of course, as happens in homicide, we got involved in all that because of a dead body. Since this is Memphis, we've got more bodies. And, I think I've got another money laundering scheme. This one's at the Midsouth Depository."

"The Depository, huh?" Lamb lowered his voice, walked across the office, and closed the door. He motioned for Marino to sit. "Look, Sergeant. This is strictly confidential. We're in the process of examining that bank."

"Any chance it's for money laundering?"

"How'd you know?"

"Happened to be at their Hickory Hills branch a few days ago. Watched a dude deposit a briefcase full of cash, in front of God and everyone."

"Ah, yes," Lamb nodded. "The blatant under-ten-thousand

transaction." He leaned forward. "But this is way bigger than one little bank branch colluding to circumvent the federal banking code's ten thousand-dollar deposit limit. We're eight months into a multi-state investigation, all focused on organized crime and their accounts in domestic and foreign banks."

"Does it involve the Gangster Disciples?"

Lamb cocked his head. "Ah…Yes. I read about that shooting at the MED. The dead shooter was a Gangster Disciple, right?"

Marino nodded. "They take up a lot of our Organized Crime Unit's time."

Lamb paused. "As a matter of fact, this investigation is focused exclusively on the Gangster Disciples. It's a major law enforcement operation. Covers almost twenty-five states."

Marino sat back.

Lamb fiddled with his pen. "Back to the Midsouth Depository. What can I help you with, without really helping you?"

"You had any dealings with Fred Dancer, the regional manager of the Depository?"

"He's really a small fish. Initial reports on his bank show money laundering and what looks like charging excessive fees to customers, particularly customers with Hispanic names."

"I've talked to him. He doesn't act like a man who's about to get closed down."

"We haven't shown our hand to any bank yet. As far as they're concerned, these are simply routine bank examinations, just like ones they've passed before. But you wouldn't believe how complicated this investigation is. This whole thing has to be tightly coordinated. We still have a few midsouth banks to finish up. The goal is to seize as much of their illegal assets as possible which means we must descend on them all simultaneously. Any whiff of an investigation and all illegally-gained funds could be instantly transferred out of the country.

"Any chance you've seen the name Leonard Owen? Pretty sure he's involved with Dancer in whatever he's doing."

Lamb reached back and pulled a file, began leafing through it. "Here he is. Good guess, Sergeant. Owen is listed on the payroll as a consultant. Used to be a Depository bookkeeper. Retired in 2007."

"Dancer impresses me as more slimeball than technician. Would Owen know enough to set up the routing of cash deposits so as to keep it under the federal radar? Would he know how to disguise inflated fees?"

"With his training, credentials and experience, he'd certainly know his way around computers. Yes. I'd think he'd be quite capable of doing all that."

Marino paused, stared at the desktop.

"Something I said?"

"Just thinking," Marino said quietly. He looked up. "We've been trying to identify someone with computer expertise, someone familiar with the Hispanic community."

"Outside of money laundering?"

"Yeah. Way outside of money laundering."

"But still involving the GDs?"

Marino nodded. Lamb frowned.

"So you need us to keep a lid on the fraud part of our investigation?" Marino said. "Just leave that to you?" Lamb nodded. "Happy to do that."

"If your murder investigation involves the Gangster Disciples," Lamb said, "it might be good to back off on that for a week or too."

Marino shook his head. "Sorry, Max. No can do. Somebody's killing children. We kinda thought we might want that to stop."

Chapter 46

Recovered Remains

Berston Funeral Home...Julia found Sales and Dawkins in the mortuary, now the staging area for body retrieval, forensic evaluation, and identification.

"Nine," Sales said loudly.

"I didn't even ask," Julia said.

"I know. But you were going to, weren't you?"

"Of course," Julia said. "Always good to have a tally of the bodies."

Rafe shook his head. "You two have been doing this a while," he said. "Right?"

Julia smiled. Sales didn't bother looking up from the remains before her.

"Okay," Julia said. "Fill me in."

Rafe pointed to a hand-written sheet on the wall. "We've ID'd four of the nine bodies:

Description	**Forensics**	**Identity**
Pre-adol female Hispanic	Broken neck BFT head	Gabriela Delgado
Adult Male black	Bullet to head	GD bookkeeper
Adult Male Asian	Bullet to head	Store owner
Adol female black	overdose	UK

Adol female white	overdose	UK
Adult female black	BFT back of head	Eve Lowell
Adult male Hispanic	Bullets to chest	Latin Kings
Adult male Black	Bullets to back	Vice Lords
Adult male Hispanic	Bullets to back	MS-13

"First one you know—Gabriela," he said. "Second body according to the Gang Unit, was a GD bookkeeper. Word is he was skimming. Third body was the owner of a convenience store and gas station. According to his family, he refused to pay GD extortion money." He stepped closer to the sheet. "The next two belong to teen girls. Overdosed, identities unknown. No match with any missing persons alerts in the tri-state area."

"Oh, sweet Jesus," Julia said, reading ahead. "Eve Lowell. Everyone's been trying to find her. We hoped she could identify the local network members who've been smuggling undocumenteds, help lead us to the creeps who hacked their system and were abducting the girls."

Sales looked up. "Blunt force trauma to the head. Could be she was bludgeoned. But the indentation in her skull is also consistent with the corner of a table or desk."

"The last three were decked out in gang colors and tats," Rafe said. "Represented three different rival gangs: Hispanic gang Latin Kings, the Vice Lords, and the El Salvadorian gang MS-13. The Gang Unit is working to identify them."

Chapter 47

The Drive

*I-40 West to North Little Rock, Arkansas...*Tagger drove his SUV. Julia rode shotgun, Marino stretched out in the back seat.

"I checked in with Rafe and Dr. Sales," Julia said. They've finished their survey of the cemetery. Nine bodies, including Eve Lowell's."

"Damn," Marino muttered. "Was kinda hoping for better news for her family."

No one spoke for several minutes.

Tagger broke the silence. "Saw Rollins at the MED. He's in bad shape, but wanted to talk, get everything off his chest. Had some heavy gambling losses. Stupidly took out a high interest loan from the GDs. Said a GD enforcer showed up at his mortuary with the body of an MPD officer. Put the officer in a casket on top of a body Rollins had already prepped for burial, and forced the lid shut. Had a list of demands. Threatened to shoot Rollins and his wife if he didn't bury the casket. Made him hire GDs as cemetery security guards, and allow the future burial of other bodies. In exchange, the GDs would let him and his wife live, call the loan paid in full, and would send Rollins a check for each body buried in the cemetery. Rollins says he never saw any of the other bodies. He assumed they were being buried at night in existing plots.

That's why he freaked out when the woman complained to him about the raised ground above her father's grave. Added to the nine the TBI found, the officer makes ten."

She nodded, turned toward Marino. "Anything on Dancer and Owen?"

"Got confirmation they're both in bed with the GDs," Marino said. "Talked to a bank examiner at the Treasury. They've got a hush-hush investigation going that involves the GDs. He's certain Dancer and Owen are laundering money for the GDs and price-gouging customers, especially Hispanics. "Owen knows his way around a computer. Have to wonder if he's involved in the hack. Pretty sure the FBI is monitoring these guys. Be good to compare dates and places."

Chapter 48

Stakeout

*7:00 PM, Wednesday, North Little Rock...*The sun's final glow evaporated and darkness settled on downtown North Little Rock. Just north of the Arkansas River, old men hung out in front of the Greyhound bus terminal, wearing ill-fitting, mismatched clothes. A black man held the pull-strings to a stuffed black plastic garbage bag. A white man kept one hand on a shopping cart loaded with a hodgepodge of unfolded clothes and blankets, a rumpled paper grocery bag perched on top. Another sat on the sidewalk, his back against the building. One paced, muttering to himself, occasionally yelling out to no one.

Weathered plywood replaced a large window. Peeling duct tape covered lettering on the front door's cracked glass. Inside was dimly lit. A TV blared from high on the wall, tuned to CNN. Waiting passengers sat in rows of plastic seats. A handful of tables and chairs were scattered near a row of vending machines, the only source of food or drink.

Julia sat on a bench near the women's restroom dressed as a bag lady— uncombed gray wig, ankle length dress, stained cloth jacket, dirty running shoes. Buses arrived, passengers filtered into the terminal. Passing women ignored Julia or gave her a wide berth. A mother and daughter came from the restroom.

"Mommy, that bathroom was gerrrosss," the girl said.

"I've seen worse," the mother said, "just can't remember where."

Marino monitored the main open area, dressed in brown coveralls, a battered Texas Rangers baseball cap, a push broom in hand. Tagger slouched down in his SUV, parked at the far end of the lot, watched through binoculars. The three had no visual contact, connected only by two-way miniature microphones and earbuds.

According to Elwood's phony itinerary, the decoy Greyhound bus would come from Texarkana through Little Rock, across the Arkansas River, and arrive shortly at the North Little Rock terminal.

"Hey, Tony," Tagger said. "You think you overdressed?"

"Very funny, smartass," Marino whispered. "You pull the next inside duty."

Crash!...thwomp!

"What's that?" Tagger asked.

"Just another satisfied customer," Marino said, watching a man fish out a soda can. "I think this was a freebee. Always helps to know just where to hit the vending machine."

A black Chevy Impala, windows tinted, turned into the parking lot. A man got out. The Impala parked nearby, engine running.

"Black Impala just dropped off a man. Entering side door," Tagger said. "Black pants, black jacket, black fedora. Can't see his face. Can't see the driver or the license."

"Got him," whispered Marino. "Taking a seat facing the arriving passengers."

"Here comes a bus," Tagger said. "I think it's ours."

The decoy bus pulled in. Passengers slowly filed into the terminal and fanned out. Some dropped into available seats, a few walked to the snack machines, others followed signs to the restrooms.

"Heads up," Marino whispered. "I count five target-age kids. Four headed your way."

"Copy," Julia whispered.

Marino's eyes shifted at the sound of rattling beads. The man in black stood, something dangled from his left hand. Marino turned away. "Dude's a priest," he whispered. "Roman collar, rosary. The whole nine."

"Perfect disguise for Mexican immigrants," Tagger said. "Can you see his face?"

"No. Hat pulled low. Black-rimmed glasses, dark beard."

Women and children drifted back from the restroom and settled in the waiting area. The priest scanned the crowd until no more people came in. He walked toward the restrooms.

"Priest coming to you, Lieutenant," Marino whispered.

Julia watched a woman and a young girl come out of the restroom. The mother stopped, dug through her handbag. "Oh, no," she said. "I must've dropped my ticket. You stay here. I'll be right back." She looked across the hall at Julia. "And don't talk to anybody." The girl nodded.

A person in black entered Julia's peripheral vision. Julia busied herself searching in her shopping bag, fingers wrapped around her Sig Sauer's grip. The priest approached the girl, bent forward and said something. The girl pointed to the restroom. He spoke again, held out his hand. The girl took it.

Julia's weapon cleared the top of the shopping bag as she stood. A stench filled her nostrils. Someone hit her hard on the shoulder. Her weapon clanked to the floor. She looked back to find a woman with an overpowering body odor, dressed like her.

The priest heard the commotion, saw the gun, released

the girl's hand, and ran.

"That's my seat!" the woman yelled, spit flying everywhere. She hit Julia again. "What the hell you doin' in *my* seat?"

Julia reached for her Sig, but the woman grabbed her. Julia turned back, took the woman by the shoulders and sat her down hard. "Take your damn seat." She picked up her weapon, and spoke loudly as she ran, "It's the priest! Running your way!"

Incoming busses queued up outside. Passengers poured into the terminal. Marino saw the priest run past but had to negotiate his way through the crowd. "Going out the side door," Marino yelled as he broke through the travelers. Julia came running behind him.

"The Impala's on the move," Tagger said. He dropped the gear shift into drive, stomped on the gas, but immediately hit the brake, the front end of the car rocked down, then back. He pounded the steering wheel. "Can't get around this friggin' bus." Tagger pushed the door open and jumped to the blacktop, stretched out his long legs, raced toward the terminal. He saw the Impala pick up the priest, and speed off.

The bus moved. Tagger returned to the car, collected Julia and Marino.

"You see which way it went?" Julia asked.

Tagger shook his head. "Damn bus."

"Get a plate?"

Tagger fumed. "I got *Butkus.* Nothing."

"They're either laying low in town, or they're on I-40 back to Memphis," Marino said.

"Six of one," Tagger said. He took the nearby entrance ramp to I-30 north for about a mile, then followed the sweeping right turn onto I-40 east, mashed the accelerator. Julia called the state police, requested an all-points on a late model black Chevy Impala.

She slid back into her seat, fists clenched in front of her. "He was right there. Two steps and I had him. Damn bag lady. Knocked my Sig to the floor, got on me again. By the time I picked up my gun, the priest was gone."

"Least we stopped an abduction," Marino said.

Julia looked straight ahead. "I couldn't live with myself if I'd let a child be taken by these animals."

Chapter 49

A Question of Conscience

*Thursday morning, the Union Station…*Teresa buzzed in. "Lieutenant. The priest from Saint Michael's is on two."

Julia punched the blinking light. "Father K?"

"Yes, Lieutenant. I have something you need to see. Something important. Any way you can meet me?"

"Sure. When and where?"

"Actually, now. I'm in your parking lot. An old brown Chevy."

Julia strode out the front door and found Father K standing next to his car, looking serious. "This is strange. Everything all right, Father?"

The priest got in without saying a word, and waited for Julia to buckle up. He turned to her. "I don't know if I'm doing the right thing. Promise me again that you will not turn in any undocumenteds."

"Father, my focus is on the murderers. It is not my intent to turn in any undocumenteds immigrants. That's as strong as I can state my position."

"Please, God," he mumbled, then started the car. "I have been praying about this for days. I've tried to convey to them the seriousness of the situation and I've done my best to assure them everything will be okay. And I'm really trusting you to do the same."

Julia waited.

Father K drove past Saint Michael's Church and parked in front of an apartment complex with peeling paint and more bare ground than grass. He punched numbers on his cell and spoke in Spanish. "We're here? Are you ready?"... He listened, then clicked off.

"Father? You're going to have to give me something to work with here. It's clear you're nervous, and you think I might mess things up. But I don't have a clue what's going on."

"You'll see. Come with me." He led her to the apartments. A door opened, but no one showed. "Wait here," he said, then walked inside. He returned seconds later and waved her in.

Julia entered a small living area. Four adults and a boy, standing as far from the front door as possible. Father K closed the door and gestured. "Lieutenant, I want to introduce you to Ricardo and Laticia Delgado, and their son Jorge.

Julia nodded, looked back at Father K. "Delgado? *Our* Delgado?"

Father K ignored her question. "Ricardo and Laticia are long time parishioners at Saint Michael's."

"And the others?" Julia asked.

"They are new to Memphis." He paused. "They do not speak English. This is Alejandro and Sylvia."

Julia saw movement behind the woman—the flash of a skirt, a small hand. "Is that a child? A girl?"

"This is why I asked you to come," he said. "This is Gabriela."

On hearing her name, a young girl peeked around Sylvia—light brown skin and lively green eyes.

"What?" Julia whispered loudly. "The Gabriela in the

red diary?"

Father K nodded, spoke calmly. "As you can see, she is very much alive."

Julia's eyes flashed. "Did you know this when I gave you the flyer?" she said, more sharply than she'd intended.

Gabriela ducked back behind her mother. Alejandro and Silvia pressed even closer to the wall.

Not looking at Julia, Father K smiled and continued to speak calmly in English. "A fellow priest called me. Said Gabriela showed up at his church. I gave him Ricardo's number. When you showed me the flyer, I recognized her name. I came here to console them. That's when I met Alejandro, Silvia *and* Gabriela."

"Okay," Julia said, imitating Father K's casual tone. "Sorry if I overreacted."

Father K nodded. "I've been worried sick since you gave me the flyer. I don't want any trouble for the new arrivals, but I can't live with the thought of any more children being killed. I decided to trust you to do the right thing."

"I'll do my best. I need to know about these events, from Gabriela."

"I've told them that you are the person who has worked very hard to find Gabriela, to help her, and to keep her safe from the gangsters."

"Will you translate for me, Father?"

Chapter 50

Mug Shots

*MPD Gang Unit...*Tagger drove south from downtown on Riverside Drive. Marino rode shotgun, idly watching a Mississippi River barge head downstream to New Orleans. They turned right on Channel 3 Drive and immediately pulled into the first building's parking area—the home of MPD's Gang Unit. "Let's hope they've got something useful on these clowns," Marino said as he released his seatbelt.

They were met by a black man dressed in jeans and a blue T-shirt, with tattoos and one diamond earring. "Hey, Brock," Tagger said, shaking his hand. He introduced Marino. "Brock works the streets. Knows all the players."

Brock led them into the conference room, gestured to the seats. "I got books of mug shots and a bunch of surveillance DVDs. Who ya lookin' for?"

"Need to know about a few GDs," Tagger said. "Tony saw a dude fully stylin' who unloaded a ton of bills in the Depository. And I was told about someone called Benji who runs the GD's loans and collections."

Brock smiled. "Bet y'all are talkin' 'bout the same dude." He dragged over a book, flipped through mug shots, then tapped his finger on a row of pictures. "This the guy?"

Marino pulled the book closer. "Can't tell. Saw him from behind. Short. Wore a cap and the latest rapper get-up."

"I've got some footage that might help," Brock said as he started to close the book.

"Wait," Tagger said, pointing to another row of mug shots. "I've seen this guy hanging around Apollo High School."

"Dillard White," Brock said. "Goes by Dill. Low level street vendor. Sells drugs." He leafed through a box of DVDs, pulled one and slipped it into a projector. A smallish man, dressed in the latest upscale urban rap clothes, appeared on the screen. "I'm thinkin' he's wearin' Flysociety or Enyce."

"I was going with Akademics," Tagger said.

"I don't have a clue about *what* or *who* he's wearing," Marino said. "But that's the dude I followed into the Depository. Thought they called him, Benny."

"That's Benji," Brock said. "'Benji' for all the hundred dollar bills he carries."

"And those guys leaning against the SUV?" Tagger asked.

"Mean SOBs," Brock said. "Yeah, Benji's quite the dude, always stylin'—kind of a walkin' billboard for the GDs. He's their main money man. Makes loans. Never without his oversized knee-breaker homeys. His homeys guard the stash and take care of collections. If you saw Benji in the Depository, you can bet his crew wasn't far behind. My guess? They stayed in the SUV because the Depository didn't want them scarin' away customers."

Tagger smiled. "Good thing his crew didn't get out of the car, Tony."

"Benji's predictable," Brock said. "You can almost set your watch by little Benji. Wound tight, like a banker. Same places, same times. We don't spend much time tracking him." He switched DVDs. "Actually, Dill is pretty easy to find too. He's more the corner pharmacist—takes orders, makes deliveries. Has a better class of customers than most, and specializes in prescription drugs."

"A better class of customers?" Tagger asked.

"Yeah," Brock said. "Most have a job, or are married to someone who has a job. They drive cars, dress better than the street addicts."

"One more," Tagger said. "Know anything about a GD who carries a Kahr Arms 'Black Rose'? Has a matching black rose tattoo on his forearm and a teardrop."

"That one's easy," Brock said, reaching for a mug shot book. "He's the dude killed in that shootout at the MED a few days back." He flipped through the photos, spun the book and pushed it to Tagger. "Torrance Rose. Liked to hurt people. An enforcer. Called himself 'The Black Rose.' Always had that little nine millimeter Black Rose special on him somewhere. An honest-ta-God *psycho.* Good to have him off the streets. Kudos to the guy who took him out.

Chapter 51

Gabriela

Delgados' apartment...Father K organized the seating. Alejandro and Silvia on the small couch with Gabriela in the middle. Julia and the priest on hardback kitchen chairs facing the couch. Ricardo, Leticia and Jorge in kitchen chairs on either side.

Father K spoke in Spanish to the new Delgado family. They held hands, nodded occasionally, did not smile. The priest spoke English to Julia, softly. "I told them you are not here to take them back to Mexico. I told them you want to know about Gabriela's kidnapping so you can find the man who killed the girl whose face is on the flyer. I asked them to tell you their story."

"Do they understand?" Julia asked.

Father K nodded. "They understand, but they're scared. I will translate while they speak."

Alejandro spoke first. "Los Zetas cartel became more violent, making more demands in our village. They killed many of our friends. We had to leave." He looked at his brother. "Ricardo sent us money and told us to find Dominic, a coyote he had used when he crossed the border years ago." He turned back to Father K. "We made our way on foot down the mountain, hiding from Los Zetas."

"They are awful men," interrupted Gabriela. She smiled

and touched her father's arm. "Papi is very brave."

A look of pride shown on Alejandro's face. "Then we rode buses to Matamoros, where we found Dominic."

"And we rode in his fine car to his big home," Gabriela said. "He had more food on his table than I have ever seen."

Alejandro smiled. "Yes, it was a fine car, and a grand home, and he had lots of food." He squeezed her hand. "What about the bathtub?"

"Ohh," she said, her eyes bright. "I did not want to get out. I smelled so pretty. And he gave me a new blouse and skirt."

Julia smiled.

"But then we had to get in the trunk," Alejandro said still looking at Gabriela. "First for practice, then for the long trip through the border crossing."

"I didn't like that," Gabriela looked up at her mother and cringed. "It was so hot and we couldn't move or talk. And those dogs, barking and growling. I was so scared."

Silvia stroked Gabriela's hair. "You were such a brave girl."

"We were in two cars," said Alejandro. "We got split up at the border. Silvia and Gabriela went to Houston right away and got on a bus. I was delayed and went to San Antonio. In North Little Rock—"

"That's where that terrible woman took you away," said Silvia, pulling Gabriela to her. She spoke fast, seemingly without taking a breath. "I will never forgive her, may she burn in hell." She looked up, blushed. "Forgive me, Father."

Father K made a sign of the cross, then smiled. He spoke in English, "Silvia described her horror at losing Gabriela. Apparently people tried to help but did not speak Spanish. After several hours Alejandro's bus arrived. A man let them use his cell phone. They called Ricardo, who drove to North Little Rock and picked them up." He turned to Sylvia and spoke Spanish at length. She nodded, "Si, padre."

Julia whispered. "What did you say?"

Father K kept his voice lowered. "I just shared what I'd told you, and asked if I had remembered correctly."

Julia nodded.

"You can ask questions now," said Father K. "I will translate, and then I'll tell you their answer."

"Okay," Julia said leaning forward, elbows on her knees. "I want to know about the kidnapping. What did the woman look like, what did she wear?"

Father K asked Sylvia in Spanish. "The woman, she was younger and taller than me. Her eyes were dark, like mine. She wore pants, blouse, a jacket, and a round black hat over her blonde hair."

Julia jumped in. "Did she speak Spanish? Good Spanish?"

"Si." Silvia smiled and pointed at Father K. "She sounded like him."

Father K smiled. "My English sounds and grammar blend into my Spanish. My guess is that the woman was bilingual: English and Spanish."

"Have Gabriela tell us about the kidnapping." Julia said.

Gabriela's face lit up at Father K's directive. Julia kept her eyes on Gabriela while listening to the English translation which the priest provided quietly.

Gabriela spoke fast, gestured and sometimes acted out the scene. "The lady said we were going to buy candy. She held my hand. Then she squeezed hard and pulled me out the door. I yelled for Mamá. I heard Mamá call my name. The woman picked me up and threw me into a car. I tried to get out, but the lady grabbed me." As she spoke, Gabriela kicked out and made a cat-like motion with her hands. "I kicked her and scratched her. Her hair moved over her eyes. She slapped my face, real hard." Her hand went to her cheek. "Then she put a cloth over my nose. I fell asleep."

Tears rolled down Silvia's cheeks. Alejandro clenched his fists.

Julia fed Father K questions. "Is she talking about a wig?"

Gabriela nodded. "Si. A wig. Yellow."

"Was anyone else in the car?" Julia asked.

Gabriela nodded. "A man. In the front seat."

Two of them. So, last night's driver was a woman? Julia thought. "What did the man look like?"

Gabriela shook her head. "I cannot say."

"She's doing great," Julia said. "Show her the flyer. Does she know this girl?"

Father K handed the flyer to Gabriela. "This girl had your diary. Do you know who she is?"

Gabriela snapped her head away, burying her face in her mother's bosom.

"Gabriela," Alejandro said gently. "Answer the Padre's question."

Gabriela turned slowly, not looking at the sketch. "I don't know her."

Julia encouraged, "But you've seen her before."

Gabriela nodded slowly. "I saw a big black man sit on top of her. She spit in his face. He got mad, hit her really, really hard. She did not move. A black woman yelled at the man. He left the room. The woman followed him. She looked back at me. I closed my eyes, pretending to be asleep."

"Ask where she was," said Julia.

"I was on a bed." Gabriela spoke faster. "The girl was on the other bed. I tried to get up but I could not move my arm." Gabriela held up her right hand, looked up at it. "A chain was on my arm. I pulled but it was too tight."

Gabriela got on her knees, acted out spitting in her hand, rubbing her wrist and pulling. "My hand came out." She rubbed her wrist. "I got out of the bed, but my legs felt like willow strips. I fell. I got up, but I could not walk good."

Gabriela looked in the distance, remembering. "I heard men talking. They were coming. I hid under the girl's bed. I saw their shoes. I saw my diary on the floor. A man picked it up. They left. I rolled out. The girl was gone."

Gabriela looked at Father K. "I ran to the window and tried to open it, but it was stuck. I pushed the window down and pulled up really hard. It opened only a little. I heard the men coming back." Gabriela paused, her eyes wide, her chest heaving.

Father K urged her on. "What did you do?"

Gabriela got off the couch. Then, standing on one foot, she laid across the front edge of the cushion, looking at Father K. She pushed off the floor onto the couch. Rolled onto her back.

"What in the world is she doing?" Julia asked. "Is she showing us how she squeezed through the window?" Father K translated the question.

Gabriela nodded, and held her head.

"And she scraped her head?"

"Si."

"And then what?" Julia asked. "That must be at least a four-foot fall to the ground?"

"I fell on my back. All my air came out."

Julia sat back in her chair. "Please tell her she's doing a fantastic job. How about we get her something to drink before we go on?"

Julia's mind raced. *Was Gabriela in the room next to the teenage girls? Is she one of the two girls they thought were dead? If T was there, she'd be a witness. That's why Beard had her killed. Where is this place?*

***

"Okay, Father," Julia said. "Let's find out what happened next."

Silvia had her arm around Gabriela as they sat on the couch. Father K spoke in Spanish.

"It was night," Gabriela said, leaning forward. "I crawled to the front of the house. I saw lights on tall poles, and big houses with trees behind them. I peeked around the corner. A man was smoking. A woman yelled. The man threw his cigarette away, and ran into the house. I asked the Blessed Virgin to protect me. Then I ran to the trees."

Alejandro patted Gabriela's knee. "You are so brave, my little one."

She smiled. "I ran as fast as I could. Climbed a fence and hid behind a tree. A car came, with a big flashlight. It shined on my shoe. I was so afraid, but he did not see me. The car drove away. I ran into the road, hid behind cars."

Silvia crossed herself twice, quickly.

"I saw a really big building. Blessed Mary told me I must go there. I ran there, hid behind a tree. The car came. The man got out with his flashlight, walked to each tree. I knew he would find me."

Julia whispered to Father K, "What kind of building?"

Father K shrugged.

Gabriela continued. "I hid behind a small building. The man shined his light. A big dog growled and crashed into the fence. It was mean. It barked loud. A light turned on and a man came with a gun. He yelled, made the bad man go away. Then he went back inside the house, and the light turned off."

She looked at Sylvia. "I could not see. I heard the dog coming. Heard the leaves he walked on, heard his breathing. I knew the dog was right beside me. I prayed to the Mother of God. She told me to hold out my hand. I didn't want to, but I did. He sniffed my hand, then he licked it. I reached up and petted him. He was much bigger than me. He knocked me over. Then he laid his head on my chest. I fell asleep."

Silvia pulled Gabriela to her.

***

"*Where is this place?*" Julia thought. *"Sounds like a neighborhood, a small stand of trees or a park. A store, maybe a church."*

Father K turned to Julia. "She says she's ready."

"The dog woke me up," Gabriela said. "Lights came from the big building. I hugged the dog goodbye. I climbed the fence and walked through the trees. Then I ran down to the building. Light came through two windows. I peeked in. A door banged open and a lady stood over me, holding a big knife. She dragged me inside."

Chapter 52

Wild Card

*Union Station...*Marino and Tagger sat across the desk from Julia.

She continued to speak softly. “Once news gets out about Gabriela, and it will, the shit will hit the fan.”

“Who else knows?” Marino asked.

“Father K, Gabriela’s family, and the three of us,” Julia said.

“With all Beard’s contacts, there’s nowhere she can hide,” Tagger said.

“There’s a part of me that thinks she’s safest staying right where she is,” Julia said.

“That could be the best thing,” Tagger said. Marino nodded.

“Okay,” Julia said. “It’s settled. She stays put. I need to tell Major Ayers. He’ll want to organize an assault on the GD house now we have a clear witness to Jane Doe’s murder. But there are things I need to do first.”

Marino cocked his head. “Meaning?”

“I want assurances she’ll be taken care of *before* we go after Beard.”

“Got an ace up your sleeve?” Marino asked.

“More like a wild card,” Julia said. “Sure hope it works.”

Chapter 53

The Prep House

Julia drove to southeast Memphis, a few blocks from the strip mall where one assault on the GD's party house had taken place. She pulled into the Church of the Resurrection driveway. A custodian greeted her at the door, and led her to the rectory, a comfortably decorated living area. A man stood. Julia judged him to be in his mid-forties, wearing a neatly trimmed beard, black slacks, and a black short sleeve dress shirt with a pastoral tab-collar, open at the neck. A slightly overweight middle aged woman remained seated beside him. Her hands clasped in her lap.

"I'm Father Court," the man said, extending his hand.

Julia crossed the room and shook his hand. "I'm Lieutenant Todd. Thanks for seeing me."

"This is our cook, Consuela Dias. Please, have a seat, Lieutenant. Would you like something to drink?"

Julia shook her head. "No, thanks." She sat on the edge of the chair, leaned forward. "I'm following up on Gabriella Delgado's visit to the Church of the Resurrection about two weeks ago." Father Court nodded. "I'm most interested in retracing her path. I want to know how she got here. Where she came from."

"Actually," he said, "the little girl showed up at the rear of our new school, across the street." He gestured, "Consuela was the one who talked to the child. And of course, her Spanish is much better than mine."

Consuela hesitated. He encouraged her. "Remember? You told me you were making breakfast when you saw a face looking through the window." He turned to Julia. "We've been having trouble with kids dumping trash all over the back parking lot. Consuela promised me she'd catch them."

Consuela barely looked at Julia. "Si. I start breakfast," she said slowly, in passable English. "I see small face look in window. I take my butcher knife and go outside to catch the child—a little girl. She did not run. I grab her and pull her into the kitchen. She was a mess—clothes dirty, hair full of leaves and grass, look like she not sleep." Consuela looked up, spoke more rapidly. "I think she was the one who go in our trash. I yell at her. But she say nothing. I turned away. That's when she talk—in Spanish. Asked me to help her."

"Help her do what?" Julia asked.

"She talk loco…crazy. She say she chase by bad men in cars, but Mother Mary protect her and tell her come to our school. Say she hid with a dog, in his house."

"A dog house?"

"Si."

"What about these bad men?"

"She say they were black. She show me her wrist and her head, all red and scratched. Say she hid in the woods."

Julia looked at Father Court. "Does this make sense to you? Is there a wooded area around here?"

"I don't know about woods, but there's a little playground called Emerald Park. It has trees." He motioned. "Just a few blocks north of here."

"Will you two come with me? I want to see the school, the park, and check out the neighborhood. Maybe something will trigger a memory of what Gabriela said. Let's start with the school."

Julia pulled into the Resurrection School driveway, drove around back. A large grassy field fanned out from behind the school. Trees lined the property which backed up to houses. Consuela pointed. "That only dog house I see back here."

They walked up the rise. Wooden fences blocked the view of backyards…all except the cyclone fence before them. Leaves rustled as an enormous Rottweiler bounded toward them and hit the fence hard. Consuela jumped. The dog issued a deep-throated growl and barked. A tall black man pushed through the back door, holding a shotgun.

Julia put her hands up. "Whoa! Police!"

The man lowered his gun and walked to the fence. "That you, Father?"

"Yes, Harrison."

Harrison roughhoused with his dog, gave him a few loud pats on his ribs. "He's a sweetheart, but he don't put up with anybody coming around. He keeps them damn gang punks away." Harrison looked up. "Sorry 'bout the shotgun. I grab it whenever Boss, here, crashes into the fence."

"Were any gang bangers here two Fridays ago?" Julia asked.

"Can't say I remember the exact night," Harrison said. "But a while back, around midnight, Boss hit that fence and began barking. Took me out of a deep sleep. Grabbed my shotgun and went a-running. Found some jerk shining a flashlight in my backyard. I was fixin' to put a load of shot in his ass. Had enough sense to leave." He motioned over the fence. "Went back to a car waiting in the school parking lot, Father. Don't have a clue what he was after. But whatever it was, me an' Boss weren't having none of it."

"You know where he came from?"

"I just figured he came from that house the other side of the park." He threw a thumb over his shoulder. "Can't miss it. The one with the ugly blue trim. Lots of 'em hang out there. Cars parked every which way. Always coming and going, busier than a damn burger joint. God only knows what goes on there."

***

Father Court and Consuela climbed in the car with Julia. She drove the short distance to the park, circled the block, then checked out the side streets. She spotted the blue-trimmed house. Julia slowed, scanned the house—no cars, curtains closed, front door ajar—then drove past. She circled back, trying to imagine Gabriela's escape route. She passed the park.

"There's the school, behind those houses," the priest said, pointing. "You can see it through the trees."

"She say Mother Mary show her the school," Consuela said. "Tell her she must go there."

Julia pulled out her cell, told Marino to meet her at the church.

Father Court spoke up. "Consuela brought Gabriela to me that morning. She seemed pretty smart for her age, and from her story it was clear she had recently crossed the border with her parents. I didn't know if she was documented or not. She did tell me the name of her aunt and uncle who live here in Memphis. I called Father Kaszewski at Saint Michael's. He cautioned me not to tell anyone, then gave me their phone number. Her uncle came and picked her up right away."

***

Marino arrived at the church fifteen minutes later. "You found the house where Jane Doe II was killed?"

"Could be," Julia said. "It looks deserted, but I didn't want to go in without backup. It's just north of us. Follow me."

Julia drove into the driveway, got out, hand on her pistol grip, and cautiously checked the backyard. Marino parked in the street and met her on the front porch. The door stood slightly open, as she'd seen earlier. They pulled their weapons, held them downward, and leaned against the wall on either side of the door. Julia yelled, "Memphis Police!"

No answer.

She yelled again. No answer.

Julia raised her Sig Sauer and shoved the door open with her free hand. It banged against the wall. She nodded to Marino, and ducked inside. She crouched and swept her weapon to the right, Marino followed immediately and swept left. They methodically worked their way through the house. Totally empty, completely clean. No furniture. No dust. Not even a scrap of paper.

"Clear!" Julia yelled.

"Clear!" Marino echoed.

He found Julia in the far bedroom, her gun holstered, hands gloved. He watched her struggle to open a window, but it stuck after rising only eight or nine inches. She squatted and checked the underside of the lower sash rail and the sill. She pulled an evidence bag and dropped in several strands of black hair.

Marino winced. "Gabriela's?"

"That's my guess," Julia said. "Some kid, huh?"

Chapter 54

Apollo Academy

Apollo Charter Academy...Tagger walked into the school, went directly to the main office, and spoke to the secretary. "I need to talk to Mr. Hendricks. Maybe someone can cover his class?"

"Oh, Mr. Hendricks isn't here today. He called, said he re-injured his back."

"Re-injured his back?"

"A student jumped him on the last day of school, over two years ago, threw him down the stairwell, broke some bones. We were still a Memphis City School then. He was laid up for months, in lots of pain, had several surgeries. The surgeries fixed the broken bones but not the pain. He was on some pretty strong meds. Didn't return to teaching until second semester the following year, but I heard he did a little volunteer tutoring. All this time later, and he still doesn't move too well. Says anything faster than a leisurely stroll is beyond him."

"Any idea why the student jumped him?"

"The boy was a senior, couldn't participate in the graduation because he failed two classes—one was Spanish. In this case I believe it was his mother who spurred him on. She was all worked up because she'd invited her relatives to the graduation. The principal held the line. The mother contacted every politician from school board members to U S Senators. She wanted her son to walk across the stage in his cap and gown, even if he didn't get a diploma. Sad, really. It's so good to have supportive parents at the Apollo, parents who value education. It makes all the difference in the world."

"What happened to the student?"

"Got arrested. And since he was eighteen, he was tried as an adult. Served a reduced sentence. But the crazy thing is, after he was released he came here to see Mr. Hendricks. I guess he's just trying to make up for what he did. They seem to get along okay, but the principal ran him off. Told him he was not welcome in the school, especially showing off his gang colors."

"Gang colors?"

"I believe the principal said he's a Gangster Disciple."

"Can I speak with the principal?"

"He's making his rounds, checking the halls, stairwells, and exits. He does such an excellent job of making sure everyone's in class and no outsiders are on campus. It's so much better than it used to be."

"Tell me about the school rules, specifically gang colors and gang signs."

"Oh, none of that is allowed." She leaned forward, spoke quietly. "Before we became a charter school, we had as many as six different gangs represented here. Kids came from all over the city on transfers, usually having been suspended from other schools. On top of that, we'd get all those kids being released from corrections, telling us they'd served their time and, by law, they had to be returned to public school. Lord only knows which gangs *they* represented. And of course, they were years behind in their school work. Never could keep up. Caused more trouble."

"But now?"

She sat up. "It's so much better at Apollo. We no longer have to take the corrections kids, or transferred incorrigible students. No gang signs. No gang colors. Even broken bones have to be covered in a gang-neutral white cast. And we have a dress code. Nothing flashy, just black slacks or skirts, black shoes, and white shirts. Trouble makers are sent back to the City Schools. The teachers and students really like it. Makes everyone feel safe."

"Would it surprise you if I told you I saw a student with a blue bandana hanging out of his back pocket?" He said.

"When? Where?"

"Two days ago, in the hallway, talking to Mr. Hendricks. About five-eight, thin, light brown skin, a medium fade hair-cut."

"So he's back."

"Who's back?"

"Dillard. The student who attacked Mr. Hendricks. I see the boy every so often on the sidewalk, just off campus. I've seen Mr. Hendricks pull out of the parking lot and pick him up."

"You talking about Dillard White?"

"Yes. Do you know him?"

Chapter 55

Wheeling and Dealing

*Offices of the Attorney General...*Sanchez and Wallace sat on one side of the table, across from Julia. Assistant DA Anne Webber opened the conference room door, carrying a worn leather binder. She wore a brown skirt and matching jacket. A wavy clump of unruly brown-gray hair bounced over one eye. She sat at the head of the table, scooted up her chair and nodded to the two attorneys. Webber pushed the hair from her eye and looked at Julia. "Why don't you get us started, Lieutenant?"

Julia took a breath. "First, I apologize for the short notice, but things are moving rapidly." Webber nodded. "The purpose for this meeting involves the Gangster Disciples, one of the area's best organized gangs. Phillip Beard heads up the Memphis area cell. The GDs are hip deep in illegal activities—drugs, prostitution, gambling, extortion, sex trafficking, and murder. The TBI and MPD have joined forces specifically to address sex trafficking. Last week we broke up one of the GD's prostitution houses that featured underage girls, all abducted and forced into service. In addition, we have uncovered nine bodies buried on top of existing caskets at the Cross On the Hill Cemetery. Analyses of these remains are incomplete. However, the first body to be recovered was that of a ten-year-old female who appears to be an undocumented immigrant from Mexico. All indications are she was killed by a GD, specifically,

Phillip Beard."

"And you have proof?" Webber asked.

Julia nodded. "We have two adolescent girls who can place Beard at the site of her murder. We have a rather unique ring that matches the impression left in the side of the murdered girl's head. We found it at the GD's residence. We believe that ring belongs to Beard. The lab is analyzing the ring for prints and DNA."

"That's not proof, Lieutenant," Webber said.

Julia smiled. "And now we have a witness to that little girl's murder." She gestured across the table. "Ms. Sanchez and Mr. Wallace are representing this witness, another ten year-old undocumented immigrant named Gabriela Delgado. Her description of the murderer matches Phillip Beard, a strikingly large black man, fond of gold accessories. And her portrayal of him backhanding the victim is consistent with the marks on the victim's head. We've since shown her a number of pictures of large black men. Gabriela quickly picked out Beard as the man she saw strike the girl."

"Where did this alleged murder take place?"

"Fox Meadows. Gabriela escaped from a house during the night, but gave us enough information to narrow down our search. A check of city records showed four houses had been purchased by the same company, a shell for the GDs. We found strands of Gabriela's hair in one of those houses."

Webber brushed away the wavy spring of hair. "Are all these witnesses illegal aliens?"

Julia shook her head. "The two adolescents are US citizens and, as foster care children, they're wards of the state of Tennessee."

Webber looked at the two attorneys. "I take it you are expecting something in exchange for the girl's testimony."

"Our young client and her parents are undocumented

aliens," Sanchez said. "Shortly after crossing the Mexican-Texas border, Gabriela was abducted and sold to the GDs as part of a sex trafficking scheme. Like the Lieutenant said, she witnessed Phillip Beard murder another ten year-old child. Gabriela's parents are supportive of her testifying to that fact in court. According to the *Victims of Trafficking and Violence Protection Act of 2000,* these events, together with law enforcement's certification of her assistance in the investigation and prosecution of an illegal act, make her eligible for U visa status. Such status would allow her to remain in the United States for up to four years and, following three years legal residence in the US, make her eligible to apply for a green card and permanent resident status."

"So you want me to attest to her cooperation in the investigation and prosecution of Mr. Beard?"

Wallace spoke up. "In addition, contingent on a waiver, her parents as derivative applicants are also eligible for U visa status, with the same provisions for work permits and green card applications."

"And you want me to facilitate the securing of such a waiver for them as well?" Webber said.

Sanchez nodded. "I'm sure you can appreciate how dangerous the situation is. The GDs are responsible for the attempted murder of the two adolescent witnesses and four police officers this past week alone." She pointed, "Including the Lieutenant here."

"So I've been told," Webber said, glancing at Julia.

"That's why the family will need to be put in the witness protection program," Wallace said.

Webber sat back, not bothering to move the hair bouncing in front of her eye.

"We have something for everyone, Ms. Webber," Sanchez said. "Including you."

Chapter 56

The House Falls

Friday morning, Southeast Memphis...Vans and police cars raced down the block from both directions. Vehicles stopped in front and behind the GDs' home base. Men and women in protective vests poured into the yard. Julia forced her way to the front of the line. They burst through the front and back doors, yelling orders.

Beard jerked to his feet when Julia burst into the room, Ayers on her heels, Tagger and Marino close behind. A woman in baby doll pajamas, sitting on Beard's lap, screamed as she dropped to the floor. Two men and three women looked up. Two stood.

"Hands on the table!" Julia ordered. She shot the men a look, pointed. "You! Sit! Now!"

"What the hell's going on!" roared Beard. "You got no right, bitch! You got no cause. You're on my turf. This is harassment."

"Actually, Mr. Beard," said Julia, holding up tri-folded papers. "Things have changed. We have a warrant for your arrest. Now, hands on the table."

"Arrest? What for?"

"Hands on the table."

Beard slowly complied.

"You're being arrested for the murder of a ten year-old girl."

"I told you last time, I got an alibi. Besides, you got no body."

"We do now." Julia pointed to a TBI agent. "Cuff him."

The agent moved behind Beard and pulled his left hand behind his back. He slipped a flexicuff on one wrist. "He's too big. Need another pair." An MPD officer tossed his cuffs. But when the agent reached for them, Beard spun and sent a backhanded fist to his jaw, knocking him unconscious.

In two steps Beard closed on Julia, slapped her arm. Her Sig flew from her hand. He wrapped his big hands around her neck, squeezed and raised her off the floor. She couldn't scream, but she grabbed his forearms, kneed him repeatedly in the ribs. He winced, bent forward and lowered her, his hands still around her throat.

The moment her feet touched the floor Julia shot both hands up like a referee signaling a touchdown. She twisted hard left, smashing into Beard's wrist, breaking his grip. Julia angled her right arm and drove her elbow into Beard's nose. He yelled, fell on his back, legs spread, hands covering his face, blood leaking through his fingers.

Julia bent over, gulped air, rubbed her neck. She stared down at Beard, her jaw clenched. She stepped between his legs, did a one-eighty. Fists clenched, she raised her leg in front of her, then kicked back hard, driving her heel into his crotch.

Beard howled and sat up. His hands flew from his face to cradle his groin.

Julia looked over her shoulder. "That's for killing little Jane Doe." She raised her leg again and sent another crushing heel into his privates, cracking his fingers as well. "And that's for Ana Sofia."

Beard lay on his side, knees up, moaning, slipping in and out of consciousness.

"And this one's for me." She lifted her foot, but Tagger touched her shoulder. "I think he got the message, Lieutenant," he said calmly. She looked up. Eyes wide, unfocused. He guided her away. Marino nodded, smiled, lowered his weapon.

Julia held her neck and stared fiercely at Beard, now curled into a ball, moaning and swearing, holding his privates with one hand, his nose with the other.

"I'll get you, bitch, he growled, staring at his bloody hand. "I swear to God. I know where you live."

She turned away as he rolled to his hands and knees, the blood from his nose dripping onto the carpet. Officers grabbed him, one on each arm, and hoisted him to his feet. Beard shrugged them off, snatched a gun from a holster, and whirled.

"Bitch!" Beard yelled.

Julia turned to see the gun rise. Her eyes opened wide as she looked down the barrel.

Bang-Bang-Bang!

Julia's whole body jerked.

The windows rattled when Beard dropped to his knees, hard. Three red spots on his shirt grew into one large circle. He fell face down with a loud *Oomph* as life escaped his lungs.

Julia turned, saw Marino—eyes focused, his weapon smoking, still pointed at Beard.

"Guess we're not going to have that stare-down after all, Mr. Beard," Marino said quietly.

***

Marino and Tagger walked Julia to the ambulance. Ayers followed. "That asshole picked her up by the neck," Tagger said to the paramedic, gesturing to Beard who was being wheeled out.

"I'm fine," Julia objected, gently stroking her neck.

The paramedic began a careful visual and fingertip evaluation. "Nothing appears to be broken, Lieutenant," he said, Velcroing a cervical collar around Julia's neck. "But you'll need x-rays to make sure. As big as that guy is...er, was, you're lucky to be alive. At the very least, you're going to be sore and bruised for a few weeks, probably croaky for a while."

"Thanks," Julia said, pulling at the Velcro tab. "I'll think about the x-rays."

"That's not a suggestion, Lieutenant," Ayers said. "That's an order. Get yourself up in the ambulance."

The paramedic smiled, guided Julia to the stretcher and strapped her in.

"No siren," Julia whispered. "The ride will be bad enough."

Chapter 57

The Neck

The hospital attendant negotiated Julia's bed through doors, hallways, and obstacles as he returned her to the ER treatment room. Ten minutes later the doctor appeared.

"From your description of the strangulation, I suspect you're taller than you used to be," she said, smiling. Julia offered no response. "Thankfully, your symptoms are not life-threatening. Bruises, fingernail-related abrasions, raspy voice, difficulty swallowing, and a beaut of a headache. Your larynx, trachea, hyoid bone, and thyroid appear to be intact. I expect the swelling, bruising, and raspy voice will continue for a few days. The cervical collar should help relieve stress on your neck. Don't be embarrassed to use it."

"Thanks, doc," Julia whispered. Whispering didn't hurt quite so much.

The doctor walked to the door, squirted antibacterial soap in her hands, looked back at Julia. "You know, we usually see this kind of attack in domestic violence cases. Seems to be a favorite macho move of the jerk husbands and so-called boyfriends proving their manhood." She paused. "The man who did this to you…Is it true you crushed his nuts?"

Julia, smiled weakly, held up two fingers. "Twice," she whispered. "Broke his nose, too."

The doctor smiled broadly. "Would love to have seen it.

Oh, by the way, there's a herd of people waiting to see you. You ready for them?"

Julia nodded.

***

Julia heard a knock and, keeping her head straight, moved her eyes to the door. Aunt Louise peeked in, smiled, then pushed the door open and led a parade into the room—Mark, Marino, and Tagger.

"Oh, sweetie," Louise said, hurrying across the room. "I heard what that horrible man did to you." She started to hug Julia, but pulled back. "Can I touch you? Does it hurt real bad?"

"Only when I'm awake," Julia managed, holding out her arms. Mark stepped up and squeezed her hand. Marino and Tagger hung back. Tagger flashed a casual *hi,* his hand chest high, splayed fingers. Marino smiled. "Just wanted to make sure you're okay, Lieutenant," he said.

"I'm okay because you saved my life, Professor. Thank you."

"Glad I was there," Marino said.

Aunt Louise's eyes brimmed with tears.

A nurse appeared, made a beeline for Julia, parting the sea of visitors. "Doctor says you can go home now," he said, handing her several forms, doctor's orders and pain prescriptions.

***

The Haven for Senior Citizens, Aunt Louise's apartment... Julia's pain meds had kicked in. She sat in the lazy-boy, only her face visible beyond the array of pillows Aunt Louise had packed around her, topped off with a brightly colored cotton throw blanket.

"Y'all go on and catch some bad guys," Julia said with a

slight slur and a weak smile.

"Our family has so much to thank you for, Sergeant," Louise said to Marino. She hugged him. Marino's eyes moistened.

"That goes for me too," Mark said. "Julia and I both owe you our lives." He took Marino's hand in both of his.

Tagger steered his partner from the room. They remained quiet till they cleared the building.

"You know he woulda kept shooting, Tony," Tagger said. "You saved lots of us." He dropped a hand on Marino's shoulder. "How are you doing?"

"Okay," Marino said as he stopped beside his cruiser. He looked down at his shaking gun hand. "I could use a drink. Maybe listen to some old tunes—Dean Martin, Sinatra."

"The music of our grandparents. You add Nat King Cole to that, and it works for me too. So, you headed home?"

"We still need to tie up some lose ends— the Lowell kid, Dancer, and Owen."

"I'll split that with you. From what you said, I have to believe the feds have been tailing Dancer and Owen twenty-four, seven. You go home, make some calls. See if the FBI can provide alibis for Dancer and Owen for Wednesday's Greyhound play. After that, just climb into your jammies, pour yourself a stiff one, and put on the records. Take your time coming into the station tomorrow. I'll pick up Elwood and we'll talk to Lowell's kid. Then I'll drop in on Hanks."

Marino nodded. "Thanks, Johnnie."

Chapter 58

The Note

Saturday...Tagger climbed the three steps to Hendricks's home in Bartlett, a small, middle-class town on the northern boundary of Memphis. He knocked hard. No response. He walked around the house, looking in windows. He saw Hendricks in the rear bedroom, slumped over a desk, a keyboard under his chest. He hurried to the back door, found it unlocked, rushed in. The smell was unmistakable—Hendricks was dead, had been for a while. An empty pill bottle lay on the floor beside his chair. Hendricks had been typing—the text began:

"I'M SO SORRY..."

Tagger called for the Medical Examiner and a crime scene team. Then alerted Marino and Julia.

***

Marino sat beside Tagger on the porch steps. They watched a red Mini-Cooper pull up. The driver's door opened and a casually dressed Julia unfolded carefully, holding one side of her head. Once fully erect, she reached up and noisily un-velcroed her cervical collar, chucked it inside the car. Gently rubbing her neck, she carefully half-stepped her way up the sidewalk.

Tagger looked at her bruised neck. "You supposed to be

out walking around?"

"Stopped taking the meds," Julia said, her voice hoarse, her speech forced. "Need something to take my mind off the pain. And, bingo. You found a body."

"Wanna sit?" Tagger said, gesturing to the steps.

Julia lifted a hand, gave a slight wave. "Been sitting."

"How's the neck, Lieutenant?" Marino said.

"I can feel every one of that bastard's fingers," Julia said, rotating her head carefully. "But I can't wear that stupid collar a minute longer. Fill me in."

Tagger smiled, tight lipped. "We made a few contacts yesterday." He looked at Marino.

"Yeah," Marino said. "Talked to the feds. They've been following Dancer and Owen for the last month. They've never left town. Looks like a rule-out for the abductions."

"I picked up Elwood and we went over to the Lowell's," Tagger said. "A real sad visit. Father and son had been expecting bad news, but I'm sure they hadn't lost hope. According to Dolan, his mother never asked him to get involved with her investigation. She only asked for advice on how someone might hack into a computer and hide their identity. Said he showed her how to use a phishing email to hook them, then how to use a string of VPNs to hide her IP address. I believed him. Elwood said that's exactly what had been done."

"So what about Sara Hanks?" Marino asked.

"Talked to her," Tagger said. "She had no alibi for Wednesday. Only said she was home with her husband the entire day and evening. Of course, he's in no shape to confirm that."

"And Hendricks?" Julia asked.

"We'd run out of suspects," Tagger said. "Came here to talk to him. Found him dead." He nodded toward the house. "Crime scene team's doing their thing. Looks like a suicide. No signs of a struggle, empty pill bottle, suicide note—a short one."

"What'd it say?" Julia said.

"Said he was sorry. Said he was a good teacher who liked kids. But oxycodone took over his life. He couldn't think of anything else but oxy and how to get more. Said he made horrible decisions."

"Horrible decisions all right," Marino said.

"Found other stuff," Tagger said. "A black Chevy Impala in the garage, heavy tint on the windows. A fake black beard in the bathroom."

"So Hendricks was the priest at the Greyhound station?" Julia asked.

"Looks that way," Tagger said. "There's more." He paused. "There's a stain on his desk and carpet. Crime scene guys say it's old. And it's blood."

"Doc Sales said Eve Lowell's head wound was consistent with hitting the corner of a piece of furniture," Julia said, her voice cracking. "Think it's her?"

Tagger cocked his head. "Been wondering about that. Let's say Lowell died in his house. Let's say Hendricks had something to do with it. He may have panicked. If so, would he have done the same stupid thing Rollins did? Reach out to the GDs for help?"

"You pay a big price for getting into bed with the GDs," Marino said. "What say you and I have a chat with his dealer? What's his name?"

"Dill," Tagger said. "Dillard White."

"Don't stay out too long, Lieutenant," Tagger said.

Marino added, "You might want to consider taking another round of meds."

Julia gave a small wave and tackled the steps.

***

They spotted Dill on his usual corner. Tagger pulled the driver's side of the cruiser up to the curb, lowered his window. "Dillard White. Need a word."

Dill touched his bulging pockets, looked around as if considering his options.

"Don't do it," Tagger ordered. "You don't want me to have to chase your ass down. That'd make me very unhappy. Not to mention my partner. He'd really be pissed if he had to run after you."

"Whaddya want?" Dill said, standing taller.

"Like I said, just a word. Now come on over here."

Dill nervously looked around, leaned back, approached slowly as if being pulled in like a roped calf.

"We don't give a shit about your stash," Tagger said. "Just wanna talk. Come on. Slide into the back seat."

Marino got out, walked around the cruiser, opened the back door, motioned him in. Dill took a final look around, got in. Marino slid in beside him.

Tagger twisted in his seat. "This is about Marshal Hendricks. You know him, right?"

Dill nodded.

"You know he's dead?"

"Heard that," Dill said quietly.

"There's a bunch of things we know. In fact, things we can prove. Hendricks was buying oxy from you—"

"Ain't true," Dill said.

"Cut the bullshit," Marino said, leaning into him, his mouth inches from Dill's ear. "No interruptions. Wait till it's your turn to talk."

Dill sat rigid, said nothing. His eyes darted from Marino to Tagger.

"Like I was saying," Tagger said, his eyes boring into Dill. "We *know* Hendricks was buying oxy from you. We know about Eve Lowell. Found her blood in Hendricks's house. Dug up her body from where you GDs buried it in the Cross On The Hill Cemetery."

Dill began to squirm, snuck a sideways glance at Marino, his face just inches away.

"We know you didn't kill anyone, Dill," Tagger said. "We're not after you. We know Hendricks was abducting Mexican girls and selling them to the GDs. What we don't know is why. But I think you know. What deal did Hendricks make with the GDs?" He stared at Dill.

"Now, it's your turn to talk," Marino said, pressing closer. "Fill in the blanks."

Dill fidgeted, licked his lips. "A while back, Mr. H called me. Sounded real upset, wouldn't say what was going on. Just wanted me to come to his house right away." He paused.

"That's a real good start, Dill," Marino said. "Keep talking."

Dill looked at Marino. He began slowly, quietly. "The front door's open. I goes inside and there's Mr. H, sittin' in a chair, cryin'." Dill's eyes focused somewhere around the dashboard. He spoke faster, louder. "Blood all over his hands and shirt. He's holding this laptop in both arms, like it's a goddamn teddy bear. He points behind him. I walk over there and see this body, a woman. Jesus! Blood all over the floor." He stopped.

"Keep going," Marino hissed.

Dill maintained his stare. "I got Mr. H a glass of Jack, got him to drink most of it. I asked him what happened. He said it was an accident. Said they were arguing over the laptop. He grabbed it. She fell, hit her head. He kept saying that I gotta help him. Nobody'd believe it was an accident."

"What about the laptop?" Tagger said. "What were they fighting about?"

Dell looked at Tagger. "Said the dead woman found out who was smuggling Mexicans into town. Had proof on the laptop. Said she was going to turn them in."

"And what did Hendricks want to do?" Marino asked.

"He wanted to blackmail the smugglers. Said he needed money for his drugs."

"Okay," Tagger said. "What happened next?"

"I called Lil J," Dill said. "He came over. Mr. H told him what was on the laptop. Lil J told Mr. H he'd take care of the body, but he wanted Mexican girls for their whore houses. Said there was a big price tag on getting rid of the body, but he'd call it even when Mr. H delivered the first girl. After that, he said, he'd pay good money for each girl Mr. H delivered. Enough to keep him in oxy for the rest of his life."

"Did Hendricks say how he'd pull off the kidnappings?" Marino asked.

Dill nodded. "Said he had a friend. Some woman. He was sure she'd help."

***

They watched Dill walk away. Tagger started the cruiser.

"*Some* woman?" said Marino. "The only one left is Sara Hawks. I don't want to believe it."

"Let's get a search warrant," said Tagger, "see what we can find."

Chapter 59

I Pledge Allegiance

Sunday afternoon, the Office of Immigration waiting area... Director Jody McNeil smiled as she looked out at the people gathered before her. Gabriela sat between her parents in the front row. Behind them sat Fathers Kaszewski and Court, along with Consuela, Ricardo, Leticia, and Jorge. Sanchez, Wallace, Julia, Tagger and Marino sat in the third row.

"Father Kaszewski," McNeil said, "would you translate for us?"

"Gladly," he said, and stood beside her.

"We are here to grant asylum to Alejandro Delgado, Silvia Delgado, and Gabriela Delgado. We are in awe of your courage and your willingness to stand up to criminals both in Mexico and here in the United States. Please rise."

McNeil walked forward and gave each a United States Visa. "Welcome to your new home." The group applauded. Alejandro's and Silvia's eyes brimmed with tears as the three hugged one another. Gabriela beamed.

"I believe we have one more presentation," McNeil said. "Lieutenant?"

Julia walked to face the family, bent forward and presented Gabriela with a gift wrapped package.

Gabriela slowly pulled off the wrapping, broke into a huge smile, and held her red diary to her chest. Silvia whispered something to her. Gabriela looked up at Julia. "Muchas gracias," she said and gave her a bear hug. Gabriela stepped back and asked Father K a question. He smiled. "Gabriela wants to know if everyone will sign in her diary."

She handed her diary to Julia.

Gabriela,

Eres mi heroína.

Love ya,

Julia Todd.

Chapter 60

Burn In Hell

*Monday morning...*Julia laced up her running shoes for the first time in four days, hopping her neck could stand the pounding of the run. Once outside, she kept her neck straight, protectively, and eased into a slow jog. Feeling nothing but minor soreness, she moved her head, turned side to side. Satisfied, she increased her pace. At the InsideOut Gym she found Girty hitting the heavy bag. "That's great, Girty."

Girty stopped. "Hey, Lieutenant. I've been practicing. I want to be ready when another creep comes in here." She stepped into a hard straight right. Pop! She pulled back as Julia approached. "Ewww! What happened to your neck?"

Julia touched her neck gently. "You should've seen it when it was just black and blue. The purple and yellow doesn't do it justice."

"Well? Did you get him back?"

Julia smiled.

"Show me what you did. I wanna be ready for anything."

***

Julia showered, dressed and drove to Otherlands. The routine felt good. She felt good. That is, until she walked into the Union Station.

"My God, Lieutenant," Teresa said. "That man made

hamburger out of your neck. How can you even stand up? Shouldn't you be wearing one of those dorky white collar things?"

"Good morning to you, Teresa. So happy to see you."

"No. Really. Your neck looks awful. Shouldn't you still be in the hospital?"

"Been there. Nothing was broken. They sent me home. I'm much better. I promise. I'm fine. Just fine."

"Okay, then. I guess I should tell you that priest from Saint Michael's called a few minutes ago. Wants you to meet him at the rectory. Said something about some kind of celebration for Gabriela."

***

Saint Michael's rectory...Secretary Alexa Torres buzzed Julia in. "I'm sorry, but Father K isn't here."

"He called and asked me to meet him," Julia said. "Guess I'm early."

Alexa stared at Julia's neck. "Can I get you something to drink while you wait?"

"Maybe some water."

"We keep a stash in the fridge. I'll be right back."

Julia heard a key inserted in the door, turned to see Father K ushering in Alejandro, Silvia, and Gabriela.

Julia smiled, shook each parent's hand. Then she dropped to one knee and hugged Gabriela. Gabriela wrapped her arms around Julia, then screamed and jumped back. She stuck her arm over Julia's shoulder and pointed. Silvia yelled something in Spanish and charged across the room, left her feet in a dive, landing on Alexa. Sylvia took her to the floor and pummeled her. Julia and Father K reached Silvia at the same time and pulled her off Alexa. Silvia continued to yell and fight them, while Alejandro helped hold her back.

Father K spoke Spanish, "What did you say? That can't be? There must be a mistake."

Gabriela ran, slammed into Silvia and held tight. Alejandro wrapped his arms around them both, and glared at Alexa. Father K seemed lost, looking from Alexa to the Delgados, and back again.

"Father, clue me in," Julia said, keeping her body between the two women.

"She says Alexa is the person who kidnapped Gabriela... in the small stone? Oh. Little Rock."

When Julia was certain Silvia would stay back, she bent down to check on Alexa, lying on her side, knees drawn up, bloody hands covered her face. "Is this true?" Julia demanded. "Did you kidnap Gabriela?"

Alexa nodded, then cried openly, hard.

Julia pulled Alexa to her feet, slapped on cuffs, and called for a squad car. She looked at Father K. "Can I use your office, Father?"

"Certainly," he said, leading the way.

Julia followed with a blubbering Alexa in tow. She steered Alexa to a chair, tears flowing, nose running. Father K pulled the door closed, returned to the Delgados. Julia uncuffed one hand from behind Alexa's back and recuffed it front of her, tossed her a box of tissues.

Alexa blew her nose, wiped her eyes.

Julia read Alexa her rights, then pulled up a chair and sat facing her, knees to knees. "That was you at the Greyhound station in North Little Rock last week, right? With Marshal Hendricks dressed as a priest?"

Alexa nodded, holding tissues to her nose.

"Is it true you abducted Gabriela for the GDs?"

Another nod.

"Was Hendricks driving the car then?"

"Yes."

"How many kids have you abducted?"

"Gabriela was number two."

"And a week ago Sunday?"

"The girl was older, stronger. Marshal hurt his back trying to get her to the car. She got away. He was in so much pain all the way back to Memphis. Said he was almost out of oxy. Started talking crazy. Said he'd get a girl even if he had to pull one off the street in Memphis. Then he got an email about another illegal coming in."

Chapter 61

Regrets

*The Union Station conference room...*Tagger and Marino were already seated when Julia walked in.

"You really got Hendricks's partner?" Tagger asked.

"Fill us in," Marino said.

"Whoa," Julia said. "Keep your shirts on. Remember my neck. Let me at least sit down."

Marino stood and pulled out a chair. Tagger opened his arms, palms up.

Julia sat, smiled. "Okay. The first thing you should know is that Gabriela was the one who identified Alexa Torres as her kidnapper. And it was her mother Silvia who chased Torres down and tackled her."

"Way to go, Mom!" Tagger said.

"Torres said she and Hendricks made four trips to North Little Rock. Gabriela was their second abduction, the third being last Sunday—"

"That the one that came in while Elwood was messing around with the wrong encryption stuff?" Tagger interrupted.

Julia nodded. "But that girl got away. Made Hendricks even more desperate. Their last attempt was for Elwood's decoy in North Little Rock."

"Who's the first kid?" Marino asked.

"She didn't know. Said Hendricks did the grab, she drove the car. Described the first girl as about the same age as Gabriela."

"Back to the beginning," Tagger said. "How'd they get started? Is it like Dill told us?"

"Torres had run away from a sexually abusive stepfather, an undocumented immigrant. She was forced into the sex trade in North Little Rock. After a few years she ran away to Memphis. A priest found her working the streets, and made arrangements to get her into a treatment program. Seems Hendricks tutored kids at that treatment program. They spent time together and hung out after she graduated from the program and got a job at St. Michael's."

"Did she know about Eve Lowell? About the laptop?" Tagger asked.

"Said Hendricks told her about the accident, and Lowell's laptop, which had information on undocumented families coming to Memphis. Said Hendricks kept the laptop to himself. Never told her who the local network smugglers were. Said Hendricks was always in pain, desperate to have more oxy. She felt sorry for him. Her hatred for her stepfather bled over to all undocumenteds, apparently enough for her to rationalize abducting kids."

"Can we assume she stole Father K's clothes so Hendricks could dress as a priest?" Marino said.

"Father K let us search the rectory. Found a suit with nonhuman hairs matching the beard from Hendricks's house."

"What about the laptop?" Tagger asked. "We never did find it."

"Torres said Hendricks freaked out last week when we almost caught him. Said she couldn't calm him down. Said he carried on about what a horrible person he was. That he didn't deserve to live. Said he insisted on stopping on the bridge and throwing the laptop into the Mississippi on their way home."

"He must have overdosed that same night," Tagger said.

Chapter 62

Debriefing

Thursday afternoon, conference room, 201 Poplar...Julia, Marino and Tagger sat along one side of the large table. Their boss, Major Williams, sat across from them along with Major Ayers, and Special Agent Dawkins.

"We've tied a bow around this one," Dawkins said. "Ten bodies unearthed from the cemetery. Each one identified. The Gangster Disciples were using the Cross On the Hill Cemetery for their body disposal. And keeping with one of the TBI's top goals, we broke up a major sex trafficking program. We didn't get them all, but we made a good-sized dent and saved a handful of kids."

"Formal charges have been filed on fourteen members of the GDs for everything from possession to attempted murder," Ayers said. "And, of course, Phillip House is no longer the driving force behind the gang." He looked at Marino.

Marino looked down.

Julia changed the subject. "We were able to identify the two people behind the abduction of the undocumented children—Marshal Hendricks and Alexa Torres."

"I know Hendricks overdosed," Ayers said. "But fill us in on Torres. How'd they hook up?"

"Torres was in a treatment program. Turns out, Hendricks

volunteered there as a tutor. They even went to a few AA meetings together—Hendricks for his addiction to oxycodone, Alexa for heroin."

"Sounds like the meetings didn't help," Dawkins said.

Julia shook her head. "Not for Hendricks. He developed a major oxy habit, costing him more money than he earned. Made him desperate."

"Is this where the smuggling comes in?" Dawkins asked.

"Right," Julia said. "Eve Lowell, one of your unearthed victims, had been investigating a smuggling network, bringing undocumenteds to Memphis from the Texas border. From what we've learned, Lowell found the local smugglers, hacked into their computer and was able to read notices about undocumenteds coming to Memphis."

"Lowell and Hendricks were friends," Marino said. "Both high school Spanish teachers and both objected to undocumenteds being allowed in the country. But they differed about how to use the laptop and its information. Lowell wanted to turn everything over to the feds, while Hendricks wanted to use the information to blackmail the smugglers. They argued. Hendricks grabbed the laptop. Lowell fell back, hit her head on the corner of a desk and died."

"Who was smuggling the undocumenteds into town?" Ayers asked.

"Torres said Hendricks threw the laptop into the Mississippi," Julia said. "Said he never told her who the smugglers were. Now, all the contact information is lost."

"So the network is alive and well," Dawkins said.

Julia screwed up her face. "Or maybe its members got scared and closed up shop."

The meeting broke up, Dawkins said his good-byes. As people were leaving, Major Williams caught Julia's eye.

Julia returned to her seat.

"How are you doing, Lieutenant?"

Julia touched her neck. "Much better, sir."

"I hear it was one hell of a fight."

"I think I'd have rather been an observer. Good thing Marino was awake."

"Indeed. Understand you got close to this illegal Mexican family, but never reported them."

"The little girl, Gabriela, witnessed Phillip Beard kill another little girl. She said she would testify and the parents agreed to let her. We knew the GDs had contacts in high places. Had to decide how best to protect Gabriela from him. I thought our best strategy was to keep quiet about the Delgado family until we got our ducks in a row."

"Turned out to be a wise decision. And the folks smuggling illegals?"

"Sir?"

"You seem awfully certain they would not continue smuggling illegals. Almost as if you had knowledge of their personal motivations. Tell me I'm not going to find out you knew who they were, but decided not to turn them in?"

"Can't imagine that happening, sir."

"That's what I thought." Williams stood. "Take care of that neck, Lieutenant." He left the room.

Julia remained seated. Took slow deep breaths.

Epilogue

Julia parked behind Molly's La Casita restaurant in midtown. No sooner had she walked inside than she was warmly greeted by the manager, Kelly Johnson. "Your guy is already here, Lieutenant. Up in the front."

Julia passed the bar and found Mark. "Running late. Sorry," she said as she settled in.

"No problemo," Mark said. "Just got here myself." He watched her for a moment. "How're you doing?"

Julia smiled. "It's always different when a psychologist asks how you are." She looked up as the waitress approached with frozen margaritas.

Mark clinked his glass against hers, took a quick sip, set it down. "So?"

"Had a dream last night." She stared into her drink. "About Gabriela and Ollie. The two girls were on the swings—laughing, talking in English, going higher and higher. They challenged one another to see who could jump the farthest. They flew off and landed exactly the same distance, rolled on the ground laughing. They looked up at me, asked if I wanted to swing. I squealed *yes* and ran to a swing. They yelled for me to swing as high as I could and then jump. I was afraid. They yelled louder, cheered for me. I took a deep breath and jumped. I thought I was flying. I felt the wind push against my whole body. It was so freeing. I landed in a heap on exactly the same place they had, and rolled. They ran over to help me up. When I reached for them, my hands were the hands of a child. They pulled me up. We all hugged and laughed." She looked at Mark. "Then I woke up."

"And how'd you feel?"

Julia paused. "Happy. …Relaxed. …Home."

"Home?"

"Yeah. It was like I belonged."

"From what you've told me, these kids are bright, courageous, and resilient. Characteristics they clearly share with you." Mark cocked his head. "I might go so far as to say none of you will ever be *throwaways* again."

Julia relaxed, slumped back in her chair, swirled the straw in her drink. She looked up, smiled. "I like that."

FACTS

Tennessee Bureau of Investigation & Vanderbilt Center for Community Studies: Research Study (2011)

In the US, on average, a child is bought or sold for sex every two minutes.

In the US, the average age for a child sold for sex is 13 years-old; some as young as five years-old.

In the US, the average length of child sexual enslavement is over 4 years.

Tennessee counties reporting more than 100 child sex trafficking cases: Coffee (Tullahoma), Davidson (Nashville), Knox (Knoxville), Shelby (Memphis).

Memphis, Tennessee

Twenty Memphis-based Gangster Disciples arrested on murder and drug charges (2015).

Terrance "T-Rex" Yarbrough of Memphis was sentenced to 44-years for ten counts of sex trafficking involving victims as young as fifteen (2013). T-Rex was characterized as controlling his victims through horrific physical violence, sexual abuse, and emotional torment.

Five Memphis individuals were indicted on federal child sex trafficking charges (2013). The U.S. Attorney's Office in Memphis has consistently ranked high nationally for its prosecution of sex trafficking offenders.

Memphis Police officer pled guilty to sex trafficking

across state lines (2013). The crime was investigated by the Tarnished Badge Task Force, composed of members of the FBI, Memphis Police Department, and Shelby County Sheriff's Office.

Operation Cross Country (2013)

An FBI sex-trafficking sweep involving 76 cities resulted in the arrests of over 150 people, including three in Memphis. Some 105 victims, almost all girls, ranging in age from 13 to 17 were rescued. The largest numbers of these victims were found in San Francisco, Detroit, Milwaukee and New Orleans.

Memphis & Jackson, Tennessee and Metro Atlanta, Georgia (2016)

A twelve-count indictment was returned on 48 alleged Gangster Disciples leaders, primarily from West Tennessee and the metro Atlanta area, in addition to seven other states. Charges included murder, attempted murder, ordering hits on rival gang members, drug trafficking, weapons trafficking, robbery, carjacking, extortion, kidnapping, wire fraud, credit card fraud, insurance fraud and bank fraud. A former Atlanta-area police officer was alleged to be a hit man for the gang and tipped off other members about police activity.

Houston, Texas (2015)

A 71 year-old madam, Hortencia Medeles, was sentenced to life in prison for her role in overseeing a sex trafficking operation involving undocumented females as young as 14, smuggled from poor villages in Mexico and Central America. Other charges included money laundering and harboring of illegal aliens. Brothel prices ranged from $65 for fifteen minutes-to-as much as $500 per hour for minors. The fees

reportedly went to individual pimps. Detailed records maintained by Medeles showed 64,296 charges and collections for use of her brothel facilities. Evidence presented at her trial indicated that the madam made more than $1.6 million in a 19-month period on fees collected for use of the rooms, etc.

Tennessee (2016)

Since 2011, the state of Tennessee has passed and/or amended over thirty-five human trafficking-related statutes and regulations, resulting in some of the strictest laws in the country. The Tennessee Bureau of Investigation coordinates with local law enforcement and several community organizations to identify, protect and support victims of sex trafficking. Each nonprofit agency has its particular service to offer. Among the services are legislative advocacy, public awareness, volunteer training, self-help groups, mental health services, and reintegration programs for the women & men, and girls & boys who escape their captors. See TBI's webpage: www.ITHasToStop.com.

The Tennessee Anti-Slavery Alliance was developed in 2017 to help coordinate with other agencies in four areas of the state: **RestoreCorps** in West Tennessee, **EndSlavery in Tennessee** in Middle Tennessee, **Second Life of Chattanooga** in Lower East Tennessee, and **Grow Free** in Upper East Tennessee. The Memphis area also has anti-violence advocacy services from Zonta International, Memphis chapter (since 1927).